"Chuck Holton's military e[xperience] . . . [and his adven-]tures lend authenticity to his writing rarely found in today's fiction or nonfiction. It is entertainment—masterfully mixed with powerful life lessons that you can use, and pass on to your friends."

> —LT. COL. OLIVER NORTH, USMC (RET), host of *War Stories* on FOX News Channel and *New York Times* best-selling author of *American Heroes*

"*Meltdown* is even more hair-raising because it is so plausible. But if I'm on the run in a hot zone, there's no one I'd rather have at my back than the men—and woman—of Task Force Valor. An explosive climax is a reminder of just Who really controls our lives and destiny. My only disappointment in turning the last page was saying good-bye."

> —JEANETTE WINDLE, author of *Veiled Freedom*, *Betrayed*, and *CrossFire*

"Chuck Holton has done it again! *Meltdown* is hot and will keep you sizzling on the edge of your seat! Keep some ice water nearby. Chuck's latest may just be his hottest! Highly recommended!"

> —DON BROWN, author of the Navy Justice Series

"There are some writers who do their research in the library and on the Internet. Chuck Holton does *his* research with a passport, a compass, and a good pair of boots. The result is a novel full of action so authentic you can smell the cordite, and characters so real that you can almost touch them. *Meltdown* is not to be missed."

> —TOM MORRISEY, author of *Pirate Hunter*

MELTDOWN

MELT

A NOVEL

DOWN

CHUCK HOLTON

MULTNOMAH
BOOKS

MELTDOWN
PUBLISHED BY MULTNOMAH BOOKS
12265 Oracle Boulevard, Suite 200
Colorado Springs, Colorado 80921

Scripture quotations and paraphrases are taken from the King James Version and the Holy Bible, New International Version®. NIV®. Copyright © 1973, 1978, 1984 by International Bible Society. Used by permission of Zondervan Publishing House. All rights reserved.

The characters and events in this book are fictional, and any resemblance to actual persons or events is coincidental.

ISBN 978-1-59052-560-9

ISBN 978-1-60142-264-4 (electronic)

Published in the United States by WaterBrook Multnomah, an imprint of the Crown Publishing Group, a division of Random House Inc., New York.

MULTNOMAH and its mountain colophon are registered trademarks of Random House Inc.

Library of Congress Cataloging-in-Publication Data
Holton, Chuck.
    Meltdown / Chuck Holton.—1st ed.
        p. cm.—(Task Force Valor ; bk. 3)
    ISBN 978-1-59052-560-9—ISBN 978-1-60142-264-4 (electronic)
    I. Title.
    PS3608.O4944344M46 2009
    813'.6—dc22
                                        2009014671

Printed in the United States of America
2009—First Edition

10 9 8 7 6 5 4 3 2 1

This book is dedicated to the one person who is most responsible for keeping me alive to see age forty:

My mother.

No other person on earth has invested more in my safekeeping or prayed more for my safety.

Thank you, Mom. I love you.

Acknowledgments

I want to especially thank my good friend Lynne Thompson (www.soccermombook.com) for her tremendous help "above and beyond" on this project. She even braved West Virginia in wintertime to make this happen.

Thanks to Olenka and Stepan Mankovska and George and Sharon Markey for taking me into their home while I visited Ukraine, and for translation and cultural consulting on the manuscript.

My various editors, Julee Schwarzburg, Ken Petersen, and Jeff Gerke, held my nose to the grindstone and ensured the job got done right even as a thousand other projects vied for my time and attention.

And to my wife, who resisted rolling her eyes at me for an entire year as I grumbled about those thousand-and-one projects.

And thank You, Father God, for using any humble work of mine to further Your kingdom. May these efforts do more than entertain—may they change lives.

Cartagena, Colombia

"HIJO DE—"

Edgar Oswardo Lerida interrupted his own oath as he dropped the hotel phone into its cradle. Two weeks and the money still had not arrived in his account. He crossed himself and kissed the three rings on his right hand, *El Padre, El Hijo, El Espíritu Santo.*

You are turning into your mother. He wasn't usually this superstitious. But now that he was so close, he felt like he should be as careful as possible to keep from offending anyone in the heavens.

Edgar crossed to the window of the spacious top-floor suite and looked down on the Cartagena harbor. He spotted the lone statue of the Virgin Mary, which stood on a column in the bay. A sense of helplessness threatened to overwhelm him like the angry midafternoon clouds bearing down on Boca Grande—the modern hotel district— from across the water.

He turned away from the window and sank onto the bed like a deflating tire. He lay looking at the ceiling fan without seeing it, traveling instead in his mind back to Panama, to the bitter wife and resentful children who doubtless thought him dead by now.

If only the money would come! He let his thoughts wander to Argentina. There he hoped to take on a new name, meet a beautiful woman, and…what? Start the process all over again? The unwelcome thought that perhaps this wasn't such a good idea after all tried to crawl into his brain for the hundredth time, but he pushed it away. There was no going back. He was no longer Edgar Oswardo Lerida, and he could never be again. His name was now Gustavo. Gustavo Soto.

He sighed. It was not good for him to be alone anymore. He'd been thinking too much. That was the problem. Another night alone in this room with nothing but the television would be worse than water torture.

Edgar—Gustavo, rather—sat up. He needed a companion. Cartagena was full of beautiful women. Why not?

He stopped at the mirror on the way to the door and ran a brush through his thinning hair. Despite being in his midforties, he was still handsome enough. And if not, well, he had money, or would shortly.

He stepped to the door and pulled it open, then froze as a jolt of adrenaline nearly gave him a seizure.

The doorway was filled by the largest man he'd ever seen. The man wore a black suit and sunglasses. Hands the size of hubcaps reached up and wrapped around Edgar's neck, lifting him off his feet and carrying him back into the room.

The large man was followed by a thin, middle-aged *gringo* in a black crew neck and leather blazer, eyes hidden behind mirrored sunglasses.

The gorilla slammed Edgar backward onto the bed, then produced a giant pistol and pressed it to his forehead. *"No te muevas,"* he growled.

The thin man spoke. "You are Edgar Lerida." It was not a question.

Edgar's heart beat triple time. Questions jumped into his mind like storm troopers. *Nobody knows I'm here! Who are these men?* But he willed himself to be calm. "You have the wrong…room," he croaked.

The gringo's grin sent a shiver through him. "Ah. We will keep the payment, then."

Recognition hit Edgar like a bucket of ice. The gringo's voice. It was he who had arranged the purchase of the remaining liquid explosive. Edgar knew better than to ask the man's name. "Did the product not arrive safely?"

"It is still in port, waiting to be released by Customs."

Is that what this is about? "You must know that is out of my control."

"Of course." The gringo waved the gorilla off. The thug stepped back and lowered his weapon, but did not put it away. "We have a proposition for you."

It was clear from the man's tone that Edgar was going to listen whether he wanted to or not. He rose to his elbows and regarded the white man. His pencil-thin sideburns were like black knives on the sides of his face, and flecks of gray in his perfectly manicured goatee were the only hint that the man might be over forty. He carried a black briefcase.

"We know that you are one of the foremost experts in the product which we have purchased," the gringo said, "as well as a master of improvised explosives in general. We need your talents for a mission involving the product." He set the briefcase on the bed. "Inside this case you will find precise instructions as to what you must accomplish. When these tasks are complete, your payment will be delivered, along with a bonus of one million dollars."

Edgar held up a hand. "Gentlemen, I am a businessman, not a soldier. But I know many people in this business. Why don't I assist you in finding someone more suited—"

"Modesty does not become you, *Señor* Lerida. Neither does cowardice. When it comes to explosives, you are an artist. Use that creativity well and you will be back here enjoying the good life in two weeks' time. There is a telephone in the case. Keep it on at all times. I will be in touch." The gringo turned and followed his gorilla toward the door.

Edgar struggled to a sitting position on the bed. "And what if I'm not able to complete the mission?"

The gringo stopped on the threshold and turned, displaying a thin smile and a reply that turned Edgar's blood to cold Jell-O in his veins. "Again, put your imagination to good use."

THE ROUNDHOUSE KICK caught Mary Walker just beneath the rib cage, forcibly expelling a grunt along with a lungful of air. She fought to suck in a breath, determined to make her adversary pay for that.

The man who had kicked her gave a wicked smile and lashed out again, higher this time. But she jerked her head back, and his foot barely grazed her cheek. She crouched and jabbed a fist at his solar plexus, but he swatted it away and clubbed the side of her head with his forearm.

Now she was mad. Her pulse pounded in her temples almost as hard as her opponent. She couldn't take much more. A step back and she could see that he was breathing hard too.

He growled at her. "Come on!"

She feigned a punch to his head, and when his hands went up to defend it, she nailed his inner thigh with a hard right kick. He grunted and grabbed for the bruised leg as she launched a high kick at his head.

But even hurt he was too quick. He ducked and her foot sailed high.

She spun around just in time to see his heel coming straight at her face.

Still spinning, Mary cocked her head to the side and caught his leg over her left shoulder as it brushed her ear. She threw her feet out from under her body and fell to her knees, taking his leg with her. His momentum combined with hers to flip him by his leg and slam his face into the mat.

She released her hold on his leg and stood up, panting. She'd won.

The man rolled over and looked up at her. "What the heck was that, Mary?"

She wiped her upper lip with the back of her hand. "I don't know, Tom. Just seemed like the thing to do."

Applause broke out from the people in the small gym. They'd stopped lifting weights or riding stationary bikes to watch the sparring match. Those who weren't clapping were now gaping at her or murmuring to one another.

Tom Harliss pushed off the mat and got to his feet, chuckling. "In ten years of teaching Muay Thai, I've never seen that move before. I'm sure it's not legal."

Mary shrugged, brushing away a strand of red hair that had escaped her ponytail. "In my job, sometimes you do whatever it takes."

Tom nodded, straightening his tank top. "Uh-huh. What is it you do, exactly?"

The beeping sound coming from her knapsack saved her from answering his question. "Just a sec." She ran to her bag and fumbled with the zipper, the gloves she wore making it even more difficult to flip the phone open once she found it. When she finally succeeded, the screen said she had a new text message. She clumsily poked a few buttons until the message came up. It read simply, "OFFICE ASAP."

Tom followed her over. "So, you want to go another round, or go out for coffee?"

Nice. The guy should have been a salesman instead of a personal trainer. She had to dig for a smile. "Sorry, they need me at the office right away." She held up the phone.

Tom's sweaty, too-tanned brow wrinkled. "It's Saturday. What do you do?"

She held the smile a beat too long. "I'm an analyst for a big insurance company. Lots of travel. No life." That second part was the truth. Besides, she knew better than to date a guy she'd just beat up. Talk about giving him something to prove.

Tom smiled like a used-car salesman. "Well, next time, then. Glad we finally got to spar a little bit. You're good!"

"Thanks," she said, picking up her bag and towel. "I'll call you when I can come in again."

She could feel him watching as she headed for the locker room. And it bugged her. Even after beating him she still felt like he thought of her as a thing, not a person. Maybe it was just how guys were.

When she stepped into the shower, the scuff on the side of her face stung where Tom's forearm had landed. She felt for a bruise below her ribs but found only a small sore spot. In a way she was disappointed. She wasn't sure why bruises were so appealing. It wasn't that she liked pain. Maybe it was just a reminder that the task hadn't been easy.

Nothing had been easy lately. A thought of Panama flashed in her mind. She turned the shower knob until the stream was almost too hot to stand.

After rinsing off, she wrapped up in a towel and set her small makeup kit on the sink. The woman looking back at her in the mirror had reddish hair that looked a serviceable brown when wet, making her feel about as attractive as Paris Hilton's Chihuahua. Her shoulders bore the freckles of too many sunburns, and here and there were fading scars, each with its own story, but none adding to her charm. Around the corners of her blue eyes were the beginnings of a few wrinkles when she squinted, but she attributed them to the stress of seventy-hour workweeks, usually trying to keep herself and her team alive. She frowned.

Get over it, girl. You're lucky to be alive.

She sighed. She couldn't change her past, but maybe changing her look would be the next best thing. She reached into her bag and pulled out the card of a hairstylist. She had been contemplating this for months. Now, for some reason, she was suddenly ready to do it.

She dropped the card back in her bag and pulled her shirt on over her head. It was time for a change.

Sunday, New River Gorge Bridge, Fayetteville, West Virginia. 0500 hours

Master Sergeant Bobby Sweeney crouched in the tall grass, making himself invisible in the predawn mist rising out of the gorge. He scanned the trail leading down to the road with the aid of a set of AN/PVS-14 night-vision goggles he had "borrowed" from his locker back at Fort Bragg.

Sweat trickled down the center of his back despite the chill air. His heart and breathing rates were both higher than they should have been after the short hike from where he'd been dropped off ten minutes earlier. But then again, that was mainly due to adrenaline, not exhaustion. No one had ever done what he was about to do.

Thirty meters in front of him, Highway 19 shot out into space above the New River Gorge, supported by a massive steel arch. Locals touted it as the longest arch bridge east of the Mississippi. But Sweeney was more interested in its height—876 feet from the roadway to the raging New River at the bottom of the gorge.

His radio crackled in his ear. "Winds at two knots, over."

Sweeney nodded without considering that his partner on this mission, Sergeant First Class Frank Baldwin, wouldn't see it. He keyed his mike. "Good enough."

"You sure you don't want to put this off for another day? Did anyone mention how many laws you'll be breaking?"

Sweeney spit. "Been planning it for a year, buddy. And I didn't drive all the way up here just to go climbing. Besides, I have a wedding to go to. It's now or never."

"How's the traffic look?"

"Oncoming lanes are almost empty. Looks good."

Frank's voice wasn't so sure. "I can't believe you talked me into this. If you get caught—"

Sweeney hit his Transmit button and stepped on the other man's transmission. "You shoulda been an accountant, you know that?"

A train whistle drifted up from far below. Sweeney's heart rate rose a notch.

Frank radioed in again. "Well, Batman, here's your chance to make history."

"Right on schedule. How long is it?"

"Hard to tell. At least fifty cars."

"That'll do. Gimme a time hack."

"All right. Here comes…in three…two…one…now!"

Sweeney flipped his NVGs up out of the way and stood. "Thanks, bro. See you at the pickup."

"What am I gonna tell the major and Phoenix if you don't make it?"

Sweeney moved out of the tree line toward the roadway. "Tell the major it was my idea. As for Phoenix…" He hesitated, thinking about the pretty CIA agent. Their relationship had been professional, nothing more. That said, he was surprised to feel a pang of…something…at the thought of not seeing her again. He pushed it away with a grin. "Tell her I was secretly in love with her and hoped to be the father of her children someday. That ought to throw her for a loop."

"You've got a sick sense of humor, bro. Just don't get yourself killed."

"Roger that."

He took off down the embankment. When he reached the blacktop of Highway 19, he was at a dead run, despite the full body harness and pack tray on his back.

Sweeney turned toward the bridge and ran even faster, right past the sign that said No Pedestrians on Bridge. Running out onto it, the span looked much longer than it had when he and Frank had driven across it the day before.

Headlights rose up behind him. Sweeney flinched as a semi thundered past on the highway, sounding its air horn. He ran as close as possible to the three-foot concrete barrier that separated the roadway from empty space over the drop. The weight of the big truck made the bridge shimmy like Jell-O under his feet.

He breathed through his nose, pumping his arms and legs in a steady rhythm. His strides were shortened by the leg straps of the parachute harness, and the night-vision goggles weighed down his Pro-Tec helmet, but none of that mattered now.

Another two hundred yards.

More headlights appeared behind him. This time it was a pickup truck with big mudder tires. Its brake lights flashed as it passed him. The passenger rolled down his window and shouted, "Yeeha! That's one crazy son of a gun!"

Sweeney gave the truck a wave and kept running.

Gotta love West Virginia. They know crazy when they see it.

He bared his teeth in a grin, every pore tingling with excitement. One hundred yards separated him from the center of the span.

He was still smiling when the spotlight hit him.

Without breaking stride, he turned his head to see the source of the beam. Out of the corner of his eye he saw the blue and red lights bearing down on him.

Before he could even cuss, an electronically amplified voice tinged with a mountaineer accent commanded, "Hold it right there!"

Sweeney glanced up ahead. Only fifty yards to the center of the bridge, but it might as well be five hundred.

The police car was closing in fast. He could hear its supercharged motor roaring up behind him. He'd never make it.

"Police! Stop where you are. You are under arrest!" The cop's loudspeaker echoed off the walls of the gorge.

Then something else echoed back…the sound of the train.

Sweeney slowed to a jog and looked over the edge. He could see the train's powerful headlight just passing under the bridge more than eight hundred feet below. Tires screeched behind him as the police car skidded to a halt.

It couldn't be over just like this. There was no time to ponder how the police had arrived so quickly. Sweeney pushed himself up onto the concrete railing. He stole a quick glance at the cop just as the man's Smokey the Bear hat popped above the door of his cruiser.

"Don't you do it!" the trooper yelled.

Sweeney smiled and held his hands high. "You know, my dad used to say that to me a lot. And you know what I'd tell him?"

He never heard the man's reply, because he had already stepped off into space.

The silence swallowed him whole. He was vaguely aware of the dark forms of the metal bridge supports as they flashed by a few feet from his head.

As he fell through a swirl of mist, he arched his body hard as he'd been trained to do, counting the seconds in his head. A thought flashed unsolicited through his consciousness—*What if you just kept counting? In six seconds it would all be over. And then what?*

But Bobby Sweeney didn't take kindly to thoughts like that— they also reminded him of his fire-and-brimstone preacher father. So he pushed it away and reached for his pilot chute. He gave it a toss and less than a second later felt the pop of his specialized navy blue base-jumping canopy as it pulled him up short.

Hundreds of people jumped from this bridge every year. Virtually all of them waited until Bridge Day, held each October. Then they could get their picture taken so they could brag about how brave they were.

But fame did nothing for Sweeney.

This was the second-highest vehicular bridge in the world. It had cut the time required to cross the New River Gorge by car from forty-five minutes to as many seconds. The logging road below was the only way out for anyone landing at the bottom. That was why most people who jumped illegally got caught—by the time they wound their way back up the treacherous old road, the police would be waiting with open arms at the top.

But Sweeney wasn't planning on landing at the bottom. Not exactly, anyway.

He got his bearings and looked around in the growing light as dawn approached. Below, the New River crashed north along the bottom of the gorge. Tall trees shrouded in early summer foliage looked like a soft coat of fur in the gloom, but Sweeney knew they hid sharp rocks and sheer cliffs, some of which he and Frank had spent the weekend pretending to climb, all the while performing reconnaissance for this moment.

The traditional landing spot was actually a parking area just below the bridge. He could see it now as a wide gray strip next to the river. Normally it was crammed with buses and soggy rafters, it being the take-out point for guided raft trips down the New. But at this hour, it was empty, which made it a great Plan B.

The body of the train was almost invisible from this height, even though the moon had not yet dropped below the rim of the gorge. Sweeney let go of one toggle and dropped the NVGs back over his eyes.

Much better. He steered out over the river for a better look. Jumping before getting to the middle of the bridge had cost him some altitude, but he could still pull it off. There the train was, lumbering along between cliff and cascading water. The engine was well ahead, but the last car had yet to cross beneath the bridge.

And just there—between his dangling feet, he could make out where the tracks crossed the road to the parking area—the gap in the trees he and Frank had seen earlier.

He heard sirens. Above and to his left he could see the flashing lights as Officer Smokey's sports car challenged the hairpin turns that led to the bottom of the gorge. Looking right, he saw another set of police lights descending the old road on that side.

Gotta hand it to them: they're persistent.

Sweeney steered his canopy toward the gap in the trees. He could easily make out the black form of the train rushing by underneath. From the ground it had looked like a piece of cake—the gap was about the size of an Olympic swimming pool. Up here, he remembered he'd never had much of a sweet tooth.

The gap was coming up fast. Sweeney dumped some air so he'd drop in just past the leading edge of the clearing. He'd get only one shot at this, and overshooting the drop zone would definitely ruin his weekend.

As he drifted down a hundred feet above the tops of the trees, a draft of cool air drawn down the gorge by the river hit him, pushing his chute back toward the water.

He wrenched the toggles to try to compensate, but he was now out of alignment. That put Plan B out of the question. Plan C—one he had failed to consider until this moment—was getting strung up in a tree like so much wet laundry until Officer Smokey arrived to take him into custody.

The rumble of the train mixed with the rushing noise of the river as Sweeney's boots cleared the tops of the trees. But the train was creating its own air currents—that was something else he hadn't considered.

He was coming in sideways. *Not good!*

As he passed over the lumbering train, he yanked on both toggles to slow his descent but felt the chute tug forward, threatening to slam him facedown on the speeding cars. He let up, hoping that the forward motion of the canopy would slow to roughly match the speed of the locomotive. And since this wasn't a passenger train, the two should have been close enough.

He pulled both toggles again just as his feet touched the metal of the slow-moving car. But the train wasn't slow enough—the sudden acceleration caused Sweeney to lose his balance and sit down hard.

But there was nothing there to sit on.

Adrenaline kicked him in the chest as he fell between two train cars. He threw out his arms by instinct, grabbing at the air. His heels bounced off something metal, and that spun him so he was falling headfirst.

The ground below was a gray green blur. Sweeney clawed the air in desperation. One gloved hand closed around something solid, and he grunted as the weight of his body tore it out of his grip.

He fell only a few more feet before the chute caught on something overhead and brought him to a bone-crunching stop that probably shortened him an inch.

His helmet hovered less than two feet above the ground, which was rushing by with terrifying speed. He couldn't have breathed if he'd wanted to, but the feeling of something tearing above him gave him more pressing things to worry about.

He groped for something to grab and found a metal ladder, but the only arm that could reach it had been badly wrenched in the fall. His right shin had been bashed on something too, but at the moment that foot was all that was keeping him from slipping under the lumbering freight car. The chute continued to tear, and he dropped another couple of inches toward the ties.

In desperation, he slid his good hand along his body until it found the protrusion that had caught his foot, then he grunted through clenched teeth and pulled himself back up on the coupling between the two cars. He sat there trying to catch his breath until one of his shroud lines slid by him, stopping only inches from the ground.

Bad. Very bad. Sweeney stopped breathing again and snatched the line away from the rushing track, carefully gathering his suspension lines to keep any of them from dropping into the road wheels. If that happened, he'd be jerked beneath the train and crushed in a heartbeat.

He gingerly pulled the quick-disconnects on his shoulders, then stood on shaky legs to roll up the rest of his chute. It would have to be repaired, but he didn't care. The rip would forever remind him of how close death had been.

He braced himself between the two swaying cars and wondered why he wasn't more euphoric at being alive. Maybe it was because he had finally grasped the insanity of what he'd just done. His legs were trembling with exertion, and a slug of fear lodged in his gut.

There's hooah, and then there's stupid. And this was way over the line.

Illuminating the dial on his watch, Sweeney realized that less than four minutes had passed since he had become the first person whom nobody would ever know had jumped from the New River Gorge Bridge onto a moving train. In the dark.

But instead of elation, he was suddenly very tired. It was all he could do to stay awake for the six-minute ride to Thurmond, West Virginia.

Have I finally done it—proven once and for all that I have what it takes? How will I know I've made it—become the man I want to be? How tough is enough?

Enough what? He wasn't sure. But clinging to the greasy frame of that rumbling freight train, he decided that he'd better figure out what he was chasing before it killed him.

Sweeney picked a spot beside the tracks and leaped from the train. He hit the ground and rolled, hugging his rig to his chest.

At 0528, Sweeney watched from the bushes as Frank's Jeep CJ-7 rolled to a stop beside the road. He keyed his mike. "It's about time you showed up."

The radio beeped in his ear. "Shut up and get in."

He stood and loped painfully around to the passenger side of the vehicle.

Frank shook his head. "I'm aiding a wanted fugitive. I can't believe you did it."

Sweeney jumped in and let out a howl. "Believe it, bro. An Alabama boy can survive!"

Frank rolled his eyes. "Apparently an Alabama boy can't think of a legal way to celebrate his five-hundredth jump, though."

Sweeney just laughed. "Let's go, Sergeant Bean Counter. Mission accomplished. No problem."

He decided to keep the almost-dying-under-a-train part to himself.

After all, he was good at keeping secrets.

2

Kiev. Ukraine. 1300 hours

MILLIONS WILL DIE.

Maxim gritted his teeth in disgust. Not at the thought of the deaths, but at the sight of what "independence" had done to the city of Kiev since the last time he'd visited.

The stocky Chechnyan leaned on the railing that enclosed the tiny balcony of the safe house, four stories above crumbling sidewalks and overgrown unkempt lawns. He wondered why nobody else seemed to get it. Capitalism wasn't freedom, it was slavery. Communism was no better. When the people of Eastern Europe had thrown off Communism like an old coat and embraced "progress," they had simply traded one master for another.

In his studies, he'd learned that both of these systems of government endeavored to separate religion from government. Such a thing was not only heresy, it was stupid—like trying to see without eyes. Both rejected Allah, instead following false and destructive systems that treated the temporal as if it were holy.

And so they will die.

Maxim's younger brother, Kyr, emerged from the run-down flat carrying a stained, olive-drab coat. His pointed nose and almost bloodless face were similar to Maxim's, but Kyr kept his half-covered by a shock of black hair that hung over his eyes. Maxim doubted if the skinny twenty-two-year-old remembered much of the violence and chaos that had engulfed Chechnya in the 1990s, when the Russian pigs had tried to crush his people—and lost.

Maxim filled his lungs to capacity, reveling in the strength of his people. They were united under an even greater citizenship—that of the *ummah*—or the faithful of Islam. Maxim felt secure in the knowledge that Islam would certainly one day rule the world, though he himself would not be there to see it. He let his breath out in a great sigh.

If we are successful, the new caliphate may be closer than anyone thinks.

The boy strained his eyes in the direction of Maxim's stare. "What is it, brother?"

Maxim laughed cynically. "The incompetence of Communism almost turned all of Europe into a radioactive wasteland in 1986. If Allah had not, in his infinite patience, seen fit to give those corrupt cultures another chance to repent, none of us would be here today."

Kyr nodded thoughtfully, but Maxim could tell he was struggling to understand. "Does this trouble you, brother?"

Maxim ran a calloused hand that was missing two fingers over the black stubble on his jaw. "No. Allah does as he wishes. We were spared then so that we could be his messengers now. It is clear that these wicked people"— he swept his arm to indicate all of Kiev— "will only continue to wallow in shallow commercialism and will never repent, unless we jar them from their self-induced slumber."

Kyr dropped his gaze to his own delicate hands, which still

clasped the coat. "I wish I could speak as passionately about it as you."

This time Maxim's laugh was genuine. "You need not be eloquent, brother. Simply be obedient." He wrapped a muscular arm around Kyr's thin shoulders. "You can start by going to pick up our companions. Their train arrives from Dnepropetrovsk in an hour."

"Aren't you coming?"

Maxim dismissed him with a wave of his scarred hand. "Go. You do not need me. I have much planning to do and am waiting for the call from our supplier. Call my mobile when you find them."

Kyr tilted his head to peer at him from beneath the shock of greasy black hair. "I need some money for the cab fare."

Maxim growled and gave him a ten-hryvnia note. "Take the subway. It's safe. And use the money you have left to get a haircut. You look like an idiot."

Kyr left the apartment, and Maxim turned back to the balcony, deep in thought. Far in the distance, he could just make out the wide Dnieper River, which flowed south from Chernobyl, bisecting Ukraine's capital city. On the far bank, the sun glinted off the statue of an enormous robed woman, one muscular arm raising a sword high in the air. The titanium figure stood over five hundred feet tall. Its purpose was to celebrate the "victory" of the Soviets in World War II.

Maxim's cynical chuckle returned. He couldn't help it. If he remembered right, the Russians had lost more than twenty million people in the Great Patriotic War.

If that is what they call victory, they will soon have another great triumph to celebrate.

Pike County, Alabama

The throaty rumble of Sweeney's Harley V-Rod echoed through the pines that lined the long driveway to his grandparents' farm, announcing his arrival. The late afternoon sunshine in southern Alabama felt good on his face, though it made him sweat beneath his black leather jacket.

He rolled to a stop at the end of the drive and killed the engine. Beside him was a new white minivan he didn't recognize. He guessed it belonged to his older brother, Stuart. *A sensible car for a sensible man.*

He pulled off his helmet and looked up at the hundred-year-old farmhouse. It was two stories tall, with weathered wooden siding that had needed a paint job for the last two decades or so. It looked the same as the last time he'd seen it, when he'd come home for Granny's funeral almost two years earlier. In a way, he was glad nobody had painted the house. It felt good to know some things didn't change.

He also knew what he would find inside—that wouldn't have changed either. He could feel the tension in his gut already.

He sighed. *Come on, Sweeney. It's a wedding. It's just two days with your family, not Ranger school.* At least he'd get to catch up with some old friends from the neighborhood who would doubtless be at the reception. Free food was free food, after all.

His leather jacket creaked as he set the sleek muscle-bike on its kickstand and headed inside.

The wooden screen door banged shut as he stepped across the

threshold. The sound and musty smell of the entryway brought back a slew of memories from his childhood, like when he and Stuart killed a copperhead snake with their slingshots and carried it inside to show Granny. The poor woman had screamed like she'd been electrocuted. The screen door had banged hard that day as she chased the two of them back outside. Sweeney grinned at the memory while the clomp of his logger's boots proclaimed his arrival.

The first person he saw was his father, sitting in an easy chair in the living room, reading the *Troy Messenger*. Something else that hadn't changed much in two decades.

Lawrence Sweeney looked up from his reading and grimaced at him. "Son, you look like a Hells Angel."

And so it begins. "Nice to see you too, Dad."

His mother came out of the kitchen, wiping her hands on her apron. "Leave him alone, Lawrence," she snapped. Then her frown turned on Sweeney. "You're late, Bobby. Now get over here and give me a hug."

"Yes ma'am." Sweeney walked over and wrapped his arms around the wiry woman. "Hello, Momma."

After a few seconds, she pulled back, a scowl still firmly in place on her features. "Now sit down and tell us what've you've been doing. It must be very important since you haven't had time to call or write."

Great. Guilt appetizers. Mom's specialty. Sweeney shrugged. "Been traveling a lot."

"Well, don't they have phones in these places? The least you could do is call." She turned and made for the kitchen without waiting for an answer, muttering like she always did. Something about a respectable job.

At that moment two identical, brown-headed tornadoes ran around the corner and ambushed him, each one taking a leg and shouting, "Uncle Bobby!"

Laughing, he noogied each of his twin nine-year-old nephews on their buzz-cut heads. "Bubba and Moose! Who stole your hair? You look like basic trainees!"

"We're gonna be Navy Ninjas!" Bubba said.

Sweeney looked down at them, grinning. "You don't wanna do that! All the Navy Ninjas get to do is peel potatoes. You want to be Army Rangers!"

The boys looked at Sweeney with wide eyes. "Really?"

"Yep."

"Army Rangers! Yeah!" The boys bolted out the front door, making machine-gun sounds.

"Don't encourage them, Robert!" his mother barked from the kitchen. "Lawrence, tell your son not to talk to them that way!"

His father looked up from his easy chair. "You heard Mother. All we need is to turn them into a couple of warmongers!"

Sweeney was formulating a sarcastic comeback when another voice interrupted from the hall. "Aw, Dad, it's okay. They'll want to be something else by next week anyway."

Sweeney turned to see Stuart grinning at him. His older brother was taller than his own five-foot-ten-inch frame and had always been skinnier, except he'd gotten sort of pudgy since the last time Bobby saw him. Stuart gave him a manly hug. "Hey, bro. Saw you come in. That's a nice bike."

"Thanks, Stu. How's the accounting business?"

Stuart sucked in a breath and ran a hand through prematurely thinning hair. "Slowing down now that tax season is over. But with all the craziness we've seen in the market, my business has exploded in the last six months."

Sweeney chuckled under his breath. "Yeah. Mine too. Where's Darrell?"

"Down at the chapel, going over the wedding music for the tenth time. Momma says supper will be ready in an hour." He winked at Sweeney, lowering his voice. "So you know they'll be home by then, or they'll hear about it."

Sweeney grunted. "I'm sure. Been hunting lately?"

"Nah, I don't get to do that sort of thing very much now that we've moved to Birmingham."

"I got a new pistol. Wanna go shoot it?"

Stuart's eyes lit up, then flicked toward their father, who was buried back in his newspaper. "I'd love to."

"Great." Sweeney turned toward the door. "Let's go practice our warmongering skills."

Lawrence pretended not to hear, but Sweeney knew he had. The screen door banged behind them as they went outside.

"He didn't mean it like that, you know," Stuart said.

Sweeney waved him off. "Yeah, whatever. I quit caring a long time ago. You ever hear anything from Shane Patterson? I haven't seen him since my first leave after basic training."

Stuart smiled, shaking his head. "I hear he's still in town. Works down at Napa Auto Parts, I think. We were holy terrors, the three of us, weren't we? You remember the time we snuck onto that golf course and almost got arrested?"

"Yeah. We thought Momma was going to be mad when we came home all muddy from hiding in that storm drain."

"Ha! I'll never forget the look on your face when Deputy Harris showed up at our house."

"She must have worn out a half-dozen wooden spoons on our backsides after he left." Sweeney walked to the motorcycle and pulled a pistol case from his bag. "I bet Shane will be there at the wedding. Anyway, here's my new Glock 37." He opened it and handed the composite black handgun to his brother, grip first.

Stuart let out a whistle. "Nice. Nine millimeter?"

"Forty-five."

"Wow. Is this a laser sight?"

"Sure is."

"Bet those come in handy."

Sweeney nodded. "I can honestly say one of these saved my life." *Though not in the way you might think.* Images of Panama clouded his mind for a split second.

"Wow," Stuart said. "Guess you can't talk about it, huh?"

Sweeney grinned as he retrieved a box of ammo from another pocket of his bag. "Not unless you agree to have your mouth surgically removed."

The two walked down the path that led to a mostly dry creek bed sheltered by pulp pines. After a moment, Stuart said, "I'd hate to have to keep everything a secret all the time. Especially if I was doing exciting things like you are."

A shrug lifted Sweeney's shoulders. "No sense talking about it. Most people couldn't understand anyway."

"Don't you have a chaplain or something?"

"No."

"Must be hard."

"What?"

"Not being able to talk to anyone. I mean, you, me, and Shane—we used to talk about everything."

Stuart had a point. The three of them had been inseparable as kids, spending hundreds of hours stalking squirrels, and anything else with fur, along this very creek bed. They never kept secrets from one another nor wanted to do so. But these days, he didn't feel like talking, most of the time anyway. Sweeney just shrugged again and jumped down into the creek bed.

"So, any women in your life?" Stuart handed Sweeney the pistol and jumped down himself.

The image of a certain female CIA officer flashed in Sweeney's mind. *Whoa. Where did that come from?*

He shook his head. "Not really. I haven't been on the same continent long enough to meet anybody since 9/11. Besides, if I spend money on girls, my Harley gets jealous."

His brother laughed, and the sound brought back happy memories. Sweeney wrestled a log up against a sandy bank. He found a few sticks and an old milk jug and propped them up on it, then set about loading the pistol's ten-round magazine.

He straightened and looked at Stuart. "So what's this girl like that our kid brother roped into marrying him?"

Stuart pursed his lips as they walked back thirty yards or so from the log. "Met her at Bible school, I guess. Not that long ago. She's a quiet little thing—Darrell seems to think she'll make a fine preacher's wife."

"God help her," Sweeney grumbled.

"What do you mean by that?"

"Ha! You grew up in the same house I did. Have you forgotten what that was like?" Sweeney slapped the magazine into the butt of the pistol and racked the slide.

Stuart looked a little sad. "Sure, I remember." He looked up at Sweeney. "But having kids of my own has made me realize that even when you do your best, sometimes things still get crooked. Dad and Momma weren't perfect, but we knew they loved us."

Something that had been simmering under the surface of Sweeney's emotions suddenly hit a rolling boil. "Sure, they loved us. Loved us enough to beat the stuffing out of us whenever we forgot to close the screen door. Loved us so much they never let us go to a movie or listen to any of that *eeevil* country music. Loved us so much that to this day I can't drive by a church without hearing Reverend Lawrence Sweeney pounding the pulpit!"

He turned and rapid-fired ten shots that made the plastic milk jug dance an Irish jig.

As the handgun's thunder echoed away through the pines, Sweeney dropped the gun to his side and turned back to face his brother. "Yeah. That's love, all right."

Stuart held both hands up like he was surrendering. "Okay, okay. You have a point. But I finally realized that being mad at our folks for the way they raised us wouldn't make my life any better. And despite Dad's legalism, now I know that there's a whole lot more to the Bible than the Ten Commandments. At some point you just have to get over it."

"I am over it." Sweeney dropped the magazine and inserted a fresh one in one quick motion. He then passed the gun to Stuart. "Now shut up and shoot."

Forty minutes later the two of them were back indoors, seated around Granddad's old chestnut table, Bobby holding hands with his mother on one side and his burr-headed nephew Moose on the other. Seated across from him were his thin, bookish little brother Darrell, with fiancée in tow; his father; and Stu and his family. Grandpa sat at the head of the table, his one remaining tuft of hair smoothed neatly over a shiny white pate that rarely saw anything but the inside of the old man's straw hat.

Grandpa spoke up, his voice shakier than Sweeney remembered it. "Let us bless God for His provision and thank Him for tomorrow's ceremony of holy matrimony between Darrell and his lovely bride."

They bowed their heads while his voice rose in volume and intensity.

"Our Heavenly Father, we thank Thee this day for our many blessings and pray Your forgiveness for the many ways in which we have sinned against Thee."

With his eyes closed, Sweeney was transported back to the front row of the Land of Beulah Independent Fundamental Baptist Church, listening to his father on a gorgeous Sunday morning when all the lucky fourteen-year-olds were outside playing baseball or hunting rabbits or doing anything besides sitting in that stifling country service.

As Pastor Lawrence T. Sweeney droned on in his prayers, he would occasionally forget that he was supposed to be talking to God and would go back to preaching—proclaiming dire warnings about the unspeakable horrors that awaited sinners who did despicable things like play cards, listen to "worldly" music, and have lustful thoughts.

And as the prayers/sermons extended in his memory, young Bobby Sweeney started thinking that if playing cards was all it took to be excluded from heaven, he didn't stand a chance. Maybe nobody else knew the images that sometimes flashed upon his mind when he thought of some of the girls at school. Maybe nobody but Stuart knew about the pack of cigarettes hidden out behind the barn. But surely God knew.

Granddad finished his prayer, one that had mercifully been shorter than usual, and Sweeney jumped at the chance to chase the painful memories from his mind by reaching for Momma Sweeney's chicken-fried steak and biscuits.

"Hey," Moose cried, pointing at Sweeney's tricep. "What's that funny writing on your arm say?"

Sweeney suddenly wished he had worn long sleeves. "Uh, that's Arabic writing. It says, 'Infidel.'"

"What's a infidel?" Bubba asked, his mouth full of mashed potatoes.

"It's a—"

"The Bible says tattoos are a sign of spiritual slavery," Darrell cut in.

Sweeney cast him a sideways glance. "Yeah. Or maybe they just look cool."

"You boys stop your fussin'." Momma's scowl was etched in stone. "You're setting a bad example for the little ones. Isn't that right, Lawrence?"

Sweeney's father looked up from his chicken-fried steak. "Er, yes, dear. It's a bad example."

Grandpa chimed in. "'Ye shall not make any cuttings in your flesh for the dead, nor print any marks upon you: I am the LORD.'"

"Leviticus nineteen twenty-eight," Darrell mumbled before stuffing a forkful of green beans in his mouth.

Sweeney sighed, willing himself not to respond. *It won't do any good.* Instead, he changed the subject. "So…anybody know if the Pattersons will be there tomorrow?"

Momma reached for a biscuit. "Heavens, no. We don't want nothin' to do with their kind."

Sweeney was confused. "*Their* kind? The Pattersons have been family friends since before I was born! Dad, you and Mr. P. have been hunting together since high school! What do you mean you want nothing to do with them?"

Stuart wiped his mouth with a napkin. "I think it's because they left the church."

Lawrence got a sheepish expression, shooting a glance at his wife before speaking. He cleared his throat. "Well, I wouldn't say—"

"That's exactly right," Sweeney's mother said. "They ran off and joined that new church on the edge of town. Calls itself 'nondenominational.'" She spit the last word out like it was made of sewer sludge.

Grandpa raised his fork. "'For the time will come when they will not endure sound doctrine; but after their own lusts shall they heap to themselves teachers, having itching ears.'"

Darrell nodded. "Second Timothy, chapter four."

Sweeney couldn't believe what he was hearing. "So you didn't invite them to the wedding because they changed churches?"

Darrell looked at him as if he was a slow child. "We wouldn't want *sinners* at our holy matrimony, now, would we?"

Sweeney blinked, then threw his napkin on his plate. He stood up. "Well, I suppose that leaves me out too."

Before anyone could reply, he grabbed his coat and stomped out the door.

When the screen banged shut this time, no happy memories came with it.

———

A six-paneled teak door swung shut behind Michael Lafontaine as he entered his hotel penthouse. He set his briefcase down with a sigh, then stopped breathing altogether when he heard a *thump* come from the direction of the bedroom.

For a second, he wished he was carrying a pistol, but that was something James Bond did when he was in a foreign country posing as an American businessman. Lafontaine actually *was* in a foreign country as an American businessman, and he hadn't carried a gun in decades.

He looked around for something with which to defend himself, but before he could find anything, a stooped old man emerged from the bedroom, pushing a small handcart.

The man looked up in surprise. "Oh, very sorry to be disturbing you, sir." The man's white turban and smock and tapered gray beard made him look like a genie, but the singsong accent made it clear he was from India. Michael guessed him to be a Sikh. "I am just to be arranging your bedroom for the night. I am told you will be leaving soon. I trust your stay has been satisfactory?"

"Yes, of course. Thank you." Lafontaine smiled, shrugging off his initial surprise. "Do you think you could ask the kitchen to send up a caesar salad and some coffee?"

"As you wish."

The servant was thorough and polite to a fault, traits that were hard to come by anymore. He pulled the door open and held it for the old man, retrieving a folded ten-dollar bill from a money clip in his pocket. He enjoyed the glint in the man's eye when he handed it over. "Your English is quite good. Tell me your name, sir."

"I am Nagar Singh," the man said. "If I can ever be of service again, please feel free to ask for me by name."

"I just might do that," Lafontaine said. He had been looking for a new household manager, though that might be more than the old man had in mind. He committed the name to memory nonetheless as Singh shuffled out.

When the door closed behind him, Lafontaine tugged off his suit coat and hung it in the closet by the door. He might be a billionaire, but he still wasn't the kind of man who would toss an eight-hundred-dollar Darren Beaman suit coat on the couch.

People thought that money made everything easy, but that wasn't his experience. Money was a multiplier—and it multiplied problems as surely as it multiplied possibilities, and both took time and effort to manage. The real trick was to turn the first into the second.

Which brought him back to the purpose of this trip. A recent chain of events had threatened to interfere with his plans, but with quick and decisive action, he had turned the problem on its head.

He loosened his tie and picked up the television remote. The flat screen on the wall flashed to life, and he flipped channels until he got to BBC News—the first station he found in English.

"...*made arrests during yesterday's demonstrations in London's financial district*," the serious-looking blond anchorwoman was saying, "*where several thousand Arabs were marching to protest comments made recently in a speech by Fenton Abrams, president and CEO of Barclays Bank in London. In the speech, Abrams referred to radical Islam as a 'barbaric belief system that is costing the British people billions of pounds a year.' In the ensuing riots, several cars were overturned and burned, and shop windows were broken before police moved in.*"

Lafontaine scowled at the television. *Unbelievable. These people have no sense of irony.*

The anchorwoman continued, her sultry voice making the mayhem sound like an ad for cologne or makeup. "*The United States Congress was back in session yesterday after their spring recess, debating a resolution to stop using the term 'terrorist,' as many believe it to be too divisive.*"

Idiots. Lafontaine fought the urge to hurl the remote at the screen. He was so tired of pansy politicians with fewer guts than a troop of Brownies on their first campout. Since when did defending freedom become synonymous with appeasing those who would destroy it? He'd recently come to the realization that no matter how much money he waved in front of these drooling morons, one simply couldn't buy backbone. And it made him physically ill.

There had to be another way.

He'd tried everything short of lighting himself on fire to convince the namby-pamby politicos to live up to their oath to defend the

United States, and while he got lots of pasted-on smiles and promises over lunches that cost more than his first car, he had yet to see one senator or congressman dare to risk offending those who were, by their nature, perpetually offended.

Not one politician or general, especially in the current administration, had the stones to publicly advocate the kind of take-no-prisoners stance against terror that would be required to chase the jihadis back into their caves for good. Instead, the Pentagon brass and politicians insisted on endless investigations into whether our troops were being gentle enough with the savages who were out to murder them. To Lafontaine, that kind of behavior wasn't just cowardly, it was treasonous.

The time had come to hit these craven critics where it hurt—in their ratings. Normally, Michael despised the press. But maybe it was time to make use of the fourth estate, to get more public in his calls for a change in the status quo.

He reached down and fished his mobile phone from the pocket on his coat. As much as he preferred to work behind the scenes, the time had come to step onto the stage. Perhaps he would even run for office himself.

A knock at the door jolted him away from his plans. *Mr. Singh must have forgotten something.* He turned and moved to the peephole. A young man stood in the hallway, shifting from one foot to the other.

Lafontaine was not used to uninvited guests. *This had better be important.* He swung the door open.

The boy was perhaps in his late teens, with black hair that was carefully combed as if he was on his way to school. The boy's striking blue eyes went wide, and he cleared his throat. "Colonel Lafontaine?"

"I am. What can I do for you, son?"

The boy seemed to falter a bit, as if he suddenly wished to be somewhere else. "Sir." He swallowed hard. "I am sorry to bother you. But would you happen to remember a woman named Mia Saldana?"

The name was like a Taser to the chest, and Lafontaine flinched, momentarily overwhelmed by the memory of the raven-haired beauty he couldn't have forgotten if he tried. Something like hope sprouted in him.

"I did know that name once. But I have not spoken with Miss Saldana in a very long time. Do you know where she is?"

The boy shoved his hands in his pockets and dropped his gaze. "Yes. I know where she is. I…I am her son."

Her son? Lafontaine knew he shouldn't have been surprised by the news that Mia had gone on to have children, but the shock of her grown child standing in front of him like this was almost too much to bear. In his mind, she was still the same beautiful young woman he had fallen in love with two decades earlier.

He looked at the boy and weighed his words carefully. "It is nice to meet you. I have often wondered where your mother went after I lost touch with her. I would be delighted to see her again."

The boy's expression fell further. "I am afraid that is not possible." His lip began to tremble. "My…mother passed away in San José, Costa Rica, three months ago."

The hope that had taken root in Michael Lafontaine's heart exploded like a pipe bomb, tearing open a very old wound. He suddenly needed to sit down. He put a hand on the boy's shoulder. "Come in, young man. Tell me your name."

The teen looked up at him with tears on his face.

"My name...is Michael."

———

JSOC Headquarters, Fort Bragg, North Carolina

Sweeney's eyes bugged out the second he walked into the cherry-paneled conference room and saw her.

"Whoa! What happened to your hair?"

Even with her hair cut *way* short, Mary Walker was still the best-looking CIA officer—or any other kind of officer—he'd ever seen. Despite being dressed in an Army multicam uniform that was anything but form fitting, she looked like she ought to be on a calendar someplace. For the moment, however, she was seated at the head of the conference table, furiously scribbling on a yellow legal pad.

She didn't even look up from her notes. "Thanks for noticing, Sergeant Sweeney. It's called a pixie cut. Have a seat."

John "Coop" Cooper was already there, sitting at the other end of the table with his arms crossed. "You sure have a way with the ladies, Bobby. I already asked her about it." His square jaw twisted into a grin. "She says she decided the shorter 'do would be easier to take care of."

Sweeney back-pedaled. "It's great. Ah...I mean, I like it." He grabbed a folder off the table and started fanning himself. "Wooh. It's hotter than Alabama in August in here. What gives?"

Mary smirked and threw a glance his way. "The air conditioner's down." She stood and picked up a stack of photos, passing them to John. "Don't worry, Staff Sergeant Baldwin back there is going to get it fixed, right?" She nodded toward the back of the room where Frank Baldwin had his head stuck inside the closet in the corner of the room. Sweeney hadn't seen Frank since the jump.

"Ow! I think I found the problem," came Frank's muffled reply.

A smirk crossed Sweeney's face. "Should we call the paramedics now or wait until he electrocutes himself?"

John huffed. "If he's as good with air conditioners as he is with e-bombs, we've got nothing to worry about."

"I heard that," Baldwin shouted from inside the closet.

Rip Rubio burst into the room, tugging at the front of his multicam uniform and grimacing. "Man, *ese,* whose idea was it to wear the salad suits? It's hot!"

"You mean nobody told you?" Mary chided. "The reason we're here is because the secretary of defense has asked for a briefing on the ITEB issue. And you can bet that he won't be alone for the meeting. The uniforms will present a positive image."

John grunted. "Wonderful. Who else will be there?"

Mary waved a hand in mock nonchalance. "What, besides my boss? Let's see, most likely we'll be looking at representatives from the NSC, DIA, FBI, DHS, NCTC, and the State Department."

"Yeesh," Sweeney groused. "It's like an explosion in a letter factory. If I'd known we were having a dog and pony show, I'd have brought my dog Bubba back from leave with me."

"I'm sure he would have been a hit with the SecDef, Sergeant Sweeney, but since he's not here, why don't you pass these out." Mary slapped a stack of folders down in front of him.

"Yes ma'am." Sweeney said, laying the sarcasm on thick.

Doc Kelly, the team's African American medic, took the folders from Sweeney and passed them on.

As Sweeney went back to his chair, he thought about the first time he'd met Mary. Once he'd recovered from the shock of the team—ODA 374, also known as Task Force Valor—being suddenly attached to the CIA, he had been angry about having been put under the command of a woman. But several months into this mission, he now had to admit Mary, call sign Phoenix, had proven her mettle, at least when it came to running interference for them in the rear so they could get the mission accomplished. So if he still hated having a woman in charge, this one was growing on him. And those full terra-cotta lips did nothing to stop it, dadgummit.

Major Louis Williams strode through the door just as the air conditioner hummed to life. A small cheer went up from among the assembled group. The linebacker-sized commander stopped and looked at them in confusion, which made Sweeney forget that he was irked, and he started laughing.

"What'd I do?" the major said, looking around.

"Frank fixed the air conditioner," John said, grinning.

"Praise the Lord," Rip added.

Now Sweeney was peeved again. Two weeks ago in Panama, something had turned Rip from a fun-loving ladies' man into something closer to a Sunday morning televangelist. It wasn't a good change.

The major just shrugged. "Well, if you think that's great, wait until you see who I brought with me." He turned and opened the door again. "Come on, son."

A clean-shaven, brown-haired giant hobbled through the door, wearing an Army PT uniform and sporting a sheepish smile.

"Buzz!" The team members jumped to their feet and crowded around one of Sweeney's best friends in the world, Sergeant First Class Henry Hogan. They hadn't seen Buzz walking since the day two weeks earlier when the weapons sergeant had taken a bullet during a reconnaissance mission on a remote island off the coast of Panama.

"When'd you get out of the hospital?" John asked, shaking Buzz's hand.

"Jus' now," Buzz drawled in his Texas accent. "'Bout a week later'n I woulda liked."

The major laughed. "Nurses got tired of his whining."

Rip slapped Buzz on the back. "I've been praying for you, bro. How's the leg?"

Sweeney rolled his eyes. *Oh, for the love of Mike!*

Buzz shot him an unsure look, then answered, "Uh, pretty good, I reckon. Got some tingling in my foot. The docs say I've got some circulation problems still, so they're sending me home on convalescent leave for a coupla weeks."

Sweeney grinned. "Slacker." Which was his way of saying, *You deserve the rest.*

Buzz smiled back. "You bet, buddy. No catfish is gonna be safe when I get home."

Frank joined the group, wiping his greasy hands on a rag. "Almost didn't recognize you without your beard."

"Yeah, got some flack about it by the colonel running the hospital. I don't think he likes Special-Ops guys much."

"Are you staying for the briefing, Sergeant Hogan?" Mary still stood at the head of the faux-cherry table with her stack of papers. "You're welcome to."

"No ma'am. Sergeant Daly's waitin' for me outside with his car. He's taking me to the airport. I just wanted to stop by before I go. I sure hate to leave before this ITEB mission is wrapped up."

The major waved his hand. "Don't worry, Buzz. We won't go winning the war on terror without you, we promise. Now go get yourself better."

Buzz nodded. "Thanks, Lou." He turned to the others. "You men be safe."

When Buzz left, everyone migrated back to the conference table and sat down.

Sweeney plopped into the seat next to Frank and punched him in the arm. "Good goin' on the AC, sport."

"Were you born annoying, or are all southerners that way?" Frank said.

"You're just jealous," Sweeney retorted.

"That's enough, you two," the major said. "The National Counterterrorism Center will be calling any minute, and I want y'all briefed first so you don't look like a bunch of fuzzy-headed yahoos when they call."

Mary pushed a loose strand of hair behind one ear and consulted her notes. "All right, here's where we stand. The bottle you all recovered from the island two weeks ago was, in fact, our liquid explosive. We still have no idea how it appeared in that jungle clearing, but it doesn't really matter at this point. Our tests show the explosive is, as we thought, a colorless chemical compound that reacts explosively with oxygen. Our labs have been working on the sample to try to determine its origin, but that's an uphill battle."

"Didn't they get anything from the lab we found?" Rip said.

"You'll recall that there wasn't much left when we were done with it," Mary replied coolly.

Sweeney shook his head. *I'd rather not think about it.* That old World War II bunker-turned-explosives-lab in Panama had almost become a tomb for Mary, Rip, and himself.

"What about the two college guys who were hostages on the island?" Frank asked. "Did they ever get found?"

"I can answer that," Rip said. "Fernanda told me the Panamanian police found her cousin and his friend tied up in the house of some *tipo* on the mainland who was working with the pirates—ferrying supplies to them on the island. I guess the guys were pretty hungry and beat up, but they'll be okay."

"Fernanda's the young lady you found on the island?" Major Williams asked.

"Roger that," John replied. "Rip's been having a long-distance love affair with her since we got back."

"It's not like that, man." Rip looked irritated. "We're just friends."

"Sure you are." Sweeney laughed. "You don't want to cheat on all your other girlfriends, right?"

The others chuckled, but Rip's response surprised him. Instead of the wink-and-nod routine, or even the bristling anger of a former gangbanger, Rip just pursed his lips and spoke quietly. "You'll see, *ese.* I ain't like that anymore."

Sweeney shook his head. *Whatever.* Rip was no fun.

Mary cleared her throat. "Anyway, one thing we did get from the bunker was that set of digital photographs that John brought out. From them, we've identified the containers that we believe held the ITEB in its original, diluted state."

"Great!" John said.

"Not exactly. Judging by the number of containers, it appears that a large amount of ITEB was distilled and bottled there. Based on what we've found so far, it appears that there is quite a bit left to be found."

"Not great," John said, frowning.

Just then the phone on the conference table rang.

Mary snatched up the receiver. "Phoenix." She listened for a moment. "Yes sir. Okay." She grabbed a remote control off the table and pointed it at the large flat-panel plasma display on the wall, switching channels until the image of another conference room appeared.

To Sweeney, the dozen serious-looking older men in suits assembled around the table reminded him of one of the deacons' meetings he'd had to endure as a kid. He recognized Secretary of Defense Nelson Brimmer—largely because the man's scowling photo was part of the chain of command display at the chow hall. He had no idea who the men around the SecDef were, however.

Here we go. Bring out the ponies!

A clean-shaven, bespectacled man, whose double chin seemed out of place on his gaunt frame, arose on the screen and addressed Sweeney's team. "Gentlemen, I'm Steven Stark, deputy director of the National Clandestine Service." He turned to the men around the table in a room three hundred miles away from Fort Bragg, where Sweeney and his team were seated, and gestured toward the monitor. "And may I present Task Force Valor. Led here by one of our fine paramilitary ops officers, Mary Walker, code name Phoenix."

Sweeney decided the deputy director would look really funny in a clown suit. The man's jowls jiggled as he continued speaking. "Phoenix, may I introduce you to Secretary of Defense Nelson Brimmer." He indicated a dour-looking man in a rumpled gray suit sitting at the end of the table.

Mary smiled at the television on the wall. "Thank you, sir. Nice to meet you, Mr. Secretary."

The hard-faced man nodded. "Yes, of course. Let's get on with it, shall we? Miss…" The SecDef consulted his notes. "Walker. What progress has your team made recently on the problem of this 'liquid explosive'?"

Sweeney leaned over to Mary. "Break a leg," he whispered.

She stabbed him with a glare, then smiled at the screen. "Thank you, sir. As you may know, two months ago a hotel was blown up in Beirut using an exotic liquid explosive known as ITEB, which stands for Iso-Triethyl Borane. This compound is used in all sorts of applications in industry, from pharmaceuticals to microchip fabrication, but it's always diluted with another chemical that keeps it from exploding on contact with air."

The SecDef waved a hand to hurry things along. "Yes, yes. And you and your team thwarted the terrorists who were planning to use it. I've been briefed on that already. What did you find in Panama last month?"

Mary swallowed but held her composure. "Mr. Secretary, the lab we found in Panama was processing the diluted chemical into its raw, pyrophoric form, then sealing it in bottles."

The SecDef grimaced and looked at her over his bifocals. "And how many of these bottles were made?"

"The intelligence we have gathered indicates there were close to three hundred."

"And how many have you recovered, Agent Walker?"

Sweeney watched Mary's confidence start to crack. "We have recovered…one bottle, sir."

The SecDef took off his bifocals and stared hard at her from the screen. "You mean in over two months of operations, your team has solved one-three-hundredth of the problem!"

Major Williams spoke up. "Mr. Secretary, I'm Major Lou Williams, the unit commander. Task Force Valor has done a great job so far. No one could've done better. Keep in mind that much of the ITEB was destroyed in the process of tracking it down. So that part is off the market."

"How much?"

Williams punted to Mary with a look.

She checked her notes. "We believe approximately two hundred bottles are accounted for so far, Mr. Secretary."

"So where is the rest of it?"

"We're still working on that, sir."

The SecDef tapped his notes. "Then it is possible that this explosive could be making its way across our borders as we speak, and could be used to kill U.S. citizens at any moment." It was a statement, not a question.

Beads of sweat were evident on Deputy Director Stark's round bald head, even on the television. He sputtered a reply. "Mr. Secretary, I can assure you that intercepting the remaining cargo is our top priority."

The glowering SecDef shook his head. "I'll agree that is very important, Steve, because as I'm sure you are aware, the current technology in use at our borders is not capable of detecting this compound. That means it would be a simple exercise to drive it onto our soil. The president will not take kindly to that sort of thing. But what if there's a factory somewhere that is cranking this stuff out by the gross? Thirty days from now we could be looking at a problem that's a hundred times larger. No, we've got to find the source."

The SecDef turned his attention back to Mary. "Agent Walker, I suggest that you and your men bring every resource at your disposal to bear to track down the source of this compound immediately to keep any more from being manufactured." He stood and dropped the handouts on the table. "Until you've accomplished that, I consider Task Force Valor a failure. Now if you'll excuse me, I have to brief the president." The SecDef turned and left the room. Several of the others followed him out.

Steven Stark's jowly face filled the screen once again, a few shades paler than it had been before. "You heard the secretary," he hissed. "I want you to make finding the source of the ITEB top priority. I will be in touch."

Mary's face was almost as red as her hair. "Yes sir."

The screen went black.

Sweeney decided he didn't really like the SecDef very much.

3

Parishev, Ukraine, Inside the Dead Zone

BIRDS FLITTED AMONG mature fruit trees laden with apples, pears, and plums. Except for their chirping, the entire village was as quiet as death. The fruit would be full and almost perfectly ripe in another few months, but no one was there to harvest it, or ever would be again.

A wooden cart approached. It was pulled by a bony black gelding that plodded along with its head down. The rasp of the wagon's wheels and jingling of the reins intruded on the stillness, and the hunched form of an old man sitting in the cart did little to add life to the scene.

Alexi Babichev's creaky joints protested as he pulled the stubborn horse to a stop. "No, Tupy, we're not going back home just yet. I want to pick some flowers for Mother."

The little horse grumbled but turned to the tug of the reins, pulling the wooden wagon toward the small church at the end of the village instead of down the path that led home.

Alexi clucked his tongue at the stubborn animal. "Oh, you're just being a *maliatko* because it's your birthday. But I know where there are some beautiful roses that will make *Baba* very happy."

The horse seemed to accept that his supper would be delayed and plodded off toward the church. Alexi dropped the reins to his lap and retrieved a flask from his hip pocket, letting his attention wander past the overgrown trees that lined the unkempt path, all that was left of the once-tidy stone-chipped lane that ran through the center of Parishev. It had never been a busy place, even before the accident, but now it was so lonely even the spirits stayed away.

"You weren't here then, Tupy. All the people left after the great fire. Nineteen eighty-six. I was much younger then…" Alexi ran his tongue over the gums where his teeth had been. They'd all fallen out in the years since the accident. Then, as now, he lived with his mother, raising vegetables on the half-acre plot behind their tiny clapboard house on the edge of the village.

"Almost everyone back then worked at the plant. But not me. I was perfectly content with the life of a farmer." He spit on the ground. "Ech. No, you wouldn't have gotten me to work at the reactor, even though the pay was better. I'd much rather live with manure under my fingernails than with the rotten stink of Chernobyl."

The sound of a klaxon drifted through the empty pines, echoing off the abandoned and derelict homes that made up the village. Alexi grimaced at the sound. "Fifteen minutes, Tupy. That's all they work now. Before, they only changed shift four times a day. Now, it's every fifteen minutes. Did I tell you the story before?"

If the horse had heard it before, he didn't complain about hearing it again.

"I remember the night it happened. It was springtime—I had a cow that was going to give birth. I was sleeping in the shed with her when the siren went off in the middle of the night. It woke me up." He waved the flask at the bright afternoon sky, his hoarse voice growing quieter. "I looked out—and there was a light, as if from a fire, only blue. It was shining from beyond the trees, back there." He motioned with his pipe.

The horse stopped walking, which caused Alexi to look up. They'd come to the church. "Ah, good boy." He stepped off the cart and moved toward a large unkempt rose bush filled with blossoms. "The soldiers came the following morning," he continued, speaking louder so the horse could hear. "Told us to pack up and get on buses. I told them I had to go back to get Mother first…"

He stopped and stared for a moment, watching the memory replay in his mind. When he continued, his voice had grown quiet. "But they wouldn't let me. They promised they'd bring her on the next bus." He spat again.

"The city is a horrible place, Tupy. I tell you, the months I spent there were the worst days of my life. I went out every day from dawn until dusk looking for Mother. I wanted to go back home, but the thought of Mother by herself in Kyiv made me stay. But I couldn't find her. Finally, when I could have no more of it, I used every kopeck in my survivor's allowance to buy a ticket on a train to Chernihiv. From there I walked home. It took two days."

Alexi cut two of the largest roses with his pocketknife. "My father gave me this knife the year before he died, when I was seventeen." He pointed with the open blade of the knife. "That's his grave over there. He was a good man, Tupy. You would have liked him."

Thunder rumbled in the distance. Tupy's tail swatted flies. Alexi stood for a moment, saying nothing, looking at his father's grave. He sighed and bent to light his pipe. It had also belonged to his father. He turned back to the horse. Yes, at least he had Tupy. And Mother.

"We'd better get home before it rains." He climbed aboard the cart. "Anyway, when I arrived back in Parishev, everything was overgrown like it is now. Nobody else came back. But Mother was here. She'd never left."

A little laugh escaped his lips. "Heh! She tricked them, she did. She's a clever woman. And stubborn too. We had regulators show up once from the government—they told us it wasn't safe and that we should leave." He gave a disgusted puff and pointed the stem of his pipe at the horse. "I told them if they thought Parishev was dangerous, they should see Kyiv. They've never been back." Alexi's laugh turned into a wheezing cough. The air was getting thick.

He turned the cart around, and as he did, he noticed a rusty silver sedan parked behind the church. Which was odd, since there had never been a car parked there before.

"Stop, Tupy. What's this?" The horse stopped, and Alexi climbed down from the cart once again. "Wait here, friend. I'm going to see what this is about."

Vandals! Will they never give up?

Alexi muttered under his breath as he marched up the stairs to the church. Looters had long since stripped the building of anything of value—but that didn't stop others from coming now and then, hoping to find something that had been missed.

A peal of thunder shook the heavy wooden door as he pulled it open. Inside, he could smell the musty air of the building where he himself had been christened. Dust swirled in a pale shaft of sunlight that pierced the room from a broken window high above. Before long, the storm clouds would block the sun entirely.

But the church wasn't empty, as it had been for years. Now there were three wooden crates piled in one corner. He couldn't make out the stenciled writing on them, but their flat green color made them appear military in origin.

Something isn't right. Alexi took a step into the church to get a closer look at the crates. As he did, a black blur came from his left and struck him in the side of the head. He cried out as he fell to his knees, dropping the pipe.

Alexi clutched his throbbing head and turned to look at his attacker. It was a skinny boy, a wide-eyed teenager with a mop of greasy black hair, clutching a wicked-looking rifle like the ones the guards at the plant used to carry. The boy was breathing hard, hands shaking as he clutched the weapon.

"Now why would you hit an old man?" Alexi asked.

The boy looked past him, toward the rear door near the vestry. "Maxim! *Giarga'oexu!*"

Alexi's head was sticky with blood. He had never heard the language this boy was speaking. "Listen," he pleaded, "there is nothing here worth taking. Everything was stolen long ago."

"*Toé!*" the boy shouted. He raised the rifle again, and this time when the butt came down, Alexi's world went black.

Fort Bragg, North Carolina

Mary arranged her notes and tried not to look as impatient as she felt as the team took their seats around the conference table. She had a plane to catch in a few hours and hadn't packed so much as a toothbrush yet. Less than three hours had passed since they'd been declared a failure by the secretary of defense.

To their credit, all the joking was gone. Task Force Valor was all business. "What's the plan, Phoenix?" John Cooper asked.

Mary was still stinging from the SecDef's rebuke. She consulted her notes. "Okay. The markings on the large metal cylinders you photographed in the lab in Panama show that the original chemical was of Soviet origin. That gives us a starting point. We have a very good network of agents in some of the former Soviet republics, and they've been gathering intel on the subject for the last couple weeks."

She hit a button on her laptop, and a map flashed on to the screen at the far end of the table. The team pivoted in their chairs to take a better look.

"We've learned that the Soviets were at one time experimenting with ITEB as an additive for rocket fuel. The lab was in Ukraine. Our agents there have been tracking down leads, and they believe they have something of interest. Remember that Ukraine was a major manufacturer of military hardware during the Soviet era. After the Communist government imploded, much of that hardware went up for sale on the black market. We believe someone got hold of the stockpile of Russian ITEB and is peddling it to arms dealers around the globe."

"Can't have that, now," Sweeney said.

"No, we can't," Mary said. "John, Rubio, and Sweeney—you are going to Ukraine to do reconnaissance and try to find the lab where the chemical was being produced. You're to see if any more exists there."

"Hey, what about the rest of us?" Doc Kelly asked. "Why are we getting cut out of the deal?"

Mary's voice dropped a notch. "Let me explain something, men. This mission is not a military one. We won't need the kind of firepower that's been required in the past. Ukraine is on good terms with the U.S. government. But, due to the urgency of the situation, we will be going in without their consent. Every extra person only increases the likelihood that the mission will be compromised."

"Not only that," Major Williams said, "but we want to have at least some of the team available in case ITEB shows up anyplace else."

Rip raised his hand. "Uh, if the Ukrainians are friendly, why not just ask them to check this stuff out? Why go over there at all?"

Mary nodded. "Good question. The short answer is time. In any former Soviet republic, bureaucracy is an art form. The remaining ITEB, if it exists in or around this lab, would likely be long gone by the time the Ukrainian military agreed to help. Not only that, but there is a very high likelihood of corruption at high levels in their government."

"So you're saying the people we would ask for help might be the very people making money by selling ITEB?" John asked.

"Exactly."

"So who will be our point of contact in country?" Rip asked.

Mary fiddled with her laptop. "Here...just a sec." A moment later, a passport photo of a young woman appeared on the screen. "This is Olenka Mankovska. She is a Ukrainian who works as a secretary in Kiev. She became a CIA asset during the Orange Revolution in 2004."

"Is she trustworthy?" John asked.

Mary shrugged. "The Eastern European desk at Langley says

she's one of the most efficient and capable people they've ever seen. Apparently in 2002, she secured a job in the Kiev office of Russian billionaire Boris Berezovsky. That gained her access to information which proved that the Russians were trying to influence the Ukrainian political process. Apparently they went so far as to have the opposition candidate poisoned."

"So she's proven her worth," John concluded.

Mary nodded. "I've been corresponding with her off and on since the start of this investigation, and she seems to have a good handle on things over there."

"Hold up," Sweeney said, sitting forward in his seat. "I understand your reasoning for splitting up the team, but in Ranger school we learned never to go anywhere without a Ranger buddy. With only three of us, we'll need one more man in case we have to split up."

Mary gave him a sly grin. "Make that one more woman. I'll be your buddy on this trip, Ranger."

All eyes turned to Sweeney. Mary expected him to object. But for once he didn't get angry or even look perturbed at the idea.

Major Williams grinned. "Did Phoenix mention that she speaks fluent Russian?"

John nodded. "Good deal. How are we getting in?"

"Commercial." Mary looked at her watch. "I've got a flight leaving in a few hours. You all will follow tomorrow." She picked up a stack of manila envelopes labeled Cooper, Rubio, and Sweeney, and passed them around the table. "These contain Ukrainian cash and some pocket litter that will make you appear Canadian. Library cards, et cetera. Tomorrow morning, Major Williams will go and pick up your Canadian passports with your real first names and assumed last names. You're traveling as tourists, so bring only a couple changes of clothes, and don't check any bags. Your gear will be sent separately, and we'll pick up weapons once we arrive."

Rip looked like he'd just eaten a bug. "Oh man, you mean I have to be a Canadian?"

Sweeney smirked at him. "Just be extra nice and nobody will know the difference, eh?"

Truth be told, it was the best Mary had been able to do with three hours' notice. She hoped it would be good enough.

JFK International Airport, New York, New York

Five hours later, Mary made her way through security at John F. Kennedy International Airport. The international concourse at JFK was always crowded, but Mary had seen worse. She got in line at the Starbucks kiosk, watching the people go by. It had become second nature—scan the crowd for threats.

She marveled at the diversity surrounding her. *New York sure attracts all kinds.* Two Goth teens with more body piercings than fingers sat head-bobbing to their iPods between a businessman in a pinstriped Brioni suit and an Indian woman in a red and green sari. She'd been trained to blend with the local population, but here that meant she probably could have substituted the jeans, T-shirt, and Under Armour baseball cap she was wearing for a silver spandex unitard and nobody would have looked twice.

A harried soccer mom rushed past, struggling to catch up to her son, a blond-headed tornado in tennis shoes that reminded Mary of a Calvin and Hobbes cartoon. When he picked up a souvenir snow globe from a kiosk, his mother cried, "David! Put that down!" A pair of lithe flight attendants who probably knew every airport on two continents chatted on their mobile phones as they waited in line ahead of her.

A gaggle of high schoolers in matching T-shirts went streaming by, herded along by a grim-faced older woman who looked like an experienced chaperone. *Probably heading to Europe for their senior trip.*

Mary smiled, remembering a similar excursion she'd joined as a teenager. The tour of Rome had opened her eyes to the wonders of adventure and fascinating history. She'd run her hands along the rough stone of ancient churches at the Vatican in silent awe. *Someone's hands carved this block…five hundred years ago!* That trip had played a big part in her decision to apply for a job at the CIA after college. She'd wanted to be where the action was—building history like those who'd carved the magnificent stones of the Sistine Chapel.

After all, women can build empires as well as men.

A stream of people emerged from the Jetway across the hall. They were, according to the digital sign above the door, passengers from flight 6619 arriving from Cartagena, Colombia. She watched them disembark in ones and twos, noting that most looked like businessmen, with a few intrepid gringo tourists sprinkled in between. Most turned right toward baggage claim, but a few made directly for the coffee line.

A voice sounded beside her. "Man! Eight dollars for a cup of coffee. Can you believe it?"

Mary turned to see a balding man in slacks and a floral print shirt, grinning at her. She put on her most disarming smile. "Crazy, aren't we?"

Why was the hair standing up on the back of her neck?

The man shrugged. "Maybe. Can't arrest a guy for being addicted to caffeine, though."

"I...er...guess not."

"Burt Poole," the man said, extending a fleshy hand.

"Nice to meet you," Mary said. "You must be from the Great Lakes area."

Burt's eyebrows shot up. "How'd you know that? I'm from Green Bay."

"Your accent, of course."

The man laughed much too loud. "I guess you got me there. Where are you from, uh...?"

"Oh, all over." She pretended to be oblivious to his name fishing and wished the Starbucks line would move faster. Unfortunately, the flight attendants hadn't moved.

"Where you headed?" he asked.

"Oh, I'm going to Kiev for some sightseeing. You?" *No harm in his knowing your destination. Just turn the questions around...keep him talking about himself and he won't be able to ask about you.*

"Hey, me too! Only I'm going to, er..." He looked sheepish. "I'm going to meet my wife."

"Oh? Is she there on business?"

"No, well, you see...we sort of met on the Internet."

The line had finally started to move. "Really? I've heard a lot about Internet dating." *Even joined one of those sites recently myself. Just out of curiosity, of course. Not that I'd admit that to this guy.* "So what do you do for a living?"

Burt seemed to brighten. "Oh, I'm in insurance."

"Sounds important," Mary lied. "So then, you sell different kinds?" She was glad to see the line dwindling in front of her.

"Life insurance, mostly. Whole life, universal life, variable life. Annuities are the big…"

Burt was still talking, but it was Mary's turn to order, so she tried to look like she was still listening while she ordered a tall soy mocha, no whipped cream. She kept nodding at Burt as she handed over a ten-dollar bill.

Finally Burt popped the question. "What kind of life insurance do you have?"

I had a feeling that was coming. "Mine is through work."

"You know, that's never enough. I could get you a good deal. You have a card or something?"

She tried to look disappointed. "Just gave away my last one. Sorry."

"No problem. Here's mine." He produced a card from his breast pocket. "Call me if you need anything. I mean, er…wait two weeks. I'll be on my honeymoon." He winked.

Oh, good grief. "Sure, Burt. Thanks!" She picked up her coffee and turned to go.

"My pleasure. And think about that insurance. You never know when you might need it. The world's a dangerous place!"

"Okay then, have a good one." *On that happy note…* Mary headed for the Internet kiosks to cancel her profile on that dating site.

After meeting Burt, her curiosity had been cured.

———

The last time he'd arrived in this city, it had been to kill a man.

Samael Berg purchased a copy of a local newspaper and donned his Serengeti titanium sunglasses before scanning the throng in the terminal. Uniformed security personnel were everywhere, but they had no reason to be concerned with him. He felt calm, secure in his meticulous planning.

Two decades of operating in the shadows had given him both the skill to pull this off and a healthy dose of skepticism about the readiness of America's bloated "Homeland Security Administration." He had cleared customs on his Israeli passport, which was in his real name. He had learned long ago that it was easiest to hide in plain sight.

He waited for a crowd of giggling teenage girls to pass and then moved across the large hallway to stand in line for coffee.

He studied the striking woman with the short red hair standing toward the front of the line ahead of him. She was obviously very athletic—he'd rarely seen a simple pair of blue jeans look so good. He would have described the man she was chatting with as an overweight American, but to Samael, whose fifty-two-year-old frame was still taut and muscular from regular exercise, putting *overweight* and *American* in the same sentence was redundant.

Happy to be hidden behind the opaque lenses of the sunglasses, he let his eyes explore the redhead's curves from behind. She was exquisite, quite well proportioned even if she was a bit skinny for his tastes. If there were more time, he might introduce himself and invite her for a drink.

Not today. Today he must rent a car and drive halfway across this enormous country to make a pickup before he could really get down to business. Perhaps he could find some companionship once the job was finished. That day would come very soon. And when it did, Samael was due for a long vacation. This operation would make him wealthy enough, though he wasn't doing it just for the money.

In the last year, the United States' commitment to Israel had cooled considerably, and he doubted the current government understood just what was at stake there. Even in this age of global interconnectedness, America enjoyed its delusion that it could protect itself by withdrawing from the battlefield and retreating to its own shores.

Samael Berg intended to shatter that false security and to show America just how vulnerable she was.

4

Near Chernobyl, Ukraine

THE ANCIENT LADA COUPE rattled along, straddling the place where a center line had once been painted on the otherwise deserted road. On both sides, the countryside was in full bloom, taking its first full breaths of the warm air after yet another long, hard Ukrainian winter. Though the land was verdant and level—perfect for farming—no plow had touched it in decades. Perhaps none would ever touch it again.

Grigor Lychenko hummed to himself as he piloted the car around the worst of the potholes. He was in an uncharacteristically good mood. This was the last time he would ever have to drive this route. The only work he would be doing today would be boxing up the few meager possessions he intended to keep from his office and bidding farewell to his co-workers.

His passenger, Dimitri Sarkhov, was napping with his head against the side window. The swarthy older man was the janitor at the office complex where Grigor had worked for the last fourteen months. The two men had met only in the last month and recently had agreed to carpool to save on fuel. Despite the brevity of their acquaintance, the man had become a friend—his only friend, he now realized. Dimitri was always interested in Grigor's stories, and the two men had shared many a beer at local taverns and *klubs*. Grigor was going to miss him.

It occurred to him that the first time he'd followed this road had been an even happier day. On that day he'd been surrounded by his wife and two young children. They'd sung songs and waved to the farmers as they'd headed for their new home. He thought hard for a moment. *That was in…1983. Yes, that was the year. Everything was different then.*

Back then, the road to Pripyat was wide and new, as were many of the cars. As a government scientist, Grigor's job had been to go wherever the USSR sent him. He had used every contact he had to get himself transferred to the military laboratory near Chernobyl. It was so much nicer than Moscow. Instead of being surrounded by grimy streets clogged with traffic, his family would be living in one of the jewels of Soviet social engineering, a nearly new city of fifty thousand surrounded by undulating wheat fields, right on the shores of the mighty Dnieper River. The streets were orderly and spacious, the air was clean, and there was even an amusement park being constructed in the center of town.

His work was to be important, as well. Grigor's wife said he'd sounded like a little boy when he'd given her the news. "I'll be the lead scientist in the lab! And the project is so important I am not even allowed to speak of it!"

What he could not tell her was that they were creating a new form of rocket fuel, one so powerful and efficient that it would catapult the Soviet space program so far ahead that her rivals would never be able to compete.

His wife had gone to work as a librarian at the large school building near their home, which allowed her to look after Myra, their school-aged daughter, and kept their infant son, John, from ever having to spend the night in the huge state-run nursery. That made them both happy, since Grigor couldn't bear the thought of his little one lost in that sea of wooden cribs along with the children of all the night-shift workers from the plant.

Life went on happily for two years, even as Grigor was called to Moscow more and more to report on his team's progress.

That's where he was when the accident happened.

When the reports came on television that there had been a fire at Chernobyl, Grigor hadn't been especially worried. There were fires and small accidents there all the time. Everyone knew that the reactor was poorly maintained. Then news arrived that the town of Pripyat had been evacuated. Nothing serious, they said. Just a precaution for the good of the workers. Those workers, he found out later, had been told to take only their identification and a change of clothes as they were loaded onto buses for Kyiv.

Then he'd received a cable that his family was in the hospital there.

Grigor went immediately to the train station in Moscow and tried to get the overnight to Kyiv. But no trains were going that direction. By the end of that horrible day, he was nearly apoplectic.

It was two full weeks before he was able to return. By the time he arrived at the hospital, his wife and beloved son were dead. His daughter was clinging to life, gravely ill from radiation poisoning.

He later found a friend from Pripyat who told him the awful story of what had actually happened. On the night the fire occurred, many of the residents of their apartment building had gone up on the roof to gaze at the beautiful blue glow emanating from the plant less than a kilometer away. What they couldn't have known was that they were staring directly into the unshielded reactor core—each of them receiving a lethal dose of radiation in the process.

In the following days, the rest of the scientists he'd had charge over, all of whom had to cross within one hundred yards of the reactor on their way home from work that night, also dropped dead of the exposure, one by one.

Grigor had never returned to his home in Pripyat. He spent every ruble he had saved and pulled every string he could think of to be given permission to take his daughter to a special camp that had been set up in Cuba for children affected by the disaster. Once there, he secured a job with a Cuban pharmaceutical company and battled depression with alcohol as his Myra lingered for five years before succumbing to lymphoma.

That was when he'd met Adela Fernandez, a no-nonsense Cuban policewoman who had awakened him out of a drunken stupor one night in Havana by dumping a bucket of ice water on him. For some reason, she took pity on him and drove him home instead of to the *cárcel*. Miraculously, they became friends, then lovers. Adela was as saucy and unpredictable as his wife had been staid and unadventurous. She was just what he needed. As far as Grigor was concerned, this fiery *cubana* had raised him from the dead.

It wasn't long after that, as they lay on the beach one night, staring at the stars, that Grigor remembered the ITEB.

Iso-Triethyl Borane was the additive they'd been experimenting on in his lab in Ukraine. In more than ten years of alcohol-fogged depression, he'd never considered that the stockpile they'd kept at the lab might still be intact. Working in pharmaceuticals, Grigor knew how valuable the chemical was. And he was the only surviving member of the team. So if the ITEB was still there, safely hidden underground in the lab, and he could find a way to get it out…he could be a very rich man. He remembered how easy it had been to convince Adela to leave Cuba and come to this desolate place. Chernobyl.

He took a job inside the "dead zone" researching the effects of long-term radiation exposure on various materials. He knew full well that, in the process, he was subjecting himself to doses fifty times higher than the average person received, even though his office was situated in the actual town of Chernobyl, more than eight kilometers from the site of the accident. In fact, the job required him to work only two weeks at a time, then rest for two weeks to lessen the risk.

That was how he'd regained access to the dead zone. He never returned to Pripyat because he knew that doing so would tear open the wounds that had only recently begun to heal. But he did return to the lab. Under the excuse of taking samples near the reactor, he found the crumbling entrance and descended the dank, rusting stairs to the bunkerlike laboratory. He found the lab looted by vandals.

His hopes soared, however, when he found the stockpile of ITEB just as it had been in 1986. Apparently the vandals had left the tall metal cylinders alone, figuring they were too heavy to haul back up the stairs. If only they'd known what the chemical inside was worth.

Though it was backbreaking work to get the heavy tanks up to his car, little by little Grigor began smuggling the chemical back to his flat in Kyiv, while Adela looked for a buyer.

There had been many obstacles to their success, but that was all behind them now. Grigor had officially quit his job, and the final payment was safely in his bank account. While he still had some gambling debts to settle, the money left over would be enough for him and Adela to move to a tropical island, buy a home, and do as little as possible for the rest of their lives.

Grigor had finally attained his dream: to know luxury like only the privileged few. The journey to get here was painful and at times desolate—like this road—but the destination was finally in sight.

He reached over and shook Dimitri. "Wake up, my friend. It is a beautiful day, and you have yet to congratulate me on my retirement."

Dimitri sat up and rubbed his stubbly face. "Ech. I still don't understand why you'd give up such a stable position. The pension can't be *that* good." He picked up a newspaper from between his feet and began leafing through it. "Where will you live?"

Grigor shrugged. "That is Adela's decision," he lied. "All I know is that we're headed somewhere warm."

"What, Crimea?"

Grigor threw a sideways glance at his passenger. Adela had insisted that they not tell anyone where they were headed. But Dimitri was his friend. Other than Adela, he was the only person Grigor felt he could trust. He grinned. *Well, why not?* "We're going to the Seychelles."

Dimitri's bushy eyebrows shot up. "Seychelles? I'd like to see how you plan to do that on a scientist's retirement. You sure you didn't win a jackpot or something?" The older man gave him a look that immediately made Grigor regret having said anything.

Grigor shook his head, careful not to put away his smile. Dimitri waved a hand at him.

"Bah! I give you six months. Maybe less. You'll be back here begging for work again before you know it."

Grigor's smile turned to a laugh. He wanted more than anything to brag to his friend how much money he'd made selling the ITEB on the black market. But he restrained himself.

Some triumphs were too dangerous to share.

Kiev

The Lada was a rattletrap. Its brakes protested as the taxi driver ground to a halt in the shadow of the most monolithic apartment complex Mary had ever seen.

The ride from Borispol International Airport outside the city had taken forty minutes, and Mary was surprised at how many ornately decorated churches they'd passed as the taxi had wound its way through Kiev. For some reason, that clashed with her view of what this former Communist state should have looked like. But then she remembered that the Soviet Union only went back to just before World War I, and the churches were obviously much older than that.

The apartment complex, on the other hand, was postmodern socialist through and through.

The driver grunted, motioning to a dark entrance on the building. Mary hadn't seen it. It was almost invisible due to the unkempt trees that hung low over the crumbling sidewalk. She could just make out a crude, hand-painted numeral four above the entrance.

"This is it?"

He nodded. "*Da*. Yunosti block. Dneprovskiy district."

She paid the driver, then went to exit the taxi, only to realize there was no handle on the inside of the door. So she waited until the driver sauntered around to her side to open it.

He stood sucking on his cigarette, regarding her with a lascivious smile as she stepped to the curb.

Mary pretended to know where she was going until the taxi had driven off in a cloud of blue smoke. Then she stopped and regarded the building again.

Seven stories high, the unpainted concrete tenements seemed to stretch to the horizon in both directions. Even more amazing was that this was only one of several such buildings, arranged like giant dominoes laid sideways. She took a moment trying to count the balconies on one floor of the building in front of her, but gave up due to the overgrown trees that were blocking her view. Nevertheless, there had to be at least two thousand apartments in each building. She shook her head. *Unbelievable.*

From the looks of the common areas between the buildings, it would take a good-sized crew of Mexican landscapers about a year to get the green space under control. In fact, if there hadn't been people coming and going from the buildings, she would have wondered if they were even livable. Several people sat on dilapidated park benches, smoking and regarding her with suspicious frowns.

She swallowed, then strode past the benches and followed the cracked walkway toward the entrance of the building, hoping the driver hadn't made a mistake on the address she'd given him. She retrieved her phone from her pocket and scrolled through her text messages until she found the one she wanted. She'd been exchanging SMS and e-mails with Olenka, their Ukrainian agent, for almost a week. Her last message read simply, "4 Lagerna St., Dneprovskiy, Level 4 Door B."

Stepping carefully around a rusted-out bathtub that was parked beside the entrance, Mary peered inside and wished she could turn around and go back to the airport. The dimly lit stairwell smelled like an outhouse, but even worse was that it brought to mind that underground bunker in Panama. She shuddered. *Was that only two weeks ago?*

The men of Task Force Valor had almost been killed saving her, and the memory of it still felt like a karate kick to the chest. How could they trust her to lead this mission? How could she trust herself? She was bright and tough, but if that wouldn't make up for her inexperience, she was in trouble. She'd failed in Panama—let herself be ambushed and held hostage by petty thugs. That mistake put the lives of the entire team at risk. She was determined to put that failure behind her.

But what if it happened again?

Approaching footsteps jerked Mary back to the present. She whirled to see a short teenage girl with bright purple hair and multiple facial piercings hurrying toward her. Mary stepped aside, and the girl brushed past without making eye contact, then went clomping up the stairs in garish patent leather boots.

Mary shrugged. *Well, if she can do it…* She took a deep breath and started up the dank, graffiti-covered stairwell.

At each landing there were a collection of shabby dark-stained doors, out from under which other smells drifted—most notably ammonia and the smell of some unidentifiable food. These mixed with the familiar sounds of crying babies and blaring televisions to make the building seem a bit less foreboding. On the fourth floor, it took only a moment to find the door she was looking for. A faded 4B was painted beside it.

Rather than knocking, Mary reached into her pocket and retrieved her phone. She keyed in a quick text message, "PHX AT DOOR," and sent it. Better to be sure she was at the right place than to pound on the door and find out she was wrong.

A moment later, she heard someone turning the locks, then the door swung inward.

Olenka Mankovska stood before her in blue jeans and a gray turtleneck under a fitted denim waistcoat. Her blond hair was long and straight, and her blue eyes shone as she smiled across the threshold. "Come in."

Borispol International Airport, Kiev, Ukraine

The Boeing 737 bounced hard as it hit the runway. Only then did Sweeney wake up. Groggy, he sat forward and raised the window shade, letting in a blast of bright sunlight. He squinted into it and saw a flat, grassy landscape that ended in rows of tall pines. For a moment, he thought he was back home in Alabama. A closer look showed him that this airport was much too large for home.

A gruff female voice came over the airplane intercom. Though he didn't understand a word of what she said, Sweeney immediately remembered where he was: on the very last row of a completely over-booked airplane that had just landed in Ukraine.

He checked his watch. *Zero six twenty. But I never changed my watch when we left Bragg…which means here it's…* He didn't know.

He peered over the seat in front of him, trying to catch a glimpse of Rip and John—somewhere way forward of his choice seat. They were supposed to pretend they weren't traveling together, which was stupid. As if three guys traveling to Ukraine would arouse suspicion. He'd Googled it before they left, and this eastern European country was famous for its "mail-order brides." *Then again, what kind of guy would actually do that?* He wondered how many of the men on this flight were headed here for that very reason.

His own dating life had been hit or miss for the last few years, limited to a few brief relationships that usually lasted just until his next deployment. For some reason, he seemed to attract women who were either incredibly needy or incredibly shallow, or both. Besides, the team had been so busy saving the world for the last few months that there hadn't been time to think of women, or much else.

Then there was Mary. Attractive? Definitely. But he was starting to see there was a lot more to her than beauty. *Yeah, like control issues. That's all I need.* As much as he wanted to talk himself out of thinking about her, something in him wasn't listening.

Mary had mentioned they'd be venturing into the dead zone around Chernobyl. They called it the "dead zone" for a reason—the radiation was still too high for it to be habitable. *Geez, this is insane. I mean, I might actually want to have kids someday...* Though that would require getting married, which was nowhere on his radar. Not for a long time.

John Cooper had been all goo-goo since running into his old pal Liz in Lebanon, and Sweeney could already tell his once-unflappable team sergeant was whupped. He and John used to go skydiving together on weekends. Now, every time they had a few days off, John was running up to Philly to see her, like some kind of hungry puppy looking for a handout. *And he stays with her grandmother...yeah, right.* Though John swore on his reserve parachute that he and Liz had decided not to touch each other until—and unless—they got married, Sweeney would believe that when Hogan wore a dress.

Sweeney had seen what marriage did to a man—besides taking up every ounce of freedom, time, and spare change, it was a black hole for one's dignity. His own father could hardly tie his shoes without "clearing it with Mother." Dad spent his whole life tiptoeing around his wife—and he'd taught his boys to do the same. Momma ran the house, and that was all there was to it. He caught himself shaking his head. *No thanks. I've had enough browbeatin' to last me the rest of my life.*

The *ding* everyone had been waiting for finally came—the signal that they had reached the gate. At once, all the passengers jumped to their feet.

Since he was last off the plane, he wasn't at all surprised at the length of the line for immigration when he entered the large, sterile reception hall. Judging from the number of people there, several other flights must have also just landed.

Too bad I don't get paid by the hour.

There were five lines in all, each with at least thirty people already waiting. Sweeney caught sight of John and Rip, both in separate lines, pretending they hadn't seen him. Maybe he was imagining things, but there seemed to be a disproportionate amount of slimy-looking men with bad suits and too much jewelry.

What kind of man would purchase a bride? Question answered.

He sighed and took his place in the line farthest from the other two, feeling his back pocket to be sure the Canadian passport was still there.

Covert operations are sooo exciting.

"Looks like this might take a while," a man's thick, accented voice said from behind him.

Sweeney turned, then blinked. Then stared. *It can't be...*

Before him stood a huge man in a long black robe, a thick brown beard covering his face. He wore a brown smock and a big, easy smile. If he didn't know better, he'd have sworn it was Buzz, pulling a trick on him.

"Sorry, did I startle you?"

Sweeney swallowed and tried to recover. "Uh, no. I...sorry, I was...ah...thinking of something else."

"That's okay. I tend to make people look twice. I'm sure the mantle has something to do with it." The big man held out his robe like a skirt, then guffawed.

What are the odds?

Despite his initial shock, Sweeney grinned. The man's jovial demeanor made it clear he had fun wherever he went, and the Friar Tuck getup made him seem anything but intimidating. His English was perfect, though Sweeney couldn't place the accent. Something not quite British.

"What's your name, son?" The man's smile was infectious.

Sweeney smiled back. "Bobby. You?"

The giant stuck out his hand. "Nice to meet you, Bobby. I'm Brother Keith Forster. I'd welcome you to Ukraine, but I only just got here myself!" He let out a laugh that had the people around them grinning too.

Sweeney smirked. "Nice to meet you. So…you're a monk?"

Brother Forster wagged an index finger. "Good guess, but no. I'm a friar of the Carmelite order."

"Sounds sticky."

The friar chuckled. "Indeed it does. Our full name is the Brothers of the Blessed Virgin Mary of Mount Carmel. I live in South Africa."

"Ah." *That explains the accent.* "So did you come to Ukraine to find a wife?"

He immediately regretted the joke, not because the friar was offended, but because the man laughed so hard Sweeney realized they were attracting attention. He decided to cut the sarcasm.

Brother Keith wiped his eyes. "Well, considering I've already taken vows of poverty and of chastity, what would be the point?"

Now it was Sweeney's turn to laugh. He couldn't help but like this guy.

The big man patted his briefcase and continued. "No, I'm here to teach a seminar on apologetics."

"I'm sorry?"

"Exactly."

"What?" Sweeney was confused.

"Oh, I thought you were making another joke!" The friar guffawed again and slapped Sweeney on the shoulder. "You know, apologetics…'sorry'…get it?"

Sweeney slapped his forehead. "Now I do."

"Apologetics is the art of explaining the notion that God exists." The friar winked at him. "I call it 'defending the obvious.'"

Sweeney's inner skeptic kicked in. He shuffled forward with the line. "But if it was obvious, you wouldn't need to defend it, would you?"

The big man gave an amused snort. "Once, when I misbehaved as a child, my mother sent me outside to fetch a switch. I knew what the switch was going to be used for, and not surprisingly, I couldn't find one!"

"Hmmfff," Sweeney puffed. "But I bet your momma found one real quick."

"Exactly. It wasn't that all the switches had vanished from our backyard—they were everywhere when I wanted one with which to torment the cat. It was that my worldview regarding switches had changed, and my desire to avoid punishment made them awfully hard to see."

"So what does that have to do with proving God exists?"

The friar shrugged. "All I'm saying is that sometimes our motivations make us ignore the obvious. But you can't change reality on a whim. If God exists or if He doesn't, your belief about it does not affect the fact."

How'd I get roped into this? Sweeney pursed his lips and tried to see how much longer he had until he got to the customs people. "Hmm…I guess that makes sense."

The friar nodded. "So then how is God obvious? That's the next step."

"Uh-huh." Sweeney wasn't sure he wanted to go to the next step.

He was glad the line was moving. Two lines over, Rip was already at the passport control booth.

The friar picked up his briefcase with one hand and made a broad gesture with the other, encompassing everyone in the terminal. "Do you realize that every culture throughout history has had a belief in the supernatural?"

Sweeney stuck his hands in his pockets. "But they've all had different gods. Doesn't that mean they're made up in our imagination?"

"That's a good point. And any particular god may be just that—a made-up figure. But the *concept* of God is universal. Even remote tribes that have virtually no contact with other cultures worship something. It's innate."

"So what does that prove, Friar?"

The friar's wide smile returned. "Have you ever known anyone who was an artist? And please, call me Keith."

"Okay, Keith. My granddad is a whittler. Does that count?"

"You mean he carved things from wood?"

"Yeah. He'd make toys and things for all us boys every Christmas."

"Fine," Keith said. "If you were to go home and see something he'd carved, would you recognize his work?"

"Absolutely. Granddad is really good."

"So, in a sense, his work would remind you of him."

Sweeney nodded, wary of where this might lead. "I suppose."

Keith spread his hands. "Well, that's my point about God. He is evident in the things He created. And mankind has sensed that since the first cavemen. Much of human history has involved the quest to get to know this Creator."

The guy was making sense—but for some reason Sweeney hated to admit it. Feelings that he thought he'd grown out of were waking up within him, like Santa Claus showing up in his car for a chat. He tried to throw Keith a curveball. "But isn't all that explained by evolution?"

"Bah!" Keith swatted the air with his huge hand. "Evolution doesn't answer anything. It creates more problems than it solves. And it only muddies the water in the discussion about God—a convenient way for people to avoid the topic."

Uh-huh. Sounds like I hit a hot button. Sweeney decided he'd better bail on this conversation before it got any more uncomfortable. "Hmm. That's, uh, interesting. I—"

"Think about this." Apparently Keith wasn't going to let him off so easy. "According to evolutionists, the very first living things were some form of a primitive single-celled organism that sprang into being out of the primordial slime. This organism then multiplied and eventually became male and female organisms that had to get together in order to reproduce. Now, consider the complicated procedure required for reproduction to occur. Since those systems wouldn't work unless they were fully formed, how did those species reproduce while their reproductive systems were forming?"

"Hmm…good question. But I'm not an expert on this stuff. Somebody probably knows the answer."

"That's what most people say. But now consider this." Keith's smile turned more clever. "What caused the *impetus* for reproduction in the first place?"

Sweeney furrowed his brow. "What?" He was now officially in way over his head.

"I mean, in the case of the single-celled protozoan, if its very existence was a complete accident, what reason would it have to continue living, much less reproduce? What would drive it to do so?"

Sweeney shrugged again. "I don't know. It just did."

Keith snapped his fingers. "Exactly. Even if that's the way it happened, and I don't believe it is, God is evident in the impetus—He's the 'reason for being' even for the lowliest single-celled creature. That's why I say evolution answers nothing. It only confuses the question."

"Huh." Sweeney didn't know what else to say.

Someone tapped him on the shoulder. Sweeney turned to see a uniformed police officer.

"Hey, *ty nastupnyi, ruhaisia*!" The man was motioning to the waiting passport control officer. Sweeney had been so engrossed in the conversation that he hadn't noticed he was next in line.

"Better get up there or they might make you stay here talking to me!" Keith said, adding yet another hearty laugh.

"Uh, right. Nice to meet you." Sweeney headed for the booth, digging in his back pocket for his passport.

The immigration official looked a little like Michael Moore, only without the baseball hat. He took Sweeney's maroon-covered passport and flipped through it.

"What is the nature of your visit to Ukraine?"

"I'm on vacation."

The agent eyed him over his glasses. "To find a nice girl, perhaps?"

Sweeney shook his head. "Nothing like that. Only sightseeing."

The immigration official's dubious look said, *That's what they all say.* Sweeney had to keep from rolling his eyes. Instead, he just blinked at the man. After holding Sweeney's gaze for a moment, the official grabbed his stamp and slammed it down on the passport like he was trying to kill it. Then he handed it back. "Enjoy your holiday," he said with a smirk.

Sweeney bypassed baggage claim, having brought only his day-pack as a carry-on. When he finally emerged from the airport ten minutes later, the air was crisp, though the sun was shining brightly.

Pretty girls stood like sentinels around each airport entrance, holding signs advertising what appeared to be matchmaking services. Several approached him, but he waved them off before they could even ask if he was interested. That they would lump him together with the leisure-suit Larrys he'd seen in the airport was enough to make him want to puke.

He pulled a slip of paper from his wallet with the name of his hotel, the Lybid. He made a beeline for the first taxi he could see, parked just behind a row of buses. The driver was leaning on his car and smoking a cigarette. When Sweeney showed him the piece of paper, the man crushed out his cigarette with a sigh, as if taking the fare was a severe imposition. He motioned to the passenger door and, without a word, climbed into the driver's seat.

Friendly guy. I should introduce him to Brother Keith.

The drive into Kiev lasted thirty minutes, during which time neither he nor the driver spoke. Sweeney was actually grateful for the silence. The more he thought about his discussion with the friar, the more it irked him. It wasn't so much the talk about origins and man's search for meaning that bothered him, it was the assertion he'd made at the beginning of their conversation. *"Sometimes our motivations make us ignore the obvious...*" Something about that idea put a bad taste in his mouth.

Sweeney was the son of a preacher. But there had come a time when he'd decided that if the religion of his parents were true, there was no way he could ever make it to heaven. He just wasn't good enough at obeying rules.

And so he'd decided to believe it was false. Now, the story of a boy looking right past perfectly good switches was stuck in his head. Maybe because it was only so much psychobabble. Or maybe because it hit too close to home.

Or maybe you are jetlagged out of your mind and just need a hot shower and something to eat besides airplane food.

When the taxi arrived at the hotel, Sweeney used some Ukrainian money to pay the driver. He went inside the hotel and presented his passport to the clerk. Five minutes later he stepped from the elevator on the fifth floor and found his room.

It was about as luxurious as an old Motel 6, with light gray paint and cheap pressboard furniture. He poked his head in the bathroom. By the looks of the tile and fixtures, it had last been renovated sometime around 1970. But he really didn't care as long as there was hot water. He was reaching for the tap when there was a knock at the door.

John and Rip were grinning at him when he looked through the peephole. He exhaled, then flipped the lock and swung the door open. "Fancy meeting you here. Are we allowed to be friends yet?"

John pushed his way inside and flopped down on the bed. "I don't know. It looked like you were having a great time with that big dude at the airport."

Sweeney ran a hand through his blond hair. "Yeah. Nice guy."

Rip spoke up. "Man, *ese*. Maybe I'm loco, but to me, he looked kinda like Buzz."

John nodded vigorously. "I thought so too. Except for the man-dress."

"I don't want to talk about it," Sweeney said.

Rip sat on the edge of the dresser. "So what now?"

John dug in his pocket and produced a cellular phone. "I just got off the phone with Phoenix. We're supposed to meet her at a park near here in an hour. That gives us time to grab a bite to eat before we go."

Sweeney groaned. The shower would have to wait.

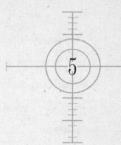

5

ALEXI TRIED TO LIFT his head, but it was too heavy. The pounding made it impossible to concentrate on anything. One minute he was trying to focus on his surroundings, the next he was back at home during a happier time.

"Quickly, Alexi. We're going to miss the wedding!"

Alexi had stuck out his stubbly chin so he could get at it more easily with the straight razor. "Yes, *Mamo*. I know. But I don't think Vasyl' will be on time either. If I know him, he will still be drunk from the party his friends threw for him last night."

Mother shuffled into the small kitchen where Alexi was finishing his shave. "Ech. I don't know what Galia sees in that *durnyk*. You should have married that one, Alexi."

"If she's dumb enough to marry Vasyl', why would I want her? Besides, she has bad teeth."

"Feh!" his mother spat. "You will never get married at this rate. Too picky!" She crossed herself and lifted the cheesecloth off the *korovai* she'd made for the wedding.

Truth be told, his mother's special bread was nearly the only reason he went to weddings anymore. At fifty-three, he was too old to dance with the girls. And besides, he hated to be away from his animals.

It wasn't that Alexi didn't want a wife. He'd always planned to marry and raise a family of his own. But he knew he wasn't much to look at, and social grace had never been his strong point, especially among the ladies. His animals were much less complicated. They were always there for him, listening, never judging. Caring for them and for his mother became the focus of his life. A wife would have simply gotten in the way.

"Are you coming, *sonechko*?" She was standing by the door, tying a colorful scarf around her head.

"*Tak*, Mamo. Just let me get my tie." Alexi picked up the worn pink towel that sat on the table next to the shaving mug and brush. He wiped the rest of the suds from his face as he rose out of the creaky wooden chair. "You go ahead. I'll cut through the woods and meet you on the road."

"All right." His mother looked up at the icon of Saint Nicholas, the miracle worker that had watched over their kitchen for as long as Alexi could remember. She crossed herself, kissing her fingertips in the old way, before picking up her bread and shuffling out the door.

Alexi remembered arriving on time at the wedding. It was held at the church, though neither the bride nor the groom ever attended services. Friends and relatives stood to observe the ceremony, since there weren't any pews. Everything went smoothly, except that the groom arrived late and already drunk, something that surprised no one. Afterward, the bride and groom went to leave their wedding bouquet at the war memorial in the center of town, while everyone else made their way the short distance to the *klub* for the reception.

Alexi followed, looking forward to the feast. The father of the bride was known for making excellent mead. And there was sure to be plenty of pork, chicken, borscht, and maybe even caviar. Not to mention Mother's beautiful wedding bread.

He slipped out soon after the dancing started, however, and not just because his cow was due to give birth anytime. In truth, he felt lonelier around all those people than he did when he was alone. He made his way home and went to the shed where the heifer was tied up. He made his bed there, intending to watch her through the night.

Sometime later that night, he awoke with a start. The ground was shaking beneath him. *What is it? An earthquake?* Fear tugged at the nape of his neck. He stood up and ran out into the crisp, moonlit night.

The air had a terrible metallic taste. Alexi spit to try to rid his mouth of it, to no avail. Then he saw the light—pale blue and intense—emanating from somewhere beyond the forest. Dread pooled in his gut. Something terrible had happened at the reactor.

Mother! He stumbled off toward the house, but without a light, he must have gone the wrong direction. He found himself pushing through a stand of fir trees, their needles tickling his face. He tried to bring his hands up to push them away, but it was as if his arms suddenly weren't there.

"Mother!"

Alexi sat up, his head throbbing. He shook the old memories from his mind. He must have been dreaming. Something was wrong. He leaned on one shaky hand and blinked at the shaft of sunlight that formed a perfect rectangle on the dusty wooden floor of the room where he had been imprisoned. It was daytime, and the metallic taste no longer assaulted his tongue, which nonetheless felt like worn-out shoe leather. Pasha, his longhaired cat, was rubbing against his trembling forearm.

"What are you doing here, Pasha?" He looked around. *Where* is *here?*

Then he remembered the youth with the gun and the greasy hair. *The church.*

A wardrobe sat against the wall across from him. Its wooden door hung askew by the lower hinge, revealing a pair of empty wire coat hangers. Two wooden drawers that must have come from the wardrobe were tossed in the corner next to a chair with one broken leg. Faded yellow walls stretched high overhead, where the single window, missing its pane, gave radiance to the otherwise dingy room.

He had never been in this room before. And there was only one room in the church that he'd never entered—this had to be the vestry.

He crossed himself twice. This was the room where the sacred liturgical instruments had been kept and where Father Andropos had changed into his vestments. Alexi had always been curious about this "secret room" behind the altar but had never dared go inside.

He looked at the closed door that led to the sanctuary, knowing it would be barricaded from the outside. Whatever the boy with the gun was after, Alexi was now his prisoner.

His skull pounded, the pain made more intense by the knowledge that now he would not be there to look after Mother.

Kiev, Ukraine. 2246 local

Grigor shuffled up the rain-slick walkway toward his apartment building as quickly as the boxes in his arms allowed. They contained the last vestiges of his life as an employee—something he planned to never be again.

He felt a surge of energy as he ascended the aging concrete stairs to the third floor and fumbled for his keys. After turning the latch, he shouldered his way inside the dark flat.

Strange. All the lights are out. Adela should have been home from the airport hours ago. She had planned to go purchase their plane tickets not long after he left with Dimitri to clean out his office.

Something is wrong. A cold, heavy weight settled in his chest. She should be here waiting. He dropped the box on a chair and flipped the light switch. The tiny apartment was much tidier than it had been that morning. His eyes narrowed. If anything, it was *too* clean.

He shrugged out of his jacket and moved through the small living area into the bedroom. The cheap compact fluorescent light did a miserable job of illuminating the room, but he could instantly see that it was worse than he thought.

Their closet door was open. All of Adela's clothes were gone.

"No!" The exclamation forced itself from his lungs as he lunged for his mobile phone. He dialed her number and paced as it rang five times. When her sultry voice came on the line, it said simply, "Leave a message."

He slammed the phone shut, then quickly reopened it. His fingers flew as he punched out the number of his bank, entering his account number and passcode into the computerized system. A balance inquiry confirmed his worst fears.

Adela is gone. She has betrayed me.

Somehow he knew he would not find her in the Seychelles, even if he tried.

And he would never see his money again.

Loading Docks, Port of Los Angeles, California, 2048 hours

The forklift rumbled down a narrow, brightly lit alleyway between two towering stacks of metal containers. Its driver, Rob Denny, deftly piloted the vehicle toward the end of the row, maneuvering the four-foot steel forks around the cones that a longshoreman had set up to mark the work area for his next job.

He spun the wheel and made a tight one-eighty before coming to a stop in front of a rust-colored forty-footer that had just come off the ship. The towering four-footed crane that had deposited the container there was rolling silently away on its solid rubber tires—each wheel powered by an electric motor. Rob tossed a tired wave at the crane operator, seated forty feet above him in a glass-enclosed control station. He figured the operator was probably as ready as he was to call it a night.

The longshoreman walked over and put one foot on the step of his machine. "How's things, Rob?"

"Fine, Ed. This the last lift of the night?" He checked his watch. "It's almost nine. If I don't get home in time for *CSI: Miami,* I'm gonna have to listen to Dory explain the whole thing to me."

Ed snickered. "Fate worse than death, huh?"

"You got it."

"Yeah, this should be the last one." Ed checked the clipboard in his hand. "Lessee…this one's a refrigerator—twelve crates of boxed beef and a pallet of…bottled water."

"Bottled water?"

"Yeah, that's what it says. The container came from Panama, so I imagine it's some highfalutin spring water bottled by hand by blind nuns in the mountains of Costa Rica or something. They'll probably sell it for six bucks a bottle."

Rob laughed. "Man, some people is just plain nuts. That's more than a gallon of gas!"

"Not for long! Let's quit jawing and get 'er done. The water comes off first and goes on that white box truck." He motioned with the clipboard to a truck whose driver was apparently sleeping in the cab while he waited—judging from the feet sticking out the open passenger-side window.

Ed continued, "Then we'll shut the container back up and let the meat truck haul 'er away."

"Good enough." Rob reached down to start the forklift.

"Hey there!"

Both men turned to see Ron Cardle, a portly man in an ill-fitting polo shirt, huffing toward them with a clipboard.

Ed groaned. "Here comes everybody's favorite Customs inspector."

Rob smacked the wheel of the forklift. "Aw…shoot. There goes *CSI*."

Ed grinned. "Well, look at it this way. We're gettin' time and a half to be here. Ol' Ron just works on salary."

"Small consolation."

Ron Cardle arrived, his polo shirt stained with sweat. "Hey, I have to inspect this reefer."

"Have at it, pal. We've got nowhere to be." Rob hated the inspector's high-pitched voice almost as much as having to miss his television program. The guy sounded like a choirboy who smoked three packs a day.

Ed threw the latches on the container. When he swung the doors back, a cool mist rolled out along the pavement. Rob wondered if Cardle had chosen to inspect this container just so he could get a little free air conditioning. Inside, a pallet wrapped in industrial-strength cellophane showed a four-foot-high load of heavy cardboard boxes. They were sturdy but without markings.

"Pull that pallet out so I can look at it," Cardle wheezed.

Rob started the lift before he answered so he could lay on the sarcasm real thick. "Yes sir, Mr. Customs Inspector. Anything you say, Mr. Customs Inspector."

He stomped on the accelerator and enjoyed watching Ed grin as Cardle practically jumped out of the way. Ed motioned that he was going to the office for a cup of coffee and walked off. Rob maneuvered the forks under the pallet faster than he should have. But who cared? It was only fancy-shmancy bottled water.

He lifted the pallet and backed out, turned ninety degrees, then dropped the load to the ground a few inches from Cardle's feet. The inspector fumed up at him, hollering something about recklessness and write-ups, but Rob pretended he couldn't hear over the roar of the forklift.

He left the machine running and motioned that he was going to make a phone call. *Gotta explain to Dory why I'm gonna miss our date night—again.* As he stalked off toward the office, Cardle was shaking his head and pulling on the top of one of the boxes.

Twenty minutes later when Rob returned to his forklift, Cardle was nowhere to be seen. The only evidence that his least-favorite person had been there was the red U.S. Customs–Cleared sticker on the pallet and the box that Cardle had conveniently neglected to re-close. *That bozo wouldn't put out the effort to breathe if it wasn't required for the job.*

The white box truck was still there, its driver apparently still snoozing up front. Rob sighed and walked over to the pallet. Inside the open box were a half-dozen glass water bottles, each fit snugly into its own padded compartment.

Nobody else was around, so Rob reached in and pulled a bottle out. It was unmarked. He figured whoever had purchased them would put their labels on later. The bottle was cold and felt good in his hand. He suddenly realized how thirsty he was.

He looked around again. Nobody would notice one bottle missing, would they? Heck, sometimes Customs confiscated a few bananas or a stuffed toy for further testing. Who'd know? Maybe a high-priced bottle of water would go a little way toward making up with Dory.

He walked back to the forklift and grabbed his lunch pail from behind the driver's seat, then slipped the bottle inside. *Call it an overtime bonus. Dory and I can have a little treat while we watch* Lost *tomorrow night.*

He put the padded lunch pail back in its place and hurried to re-close the box. If anyone noticed the bottle was missing, they'd blame it on Customs.

Then he went to wake up the truck driver.

————

Los Angeles, California

How could this have happened?

Edgar Oswardo Lerida—going now by the name Gustavo Soto—paced in front of the run-down forest green Ford Expedition. He had found the vehicle just as his instructions had said he would: in the outer parking lot of LAX. Whether or not its registration and tags were legitimate, he had no way of knowing. But the vehicle had been scrupulously cleaned before his arrival and appeared to be in good running condition. His new "employer" was thorough, he had to admit.

That said, this was not the way things were supposed to have worked out. He should have been happily enjoying his retirement in Ecuador or Argentina. Now, every moment was filled with a gnawing dread that felt like a truck tire around his neck. In the last twenty-four hours he had alternated between debilitating fear and blind fury— unable to decide if he should go through with the mission the gringo had given him, or run for his life.

In the end, his bank balance had made the choice for him. If he would ever be truly free to live as he desired, he needed the money this job would provide. And since it was obvious the gringo had the power to find him, running would be futile. He was better off proving his worth by completing this assignment, even though on the surface it was almost suicidal.

But Edgar still had his wits—and they would serve him now as they had all his life. He would find a way to do what must be done, with minimal risk to himself. *But once this is finished...* He would make sure they never found him, and he would happily never set foot in the United States again.

He got into the Ford Expedition and drove to the designated self-storage warehouse just north of Los Angeles.

An hour later, a dilapidated white refrigerated van pulled into the climate-controlled warehouse. Edgar—Gustavo Soto—was smoking a cigarette and waiting. "You're late," he said when the truck driver stepped out of the van.

The driver, who looked to be a twenty-something college kid, yawned. "Yeah, man, got held up by Customs."

Edgar stiffened. "Was there a problem?"

The driver jerked his thumb toward the truck. "Don't think so. Standard inspection, I think. Sign here." He held out a clipboard with a bill of lading affixed to it.

Edgar scribbled an indistinguishable line across the bottom and handed it back. "May I pay you in cash? I'm going to be leaving soon."

The driver looked confused. "Uh...usually people just send the payment to the office."

Edgar smiled. "I'm very busy. If you'll carry the payment in for me, I would be very appreciative. I'll add fifty dollars for your trouble."

The driver brightened appreciably. "Sweet. I'm your man."

Edgar climbed into the truck to inspect the boxes of bottled liquid.

They were heavily padded, as they had been when he'd loaded them two weeks earlier in Panama. Remembering that he'd never planned to lay eyes on them again sent a stab of anger through his chest, but he forced himself to ignore it.

Once the driver had helped him transfer the boxes to the storage unit, Edgar produced a wad of greenbacks from his pocket and handed over the whole amount. "Here you are, then. It's been a pleasure doing business with you."

The kid wiped a trickle of sweat from his brow. "What's in these things, anyway?"

"Just bottled water."

"Awesome. I could use a drink right about now."

Edgar had a better idea. "Ah, but a beer would be better, no?" He walked back to the car and retrieved a paper bag from the front seat. "Here. On me."

"Oh, you totally rock, dude. I mean, you are the bomb!"

Edgar just smiled. It was probably better not to respond to that comment.

After the kid left, Edgar hurriedly filled the back of his SUV with cases of the product. His instructions were very clear—he would take half of the cases with him, and the other half would be left in the storage facility. What would happen to them, he was not told.

That was fine with him. The less of the product he had to handle, the better.

———

The sounds of traffic invaded the otherwise idyllic city park where Task Force Valor waited for their ride.

Sweeney was chewing pumpkin seeds he'd purchased from an old woman at the park's entrance. He spit a shell on the ground. "So what are we waitin' on?"

He and John Cooper were sitting on a bench overlooking a bubbling fountain somewhere in Kiev. Rip was wandering around across from them, snapping photos with his digital camera.

John checked the telephone Mary had issued them. "Last message I got from Phoenix said to come here and wait for her."

Sweeney tossed another seed in his mouth. "Sheesh. Hurry up and wait."

"Par for the course."

"You really think we'll find this lab where the ITEB was brewed?" Sweeney asked.

John shrugged.

A shout came from the other side of the large fountain. Sweeney's head jerked around in time to see a skinny youth with a shock of scraggly brown hair sprinting toward them.

A split second later, Rip came barreling around the side of the fountain as well. That was when Sweeney noticed Rip's camera clutched in the teen's fist.

"Get him!" Rip yelled.

"Hey!" John jumped up and rushed the teen, but the thief saw him coming and changed course. Sweeney was on his feet too, moving to block the kid's escape. The skinny thug had picked the wrong people to mess with.

He was fast though. No doubt about it. When John lunged for him, the kid dodged out of the way and somehow avoided Rip at the same time. But then he turned and came straight at Sweeney.

Sweeney squared his shoulders and got ready to tackle this punk like he'd learned to do in high school football. *This is going to be fun.*

But the miscreant had other plans. Holding the camera by its strap, he whipped it at his blocker. Stars exploded in Sweeney's head as the heavy object smashed into his left eye. He grunted in pain and dove blindly at his attacker. He felt his shoulder connect with the thief's hip, and he wrapped his arms around the thug's body and held on tight. The attacker made it two more steps before Sweeney's weight drove him to the ground.

The kid kept flailing wildly with both fists and feet, one of which connected with Sweeney's jaw.

Okay, now I'm mad. Sweeney pinned the would-be thief's face to the concrete with his left hand and pulled his right fist back. One well-placed punch could knock the kid cold. But that would be too nice. He was going to make this idiot hurt.

Then someone grabbed his arm. Sweeney jerked his head around and saw Rip. "Let go, Rip!"

Rip's face was serious. "It's okay, Bobby. Let him go."

Still sitting astride the struggling punk, Sweeney couldn't believe what he was hearing. "Are you nuts?" He pulled his arm away from Rip, pointing to the shattered pieces of his camera on the ground. "You see what he did to your camera?"

"It's okay, bro. I forgive him."

Now Sweeney was even madder, but he'd forgotten about the kid. He got up, and the thief scrambled away and disappeared into the park.

Sweeney spit blood on the ground. "I've had about enough of

this sanctimonious horse manure." He put his face close to Rip's. "I don't know what happened to you in Panama, but you need to snap out of it. Your namby-pamby attitude is going to get one of us killed."

He watched the anger rise in Rip's face, turning it red as the muscular Latino worked his jaw muscles. Rip spoke through clenched teeth. "I'm a different person now, *ese.*"

Sweeney cussed again. "That's what I'm afraid of."

John had been watching the exchange and finally spoke up. "Knock it off, you two. Phoenix is here."

Sweeney kept his gaze burning into Rip. *Go ahead, say something else.* But the once-fiery staff sergeant instead took a deep breath and dropped his eyes to the ground, then bent down and began picking up the pieces of his camera.

A horn beeped from the street. Sweeney turned to see a boxy, dark blue four-wheel drive stopped at the curb. It looked like a Russian version of a Land Rover. He could just make out Mary in the passenger seat.

John motioned with his head. "Let's go."

Sweeney walked back to the bench and picked up all three of their daypacks, then marched toward the waiting vehicle.

Once they'd all piled in, Mary turned in the passenger seat to look at them. "What was that all about?"

Sweeney and Rip, sitting on opposite sides of John, said nothing. John answered for them. "Nothing. Someone tried to steal Rip's camera."

Mary looked as sympathetic as Sweeney had ever seen her. "Oh, I'm sorry. Petty theft is bad here. Are you okay?"

Sweeney wiped a trickle of blood away from his mouth. "Fine."

Mary raised her eyebrows at him. "O...kay. Then let me introduce you all to Olenka." She motioned to the golden-haired woman sitting in the driver's seat. "She's our point of contact here in Kiev."

The girl looked at them with a shy smile. "Hello. Nice to meet you all. Phoenix has told me all about you."

Despite his lingering anger and the eye that was starting to swell, Sweeney couldn't help but notice that the well-proportioned Ukrainian agent was, well, one description that came to mind was *absolutely smoking hot.* That meant there were now two beautiful women on this mission. *If one of them wasn't in charge, this wouldn't be half bad.* He stuck out a hand. "Nice to meet you, ma'am. I'm Bobby."

Mary rolled her eyes. "Sergeant Sweeney is our weapons expert. And this is John Cooper, the team sergeant."

"Hi," John said with a little wave.

"And behind you is Sergeant Rip Rubio. He'll be handling communications."

"Ma'am." Rip gave her a solemn nod in the rearview mirror.

Phoenix continued, "Olenka's call sign will be Orange One."

"Like the Orange Revolution." Sweeney nodded, hoping Olenka would be impressed with his grasp of Ukrainian history, even though it consisted of hastily reading Ukraine's Wikipedia page the night before they'd flown out of Bragg.

"Right." Mary turned to Olenka. "Why don't you fill the guys in on what you were telling me at the safe house." Then to the team she added, "That's where we're headed now."

"Are we staying there tonight?" John asked.

Mary laughed. "No way! Wait until you see it."

Sweeney wondered what that meant. He rubbed the sore spot under his eye.

Olenka took a sip from a water bottle as she pulled away from the curb, then began to speak. Sweeney found her accent mesmerizing. "We've been targeting the scientist Grigor Lychenko with surveillance for a number of weeks, and we believe he is the source of the chemical that you have been seeking."

"Wait," John said, "I thought we were trying to get to the lab where the stuff was made. Who's this Grigor guy?"

Olenka turned right, then looked at them in the rearview mirror. "Grigor Lychenko was once the top scientist in charge of a lab near Chernobyl that we know was experimenting with the substance.

"One of our agents has befriended him," Olenka continued. "It appears that Dr. Lychenko has been spending much time at the casino recently. He may be able to lead you to the remaining product and tell us if any more is being made."

"Great. Where do we find him?" Sweeney asked.

"I have another agent working on that," Olenka said. "Hopefully we will know sometime tonight where he is."

Ten minutes later, Olenka unlocked the door and led them into the safe house. To Sweeney, it looked more like a safe walk-in closet. He'd never seen such a small apartment.

"So, Olenka, do you live here?" John asked.

The pretty blonde shook her head. "No. I live on the other side of the river."

"Oh."

Sweeney had seen minivans larger than the living area they were crammed into. It was adorned with a small table and chair, a television, and a short tattered couch, which in the States would have barely qualified as a loveseat.

Sweeney nudged John. "The folks at the agency must be real big spenders, huh?"

Mary smiled. "You should see the bathroom. If you're sitting on the toilet, you can touch all four walls with your head!"

Olenka spoke up. "Actually, this is a fairly large apartment for Ukraine. Sometimes two families would share a flat this size."

Sweeney whistled and shook his head in amazement.

Mary cleared her throat. "Okay. Down to business. Olenka's contact has been getting to know our scientist for the past month. He's going to try to set us up with Dr. Lychenko sometime in the next twenty-four—"

A ringing coming from the direction of Olenka's handbag interrupted her. Olenka fished her phone from it and looked at the caller ID. "That's Dimitri now." She flipped the phone open, squeezing past Sweeney into the tiny kitchen.

Mary watched her go, then continued. "We may have a mission sooner than we expected. Our gear arrived this afternoon in a diplomatic pouch from our friends at the Irish embassy." She pointed to a black duffel bag next to the couch. "That'll have our commo and night vision and a few other things."

"How about weapons?" John asked.

Mary nodded. "We're good to go. Olenka has Russian SR-1 pistols here for all of us, and some bigger guns at another safe house if we need them. But remember, you aren't here as soldiers. We're just collecting information. If we get in a firefight, the only army you'll see will be wearing the Ukrainian flag. So stay as low profile as possible."

Sweeney bit his tongue to keep himself from saying something like, *Well, duh!*

Olenka returned with a serious look. "Okay. Dimitri has arranged a meeting with Lychenko tonight." She appraised the team and frowned. "But you can't go dressed like you are."

Rip looked down at his own khaki slacks and polo shirt. "What's wrong with these clothes?"

"The meeting is at a high-end nightclub on the river. Only do not worry, I can get outfits for you before the meeting." Olenka produced a pen and notepad. "May I have your sizes, please?"

6

THE STREETLIGHTS FLICKERED on as Grigor coasted his rattletrap Lada to a stop across from the Dnieper River. The car's engine died with a cough—a fitting commentary on the state of his life. He laid his head on the steering wheel and sighed. All of his worst nightmares had become a reality in the last twenty-four hours.

Adela was gone. *How did I not see it coming?* He was a fool to ever believe that a woman so young and beautiful would want him for anything more than money. And now she had what she wanted. All of it. Seeing the proof in the zero balance when he checked his account had literally sucked the breath from his lungs. In the space of a day, he'd gone from astoundingly rich to penniless.

And now I'm as good as dead.

The mafia would be looking for him soon, if they weren't already. That he'd ever taken a loan from them was a further monument to his stupidity. They would find him—he was sure of that—and when they did, his life would be over, most likely in a slow and agonizing fashion. The panic that had first gripped him when the realization had hit was gone, replaced by a sickening heavy dread, like a bag full of sand in his gut.

The only thing he had been able to think to do was call Dimitri and ask for help. Though he hadn't known him for more than a few weeks, the short Russian man was the only person he could call a friend.

Rolling his head to one side, he could make out the blue and yellow neon lights of the floating-barge casino across the street. Dimitri had assured him it was a safe place for them to meet, and had given him a sliver of hope. He'd promised that he knew someone who could help.

"Just make sure you aren't followed," Dimitri had instructed.

But Grigor was a scientist, not a spy. He had no idea how to know if someone were following him. *Come to think of it, why would a janitor be concerned about such things?* No matter, he was here now, desperately trying to stoke the fires of hope that somehow his friend would be able to help him.

Out of the darkening sky, heavy drops of rain began pelting the car's metal roof. Their *pop-pop-pop*ping made Grigor sit up. He turned off the headlights and yanked the keys out of the ignition, hurrying to get aboard the casino barge before the rain began in earnest.

He dodged between two cars and dashed across the street, running down the sloping drive that led to the berth where the casino was permanently moored. In all the nights Grigor had spent gambling over the past year, this was one establishment he'd never visited, because if the huge boat's shimmering exterior was any indication, the games within were far too expensive.

An enormous bouncer stood inside a booth near the entrance to the pier. Panic gripped Grigor once again as he realized there might be a cover charge to enter the casino. He had but a few hryvni in his pocket, hardly enough for a drink, much less entrance. But the guard simply waved him inside with an expressionless nod. Grigor then saw the sign announcing that the cover charge went into effect after 9 p.m. His watch told him he'd gotten there with only thirty minutes to spare.

He crossed the short gangway and entered the boat. Inside, he was at once bombarded by bad American rock music. Aside from plush gold carpeting and a hostess in a too-tight white suit coat, the brightly lit entry salon was empty. He nodded to her and asked, "De bar?" She gave him a coy smile and pointed the way.

The music got louder as he entered a large room with a low ceiling, lit exclusively by the disco lights on the dance floor. As his eyes began to adjust, he saw about two dozen women whose appearance suggested that they were for sale. The ladies that weren't standing at the bar were clustered around five or six well-dressed men seated on overstuffed couches around the room. The men sipped mixed drinks and looked up at Grigor as if he'd just stolen their wallets. The dance floor was empty. A blue neon light behind the bar cast a pallid hue on those standing nearby.

The panic started to seep back into his brain. He was turning to flee when a voice sounded above the din, coming from the shadowy corner nearest to him. "Grigor!"

He squinted in the direction of the voice and could just make out the squat form of Dimitri sitting at a table all alone. The Russian waved him over. "Come, sit down before you fall down."

Grigor hurried to the table and took his friend's advice. "I got your message."

"Obviously. Vodka?"

Grigor nodded. The thought of drinking himself under the table wasn't unattractive at the moment. "Dimitri, Adela has left me."

His friend gave a sad nod. "You said as much on the phone. I'm very sorry to hear it."

"That's not the worst of it. She took all my money. And I have debts, Dimitri…" He paused for a moment as the words choked him. "Big debts."

Dimitri nodded and stared into his drink. "I know someone who can help. They are foreigners…and they might be able to fix your problem. I took the liberty of contacting them so that you could meet them."

"Foreigners?" Grigor was suddenly suspicious. "What foreigners?"

His friend stood, looking past him toward the door. "Here they come now."

Mary swallowed her discomfort and hooked her arm through Sweeney's as they followed Olenka and John into the dim dance club of the floating casino. Rip was stationed outside. She took some comfort from the bulge of his bicep beneath the hastily purchased suit coat. She forced a smile and whispered to Sweeney, "Just act natural."

Sweeney's grin in return was as fake as her own. "You've gotta be kidding me. This is insane."

It was hard to disagree. When they'd received the call at the safe house three hours ago, telling them where to find their scientist, Mary had been hoping to fall into a jetlag-induced nap. Instead, they'd rushed around in frantic preparation for this meeting. In the short time between then and now, Olenka had left and returned with a minidress for Mary that had made her gasp out loud, plus two black suits for Sweeney and John, to their great consternation.

And here they were at a place called the *River Palace,* which, from the looks of tonight's partygoers, was having a seminar for working girls. Mary suddenly felt even more uneasy in the minidress. And the high heels were killing her. In her CIA training at the Farm, she'd been to mock diplomatic parties where they dressed up and learned to mingle with foreign dignitaries to glean certain information. But they'd never done anything like this.

Sweeney chuckled. "Hey, relax. With that dress on, at least you fit in."

"Shut up," she said through her pasted-on smile.

"Rip will be sad he got left to stand guard outside. He could probably have started a Bible study with some of these nice young ladies."

John overheard. "At ease, Bobby. Stay on your toes here; this place doesn't look friendly."

Olenka nodded toward a short, stocky man with a comb-over and a shadow of a beard. He was sitting at a corner table with a gangly man whose coat was draped over his shoulders as if he were a wire hanger.

That must be our scientist, Mary thought.

The shorter man got up and approached them, smiling and speaking to Olenka in rapid-fire Russian, which Mary understood most of.

Olenka began to translate for John and Sweeney. "This is Dimitri. He has spent several weeks getting to know the man at the table there. He's Dr. Grigor Lychenko, the scientist you were briefed about earlier. Dimitri says Grigor is in trouble with some men who loaned him money. He was supposed to pay them back today, but his fiancée stole all his money and disappeared."

"And now the mafia's after him," Sweeney quipped. "That's wonderful."

Olenka didn't catch his sarcasm and gave him a confused look. "No, that's bad."

"Come, let us sit down," Dimitri suggested.

John and Sweeney secured some empty chairs, and the four of them crowded in around the table.

The scientist regarded the four newcomers with a look just one step away from panic. "Who are you?" His high-pitched Russian was tinged with fear.

Mary looked Lychenko in the eye and addressed him directly in Russian. "We're friends of Dimitri's. He told us about the trouble you are having, and I think we can help."

Lychenko swallowed hard. "You are Americans?"

She shook her head. "That is not important right now. We need to get you someplace safe. But first, you must help me so that we can help you."

A hint of suspicion mixed with the desperation on Lychenko's face. "What do you want from me?"

Mary pinned him with her gaze. "Tell me what you know about Iso-Triethyl Borane."

The scientist's eyes opened wider when she named the explosive. Then, with visible effort, he regained his composure.

"Looks like you struck a nerve," John whispered.

Lychenko looked at Mary. "If you are looking for this chemical, I cannot help you."

A ball of ice formed in the pit of Mary's stomach. *He thinks we're here to prosecute him for selling it.* She racked her brain for a way to salvage this. Sweeney and John were shifting in their seats and exchanging glances with each other.

Mary flashed a smile to put him at ease. "I think you misunderstand, Dr. Lychenko. We know that you once worked in a lab that was experimenting with ITEB. There must have been a substantial amount at the lab. All we want to know is where it is or who has it now."

Grigor shrugged and spread his hands. "I'm sorry, I really do not know."

Mary looked around and tried to think of a way to draw the scientist out. Olenka and Dimitri were holding a quiet conversation while John and Sweeney scanned the room. Mary hoped they had their minds on security, not on the busty bleached blondes who were casting glances at them as if she and Olenka were stealing their business.

John put a hand to his ear, then looked up at Mary. "Rip says we may have company. Let's hurry."

Mary turned back to Lychenko. "Do you remember the location of the lab in Chernobyl?"

He hesitated a moment and then nodded.

"Good. Take us to it, and in exchange we will ensure that your debt is repaid."

A flash of hope in Lychenko's eyes quickly clouded over. "That would be impossible. The lab is inside the dead zone. There are guards on every road, and no one is allowed in without authorization. Besides, there is no—"

"Look out," Sweeney muttered. "We've got trouble."

Mary turned toward the door and saw what Sweeney was looking at. Three huge men had just entered. They looked like pro wrestlers. One wore a silver double-breasted suit and sported shoulder-length brown hair. The second wore a blond crew cut with diamond earrings, with his dress shirt open at the collar. The thug in the middle wore a black suit and a ponytail. All three were staring hard in their direction.

"Stay calm," John said.

The three men walked over to them.

Mary stole a glance at Lychenko and saw his face almost melt in terror when he saw them coming. *Not good.*

One of the men, the one with his black hair greased back into a ponytail, addressed Lychenko. "*Privyet,* Grigor. Did you think you could run away from us without paying your debts?"

Lychenko stammered a response, his eyes pleading as they darted from Mary to the men.

The longhaired thug was rubbing his stubbly beard and paying more attention to Mary than he was to the scientist. He said something to her that needed no translation, then reached down and ran his fingertips up her arm.

Before he reached her shoulder, Sweeney was on his feet, tipping his chair over backward. Somebody screamed. Mary grabbed the jerk's thumb and twisted until he bellowed in pain. He pulled away and reached into his jacket. John jumped up and drove a fist into Mr. Ponytail's Adam's apple.

"Gun!"

Mary jumped to her feet and caught a glimpse of the blond man's bejeweled fist clutching a huge .44-caliber pistol. She felt the fire explode from the barrel.

The round missed her, but the deafening roar was almost as bad as being shot. She grabbed the edge of the table and drove the heel of her stiletto into his groin. He gasped and dropped the gun, clutching himself.

Maybe these shoes aren't so useless after all.

Sweeney had his arm around the neck of the longhaired thug and looked to be trying to pull his head right off. John kicked Ponytail Man in the knee and grabbed his arm as he produced his own silver-plated automatic pistol, which spat flame and shattered a nearby window as the man's legs buckled.

"Go!" John shouted. "Get out of here!"

Mary turned to grab Olenka and stopped at the sight of Lychenko. He was still seated. His head lolled to one side. Blood covered the wall.

She'd seen enough. Mary snatched Olenka's arm. "Get up!" The terrified girl complied, and they made for the door.

John was already up and shoving his way through the screaming throng like a rhinoceros, yelling for her to follow. Everyone was trying to get out at once. She couldn't see Sweeney. Pulling Olenka behind her, she grabbed John's sleeve. "Wait! We can't leave Bobby!"

"He's coming! Just go!"

Another shot rang out. A tsunami of panicked humanity headed for the exit, and there was no going back.

They surged through the luxurious entry salon, then shouldered

their way down the gangplank and into the crisp night air. Only
when they reached the street was she able to stop and look around.
No Sweeney.

Please, no!

John stopped too, panting. "You stay here. I'll go find him."

She grabbed John's arm again. "Coop, no! You can't go back in
there!"

Rip ran up to them, breathing hard. "What happened in there?
Where's Bobby?"

Sirens sounded in the distance. The emotions on John's face were
darker than the night sky. "Rubio, you get to the car with the girls.
I'm going to find him."

Mary grabbed his arm. "No, you're not. Look." She nodded
toward the door. A dozen black-suited security guards had locked
down the entrance to the ship. Each brandished a boxy metal
machine pistol.

"Uzis," Rip muttered.

"Casino security," Olenka said, her eyes wide.

John shook his head, eyes smoldering. "Never leave a fallen com-
rade. I'm going to find him."

Before Mary could stop him again, the tall team sergeant disappeared into the crowd.

Sweeney struggled to the surface of the water and swallowed a mouth-
ful of the most disgusting liquid he'd ever tasted. This was turning out
to be a really bad day.

It got even worse when a fusillade of bullets smacked the dark river around him. He sucked in a ragged breath and submerged again, then swam blindly toward the sound of the shooting, hoping his assailants would expect him to do the opposite. When he bumped into slimy metal, he'd found what he was looking for—the hull of the floating casino.

If I get under them, they won't be able to see me.

The men above were leaning out the shattered window that seconds earlier had served as his exit from the boat.

Sweeney came slowly to the surface and exhaled, feeling the weight of the ridiculous suit as he trod the frigid water, trying to breathe. He suddenly remembered how much he hated swimming.

The shooting had stopped—though he couldn't be sure if they had left or were just switching magazines. *Either way, I've got to get out of here quick. Nobody said anything about swimming.*

He started a breaststroke for the bow of the boat, then swam faster when he heard the sirens.

How much are they paying me for this?

From his current position he could see several smaller craft tied up to the long wooden boardwalk that ran along the water's edge. The closest was a midsized cruising yacht. He sucked in another ragged breath and pushed off the prow of the casino ship and aimed for the rudder of the cruiser.

When his lungs were ready to burst, he floated to the surface, half expecting another hail of lead. Instead, the sirens had gotten louder, and a quick look behind him convinced Sweeney that his assailants had decided it was time to leave.

He pulled himself around the stern of the yacht, then pushed across to the next boat in line, a smaller craft. Continuing from one boat to the next, he put a hundred yards between himself and the casino before pulling around to where the vessels met the six-foot retaining wall at the shore.

A boardwalk floated just above the waterline and included a short pier that jutted ten meters out into the river. To his left, a streetlight illuminated a stairway leading up to the street. Anyone who had been in the vicinity was now crowded around the casino a football field's length to his right, craning to get a look at the action.

Sweeney floated next to the boardwalk and considered his options. The team had discussed plans for every contingency before leaving the safe house an hour earlier. They had agreed to meet at Olenka's car, parked two blocks away on a side street, within ten minutes, if they got separated. If that didn't work, they were to make their way back to the safe house however they could.

If he hurried, he might still make it to the car. That would be marginally better than trying to hail a taxi in a soaked black suit that now made him look—and smell—like a wet skunk.

He was just about to pull himself up onto the dock when heavy footsteps sounded close by. Sweeney held his breath and ducked under the floating structure. He looked through the wooden slats and saw a shadow pass in front of the glow of the streetlight.

He dared not exhale. His heart thumped harder with each successive beat. The sirens had stopped, and the only sound Sweeney could hear now was the rhythmic lapping of water against the dock.

Then he heard a harsh whisper. "Bobby!"

John!

The breath exploded from his lungs. "Coop! That you?" He ducked back out from under the dock to see his team sergeant standing over him.

"Oh, thank God." John dropped to one knee and offered Sweeney his hand. "I thought you were a goner, buddy."

Sweeney grabbed John's hand and let him pull him up onto the dock. "That makes two of us."

7

Parishev, in the Dead Zone

A LIGHT RAIN PATTERED off the wooden shingles on the derelict church. Maxim could feel it dampening the shirt on his back while he knelt outside with his face to the ground. Though his morning prayers would have been drier if he'd stayed inside, he never even considered it. *I would not offer prayers to Allah from inside the church of the infidel.*

Besides, it was much cooler out here—and the rain actually felt good on his neck after a long night inside, coaxing as much heat as possible out of their twin propane burners. If the mixture wasn't prepared in exactly the right way, it would not perform as needed and their entire operation would be a catastrophic failure.

He preferred a catastrophic success. In fact, there would be no success without the catastrophe.

Maxim realized he had long since finished praying, and sat up. There was a row of pine trees in front of him—to the east toward Mecca. Behind him lay the remnants of the village. So far, it had served their purposes well.

He looked down at his scarred hands, calloused from many years of carrying an RPG or AK-47. The two fingers he was missing had nothing to do with battle, though. They had been severed in a motorcycle crash. He'd spent his youth fighting the Russians who massacred his people wholesale. In fact, he could no longer remember a time when he hadn't been at war.

But that was the essence of jihad, was it not? To struggle. He never believed he'd live long enough to teach others. But Allah had not seen fit to allow him to die a martyr just yet. *Perhaps soon.*

The sound of boots swishing through the tall grass reached his ears. He stood and saw Kyr clomping toward him, carrying his AK-47 as if it was a suitcase.

Maxim sighed. "You must be ready to fire your weapon at all times. It does no good like that. And look around you for once. The enemy won't be under your feet."

The boy looked up with an apathetic stare and did nothing with the weapon. "I have checked the entire village. No one is there."

Maxim frowned. "The old man will not stop beating on the door and complaining about his mother. Where is she?"

Kyr shrugged. "Maybe she is hiding. How should I know? But if that old man still has a mother, she can't possibly be a threat to us."

"Don't underestimate them, brother. In Kiev I saw an old woman working on a road crew—with a pick, no less."

Kyr just shrugged again.

Maxim continued, "Omar, Ayad, and Khamzad should be finishing the last batch now. Tomorrow is our moment of glory." He indicated the prayer mat he'd just left. "You should not neglect your prayers, brother. Today, especially."

Kyr's sulkiness returned. "I don't even understand the words. Why can't we pray in our language?"

"The Qur'an was revealed in Arabic. We speak the word of Allah back to him."

"What kind of God isn't even able to learn a second language?"

"Hold your tongue, boy! Allah is not mocked."

Kyr's face fell. "I am sorry, brother. You are right, of course. It's just…" His voice trailed off.

"Just what?"

The young man peered out at him from beneath his long bangs but did not speak.

He didn't have to. Maxim could see the fear etched on his brother's face. "You are afraid to die. Is that it?"

Kyr just shrugged and turned away.

Maxim smiled and walked to him, sliding his burly arm around the boy's shoulders. "Think about this, Kyr. When we die, Allah gauges our good actions against our bad ones. If by chance your selfish deeds outweigh those that please him, hope for you is lost. But you know there is one way to be assured of heaven."

Kyr nodded. "To die for Allah. I know."

"Yes, that's right. And when you arrive in Paradise, who will be awaiting you there?"

His brother's look turned bashful. "Houris."

Maxim smiled. "Virgins, yes. All the pleasures your heart could ever hope for. Tell me, brother. What have you here on earth to compare with that?"

Kyr shrugged.

"That's what I thought. Perhaps, when you pray, you can ask for the knowledge of what to do with all those beautiful young ladies when you see them." Maxim laughed and slapped Kyr on the back. "But don't think too much about it now, brother. Now is not the time for lustful thinking."

Maxim turned and walked toward the church. Pushing the images of dark-eyed virgins from his own mind.

Now is the time for action.

San Jose, California

The mature shade trees lining Post Street in downtown San Jose also just happened to conceal most of the parking lot from the security cameras on the office building next door. The streetlights too—now lighting up the night—were only marginally effective in illuminating the parking lot, also because of the trees. Whoever had compiled the list Edgar held in his hand had certainly done his homework.

His cell phone chirped. The caller ID said simply, "Anonymous."

Edgar lifted the device to his ear. "This is Gustavo."

The voice that responded sent a chill down his spine. It was the gringo. As before, it was *über* professional, with just a trace of a European accent that Edgar couldn't quite place.

"Now that you have possession of the product," the gringo said, "how long until it reaches the market?"

Edgar switched his phone to the other ear and checked his watch. "By sunup you should hear about it on the news."

"Very well. It is very important that the objectives be accomplished with a maximum of precision and care. Nothing can go wrong. I want complete redundancy."

Edgar's chest tightened. He didn't like the suggestion that he might not get the job done, though he knew there were a thousand things that could happen that he couldn't possibly plan for. But to be tactful, he said, "Precision in matters such as these is easier said than done. There are always risks."

"And that is where your expertise comes in." The intensity of the gringo's voice rose a notch. "Do the job as instructed and you have nothing to worry about."

Edgar knew that was a lie, but he was not the kind to argue. "You will not be disappointed."

"I will be waiting for the news." The line went dead.

Edgar flipped his phone shut and dropped it into the pocket of the faded blue coveralls he'd picked up at a thrift store that afternoon. He grabbed the tool bag that contained four one-liter glass bottles and a cordless Craftsman Sawzall with an offset blade.

Stepping out of his Ford Expedition, he surveyed the parking lot in the dim halogen glow. It was hemmed in on three sides by high brick buildings. Between two of them he could just make out the top of another building—this one completely covered in golden glass and lit up like a monument.

In a way, it was. The golden tower hosted one of the most important rooms in all of Silicon Valley: the Metropolitan Access Exchange–West. The exchange was like a mammoth interchange on the information superhighway, a switching point through which passed up to forty percent of the entire nation's Internet traffic.

Some of that traffic might have even belonged to Edgar as he'd researched the site from a truck-stop Internet kiosk that morning. He'd learned that security on the network access point was virtually impenetrable. The vast array of switches was housed in a climate-controlled steel cage. Getting in was out of the question.

But Edgar didn't need to get in.

He looked up and down the street to his left, noting a row of boutique shops and a small delicatessen, all of which were dark at this hour. He sauntered around to the opposite side of his SUV and immediately found what he was looking for in the street—the manhole cover.

Just as his instructions had noted, the cover was bolted shut. Not wanting to waste any time, Edgar pulled the Sawzall from the bag and immediately set to work cutting the bolts. The diamond-tipped blade had been expensive, but it made short work of the galvanized steel fasteners. Within two minutes he was prying the manhole cover open. He kissed the three rings on his left hand and dropped down into the hole.

Only when he had climbed partway down the metal ladder into the storm drain did he switch on his LED headlamp. The dark concrete passageway was much cleaner than he'd expected—no rats or spiders that he could see. Just a trickle of relatively clear water in the bottom of the tube, which ran roughly east-west.

Crouched low to keep from scraping his head, Edgar lugged the black tool bag behind him, his shoulders quickly tiring from the weight. *I'm too old for this kind of work.* His increasingly strained breathing mixed with the sound of his footsteps to echo away down the tunnel. After several minutes, he stopped to rest, sagging against the curved concrete wall.

An idea formed in his mind, a possibility that might relieve him of some of the heavy lifting this job would obviously require. Though he hadn't been to the United States in years, he knew people back in Colombia who had contacts here. Perhaps when this job was done, he would make some inquiries.

He stood and sucked in a great breath of stale air. First he had to successfully check this site off the list.

Fifty meters farther he found what he was looking for—the grate that led to a subterranean air duct. A low hum sounded through the grate, and even with his gloved hands he could feel the pull of air as an unseen ventilation system sucked stale air from the storm drain.

Smart. By taking air from underground, the system does not have to work as hard to cool it. Down here the temperature stays constant. A faint smile formed on his lips. *The gringos are always so worried about saving energy…*

Yes, the gringos were worried about a lot of things that the rest of the world could not afford. They opposed genetically enhanced food that would increase yields and possibly rid the world of hunger. They outlawed smoking in most places in their own country while allowing cigarette companies to export their deadly product around the world. They didn't mind if people in other nations died from cheap cigarettes, so long as they got their tax revenue.

He set the bag down on the floor and produced the Sawzall, using it to make short work of the grate. Then he took out three of the glass bottles and, with great care, slid them through the hole, stacking them like wine bottles in a cellar.

He brought out a cheap plastic bowl and a bottle of glass-etching solution he'd purchased at a stained-glass supply store on the outskirts of town. After pouring the etching liquid into the bowl, he carefully set the last glass bottle upright in its center. Almost immediately, a wisp of chemically generated smoke appeared as the hydrofluoric acid in the liquid began to eat away at the glass.

Edgar replaced his tools in the bag and hurried down the pipe the way he had come. The diluted acid solution would take at least four hours to eat through the glass. At which time the liquid explosive would be exposed to air.

By then he planned to be very far away.

Stescyna Village, North of Kiev

Olenka's blue SUV rolled into the small village just after 2 a.m.

Because Mary's internal clock was still on eastern time, she was wide awake. She wondered how the rest of the team had been able to crash out in the back during the two-hour drive north from Kiev. She smiled at Olenka and jerked a thumb toward the sleeping trio behind them. "I wish I could fall asleep so easily."

Sweeney lolled, snoring by the window in his sweatpants and T-shirt. John and Rip still wore what they'd had on at the nightclub, as did Mary and Olenka. At Olenka's urging, they had stopped at the apartment for only a few moments to grab their things before heading out of town.

"Perhaps it's their training," Olenka said.

Mary huffed. *Sure, like the three of them just graduated from sack-out school.* She stifled a yawn. "Or maybe they're just tired. Especially Sweeney, after his swim."

Olenka grimaced. "I'm very sorry about that. I should have insisted that we meet somewhere private. But I didn't want to blow Dimitri's cover and lose our scientist. I'm just glad Dimitri got away safely."

Mary shrugged. "Obviously those goons were following the scientist. I don't think it would have mattered much where we scheduled the meet." She shuddered as the ghastly image of the gore-covered Grigor Lychenko flashed again in her mind, as it had almost constantly since they'd escaped the casino.

Olenka shook her head. "The mafia in Kiev is very powerful. It was a good decision to leave the city, I think. Oh, here's the place now." She pulled over, the headlights illuminating a flimsy gate made of barbed wire strung between two wooden poles.

"I'll get the gate," Mary said, opening her door.

The cool night air felt good against her legs as she wrestled the floppy gate out of the way. Olenka pulled through, and Mary closed the gate before jumping back into the car. When she slammed the door, she noticed that all three commandos in the backseat were stretching and rubbing the sleep from their eyes.

"We're here," she said.

"Where's here?" Sweeney asked.

"The village is called Stescyna," Olenka said.

"Chechnya," Sweeney repeated.

Olenka stifled a giggle.

Situated well back from the road, the house was made of brick and had a small detached shed. Olenka threw the vehicle in park.

Mary turned to her passengers. "Let's get inside, and I will brief you on what Olenka and I discussed on the ride up."

"Roger that," John said, unfolding his tall frame from the backseat.

Rip stepped out of the SUV, put both hands in the small of his back, and groaned. Mary stepped out too and was crossing in front of the vehicle when a large red mutt bounded up, barking savagely. Adrenaline surged through her already-shot nervous system and she yelped, jumping onto the hood of Olenka's car. Rip dove back into the vehicle.

Then Sweeney appeared from her left. Facing the dog, he held out one hand. "Whoa, there, big guy. What's your name, huh?"

The dog exchanged his bark for a growl, baring its teeth at Bobby Sweeney, the muscular sergeant from Alabama.

"Hey, now," Sweeney said, "that's all right. Yeah…it's okay. We're friends, see?"

The dog licked its lips, then looked from Sweeney to Mary.

"Come on, boy." Sweeney's voice had a friendly, singsong quality to it.

It worked. The dog's tail dropped, and it tentatively sniffed the soldier's hand.

Mary forgot her fear and gaped at Sweeney. "That was amazing!"

"Nah," Sweeney said. "You just surprised him. He was probably sleeping." He looked up at Olenka. "What's his name?"

She shrugged. "He came with the house. I don't think he has a name."

Sweeney scratched the dog behind the ears. "A dog's gotta have a name. Let's call him Big Al."

"Big Al?" Rip said, venturing back outside the vehicle. "That's a dumb name."

Sweeney straightened. "Big Al happens to be the name of the

Crimson Tide mascot, bud. So watch your lip or I'll have Big Al bite it off."

Rip eyed the dog and gave it a wide berth as he moved toward the house. Mary climbed down from the hood of the car. "Thanks, Bobby."

"Don't mention it."

They waited while Olenka unlocked the front door, then left them to get some equipment from the car while they entered.

The old wooden floors in the entryway creaked under their weight. To the left was what Mary would have described as a sitting room, though the furniture was draped with sheets and dust covered everything else.

"Nobody's been here in a while," Rip said.

"Thank you, Captain Obvious," Sweeney joked.

At the end of the short hall was a dining area with a table and six chairs. "Let's go in here, and I'll brief you on our plan," Mary said.

Rip handed out energy bars from his personal stash while they took their seats. "I've got a couple of bottles of water too," he said, handing one to Sweeney.

Sweeney looked up at him. "Thanks, bro. I guess I'll forgive you for making fun of Big Al."

"Okay," Mary said, "while Olenka gets the map, let's go over what we know. Our late Ukrainian scientist confirmed that the ITEB came from a lab inside the exclusionary zone around Chernobyl. So we're back to the original plan: find the lab. Olenka says she knows the lab's approximate location. The plan I worked out on the sat-phone with higher is to make a quick reconnaissance into the area to find the lab and see if there is any ITEB remaining there.

"The mission is simple," Mary continued. "We're going to bypass the town of Chernobyl proper and head straight for the site of the underground lab. If the lab is empty, we'll leave immediately. If not, we'll set timed charges to blow whatever remains and then leave—making sure to bring back a sample for our forensics people. Either way, we want to get out of the dead zone as soon as possible. I estimate the entire trip will take five to six hours."

"That guy ain't going to be selling any more of the stuff anyway," Sweeney said. "Why not take his word for it?"

Mary folded her hands, trying not to be offended at how casually Sweeney was handling this. "Because if the chemical is still there, someone else could steal the rest of it and this whole nightmare will start all over again."

John nodded. "Fair enough."

Olenka bustled in, toting a black duffel bag and a rolled-up map. She set the bag on the floor while Mary unrolled the map on the table. John grabbed Sweeney's half-empty water bottle and used it to hold the map down.

"Take it away, Agent Orange," Sweeney said.

John snickered. "Maybe we should rethink that call sign."

"Be serious, you two," Mary said. Orange One was a perfectly good call sign. These jokers would figure out a way to twist anything into a gag.

Olenka was oblivious to the "Agent Orange" connection. "Right," she said, "let me see… The reactor is here." She set a dusty saltshaker in the center of the map. "Pripyat is here, about a kilometer away. It was once a large town, very modern. I went there once about six months ago. It's very strange to see. Everything was left when the people were evacuated. Some of the apartments still have dishes on the tables and family photos on the shelf. It's as if the town was frozen in time."

"Where is the lab?" John asked.

"We believe it was about halfway between the reactor and Pripyat, along this road." She traced the route with her finger.

Rip raised his hand. "Am I the only one that isn't real excited about going into a highly radioactive area?"

No, you are definitely not the only one, Mary thought, though she wouldn't say so out loud.

Olenka nodded. "That's understandable. But you shouldn't be too worried as long as you get in and out quickly. Radiation exposure is measured in units called millisieverts. We all absorb radiation every year—somewhere around one-point-five to two millisieverts. This comes from the air, from the ground, from flying on airplanes, getting x-rayed when we visit the doctor, and many other things.

"People who work in Chernobyl are receiving approximately ten millisieverts per year. This may heighten their risk of some kinds of sickness, but most of them stay very healthy."

"So spending a half a day inside the dead zone isn't going to kill us," Sweeney said, looking relieved.

"Don't worry, bro," Rip said, patting Sweeney on the shoulder. "God will get us through."

"Thank you, Reverend Rubio!"

"Focus, gentlemen." Mary was having a hard time not being peeved. She couldn't see why Sweeney was giving Rip such a hard time. Sure, he'd gotten religion in Panama. But from everything she could see, the change was mostly good.

Olenka raised an eyebrow. "The biggest danger is that you could ingest radioactive particles and therefore continue to be exposed once you leave. This is why we must plan for you to wash and change clothing as soon as possible after you leave the zone. Also, while you are inside, you must take great care not to inhale or swallow any radioactive particles. Also, most of the radiation has been washed from the roads by the rains. But if you travel cross country you will be exposing yourselves to much higher levels of contamination."

"So stick to the roads whenever possible," Mary said. "Got it?"

Olenka reached into her duffel bag and produced several electronic devices, which she laid on the table. "I have some items here that will be useful for you. First, we have two global positioning units. I've already programmed waypoints that will help you on your journey into the exclusion zone and out again."

John slid one of the GPS units to Rip. "Rubio, geekery is your department. See if you have any questions. Bobby, you take the other one."

Olenka picked up another device, this one made of dark gray plastic. "This device will help me keep track of you while you are on the mission."

"Looks like a GPS without the screen," Rip noted. "What is it?"

Olenka set it on the table. "It's a personal locator beacon. It plots its position in real time and broadcasts that signal. I can receive it and track you on my computer."

"Like the Blue Force Tracker," Rip said.

"Yes," Mary said with a nod. "Only much smaller."

"What is a Blue Tracker?" Olenka asked.

John answered. "Something U.S. forces have been using for years to help us keep track of one another. Keeps us from shooting good guys."

Sweeney picked up the unit. "Frank was talking about these the other day. Climbers and hikers are using them as emergency transponders in case they get lost or have a problem."

Olenka nodded. "Same technology here, only this one is more powerful than consumer models. I should be able to watch your progress in real time, which will allow me to help you if there are any problems."

John's eyebrows went up. "You've got to like that. What's our security situation?"

"I can answer that one," Mary said. "The Ukrainian army has a detachment of soldiers stationed around the reactor itself. They are known to run infrequent patrols in the surrounding area. As you know, we're not going in with the consent of their government, so it's imperative that we not attract attention."

"Are we carrying weapons?" Sweeney asked, mouth half full of power bar.

Mary nodded. "We are. Olenka has some Russian paratrooper AK-74s for us. But they are only to be used as a last resort for personal protection. Got that?"

"Wait, how exactly are we supposed to sneak into the dead zone without anyone seeing us?" Rip's brow was knotted with concern.

Olenka answered. "There are many entrances to the dead zone that are, you would say, unauthorized. Even now, many people enter the area looking for anything of value. Since the paved roads going into Chernobyl are all guarded, the looters simply use these old farm roads. That's how you'll get in."

"With what? Are we taking your car?"

Olenka shook her head. "We have something much better. Please follow me and I will show you." She turned and marched out of the room.

Task Force Valor followed her outside and over to the small shed. The blond Ukrainian agent removed a bright new padlock from the door, then slid it open and clicked on an overhead light, revealing two brand new Polaris all-terrain vehicles.

"Four-wheelers!" Sweeney exclaimed. "Why didn't you say so? I've been driving these things since I was five years old!"

Mary sauntered up next to him with a devious smile. "That's great, Bobby. But on this mission, I'm driving."

8

Great Falls, Virginia

A SOFTLY TICKING grandfather clock outside Michael Lafontaine's study was the only sound in the mammoth house at this hour of the night. The housekeeper had left hours ago, and the quiet made this the most productive time of his day.

Lafontaine, a former Army colonel, sat in his small office at an antique cedar desk, clad only in a pair of running shorts and a tank top. His attire might have appeared out of place in the luxurious setting had anyone been there to see it. The desk was bare except for a brass lamp and the yellow pad upon which he was scribbling.

If there was one thing Michael's father had taught him, it was the importance of removing distractions, something the desk, the spartan office, and even the fact that there was no wife and family cluttering up his house, attested to. Michael had taken his father's no-nonsense philosophy to heart at a young age, and it had enabled him to succeed where others had failed, creating several fortunes of his own since then.

But now there was a major distraction in his life, and there was no possible way to ignore it. So he had to figure out a solution that would be tenable for a man who had always kept himself free of relational entanglements.

But for a brief time twenty years earlier.

She had been absolutely ravishing, with cocoa-colored skin and striking eyes as blue as his own—a distinguishing feature of the Costa Ricans whose grandparents had emigrated from Italy some thirty years earlier. Her jet black hair had hung in light curls down to the small of her back, and she'd had a mischievous smile that had captivated him from the first time he'd seen it.

More intriguing than her looks, however, had been her brain. She had a very linear way of thinking—something he'd not found before or since in a woman—and it had enabled them to spend countless hours, over cups of aromatic *café con leche,* discussing the Nicaraguan mess, the Contras he was there to train, and the merits of stopping the Communists before they obtained a foothold in the region.

She had challenged him to step outside his gringo way of thinking, to see America as more than the United States, and to work within the local culture instead of trying to superimpose his own onto it. That process had since allowed him to succeed, where others had not, in motivating men who were not Americans to fight for America. And he owed that success to her.

Then, they had become lovers, and it had ruined everything. The intellectual side of their relationship had been drowned out by the heavy drums of passion. Not long after that, she had simply disappeared. Not even the great sums of money he had spent trying to find her had picked up the slightest trace. It was as if she had been nothing but a dream.

Now he knew why she had left. And the answer ignited an inferno deep within him, a rage that threatened to consume him.

But Michael Lafontaine was more disciplined than that. He would not allow a betrayal to ruin him. Instead, he had made a decision that would make up for all the lost years. But it would be costly. Yes, very costly.

Money, however, was the least of his concerns. He'd long ago come to understand that striving after money was a life-sapping, meaningless exercise in passivity. And Michael was anything but passive.

He turned and removed a thick book from the shelf behind the desk. *Atlas Shrugged,* by Ayn Rand. He had read the story for the first time as a Firstie at West Point, and the author's objectivist philosophy had changed his life.

The story was prescient, written in the 1950s about a United States of America where hard work and personal initiative were punished. A place where those who supported the economy by their industry and wit were slapped with punitive taxes as if they, the "evil rich," were to blame for society's ills. In the end, all the moguls of industry simply disappeared, taking their initiative and hard work with them.

The longer he lived, the better that idea sounded.

He flipped to a well-worn passage near the middle of the book. One of his favorite quotes was highlighted in yellow:

Americans were the first to understand that wealth has to be created. The words "to make money" hold the essence of human morality....

Until and unless you discover that money is the root of all good, you ask for your own destruction. When money ceases to be the tool by which men deal with one another, then men become the tools of men. Blood, whips and guns—or dollars. Take your choice—there is no other—and your time is running out.

Michael closed the book and sighed. Money was a tool that allowed one to build, create, and shape one's world. And it was only in building and shaping that a man could feel truly alive. Collecting tools for the sake of owning them was foolish. Using those tools to construct a meaningful existence was as close to godhood as he ever hoped to get in this life.

Lafontaine was no pantheist, however. He believed strongly in the merits of religion. He made a point of attending the Catholic church near his home whenever his schedule allowed. It helped remind him of the things that were truly important—keeping a sense of one's own smallness in the scope of the universe, helping one's fellow man, and making a difference in the world for good.

These were the things that motivated Michael Lafontaine. They were the tenets that made him so driven. And he had no doubt that if there was a God, He would ultimately be pleased with Michael Lafontaine, if He bothered to care. For his part, Michael didn't spend much energy thinking about it.

The clock in the hall chimed once. Time for his workout. Michael rose and exited the study, padding silently through the marble entryway and down the stairs to his basement workout room. There, he stepped onto the Landice L9 treadmill and hit the Quick

Start button. The integrated flat-panel LCD came to life at the touch of another button, tuned perpetually to the BBC.

The polished announcer was reporting on the Russian president's recent visit to Cuba. Lafontaine started jogging as the treadmill initiated his thirty-minute program.

The announcer moved to a new story. *"A large fire this morning in downtown San Jose, California, has caused a major disruption in Internet traffic around the country. The fire is being scrutinized by federal investigators after an anonymous phone call linked the suspected arson to a radical Islamic group."*

Michael turned the volume up a little as he jogged. Grainy images of what looked to be an office building backlit by a leaping pyre of flame flashed across the small screen.

"Santa Clara County fire investigators told reporters that the U.S. Federal Bureau of Investigation was sending a team to determine the validity of the claim. As yet, no injuries have been reported. In other news..."

Michael stabbed the Mute button on the television and kept running, his mind now outpacing the treadmill. He'd known for years that this day would arrive—that another terrorist attack on U.S. soil was only a matter of when, not if. He'd talked about it with congressmen, senators, anybody who would listen. It was time for America to stop believing that the ridiculous Department of Homeland Security could protect it from the barbarians.

As much as he hated the spotlight, he knew it was time to go looking for it. The perfect sound bite was already rolling around in his head.

America is burning, and it's time to hold our politicians' feet to the fire.

Sweeney wrapped his arms around Mary's waist and held on for dear life. The flat Ukrainian countryside flew by in dark greens and blacks as she piloted the Polaris MV700 all-terrain vehicle down a disused back road an hour before sunrise.

"I can't believe you jumped out the window of the casino!" Mary yelled through the closed face shield on her motorcycle helmet.

Behind her, Sweeney yelled back, "I can't decide which I like less…that we're driving into a nuclear wasteland or that I'm being driven there by a girl!"

"Keep running your mouth and the radiation will be the least of your worries," Mary shot back.

Sweeney chuckled. "Remind me to teach you how to really drive one of these things sometime."

In response, Mary gunned the big ATV even harder as they climbed out of a small washout, catching air momentarily at the top. Sweeney grunted and held on tighter to the ATV's reinforced frame with one hand and the shortened AK-74 assault rifle with the other. He found he was smiling. Despite the banter, or maybe because of it, he couldn't help but like the feisty CIA officer.

Up ahead, John Cooper turned his ATV left to follow the muddy track. It ran beside a dense row of pines separating one dormant farmer's field from another. Rip Rubio was doing his best to stay on behind John while clutching a bolt-action Soviet Dragunov sniper rifle.

They'd left Olenka's country safe house well before dawn, following the route she'd programmed into their handlebar-mounted

GPS units. The team made their way past dark farmhouses and quiet dachas—the quarter-acre gardens each family used for food.

The back roads had eventually narrowed to a rutted two-track, what their Ukrainian agent had called "the worst kept secret of the dead zone."

When Olenka had explained that looters still scoured the dead zone for anything they could haul away—from scrap metal to furniture—Sweeney had been incredulous. He imagined whoever was buying the looted goods was either unsuspecting or unconcerned that the products were still saturated with radiation.

As the light grew, the rain of the previous night combined with the brisk morning air to spawn a low-lying ground fog that made Sweeney shiver, despite his black Gore-Tex jacket. At least the fog obscured their passage from anyone more than a hundred yards away, though that probably didn't matter. The two structures they'd passed in the last couple kilometers had been in ruins—the roofs collapsed in on the houses, whose crooked window frames now stared vacantly at the overgrown landscape.

John pulled his four-wheeler up short and waited for Mary and Sweeney to catch up. Mary braked to a halt beside him.

Sweeney flipped the face shield up on his helmet. "What's up, Coop?"

John pointed up ahead. "I'm guessing that's where the dead zone begins."

Sweeney leaned to look around Mary. Barely visible through the fog ahead, the trail ended at a shiny new barbed-wire fence. Beyond it, several large trees had been felled across the road.

Rip piped in from where he sat behind John. "Man, it looks like the government has been out plugging holes, you know? How are we gonna get through that?"

"Can we go around it?" Mary asked.

John reached up and shut off the Polaris. "Let me go check it out on foot. Sweeney, come with me."

Mary killed her motor and hopped off the cycle. "I'm coming too."

Sweeney swung his foot over the seat. "Whoa, little lady. John's calling the shots here."

The CIA officer yanked off her helmet, exposing a very red face. "I am in charge of this operation, Sergeant Sweeney. And don't ever call me 'little lady.'"

Before he could respond, John stepped between them. "Hang on, Mary. I'm not trying to take over here. We just need to stay with a buddy in case anything happens. Tell you what, Sweeney and Rip will stay here and you and I can go check it out."

Sweeney would have objected, but he knew he'd look like an idiot contradicting John after he'd just asserted his authority. Mary, however, seemed placated by the offer.

"All right," she said. "Sure, John. Let's go."

With only a nod at Sweeney and Rip, John unslung his AK-74 and stalked off to inspect the roadblock.

Sweeney watched Mary's slender frame hurrying to catch up with John, then turned away, fuming.

Rip blew into his hands to warm them. "You don't like women much, do you, bro?"

Sweeney was surprised by the question. "What, because I don't want some chick with no combat experience getting us killed?"

Rip pursed his lips. "It's not just her, you know. You almost did cheetah flips when we were in Lebanon and Coop brought Liz out of that refugee camp. And you weren't happy when I showed up with Fernanda in Panama. Is it *all* women that bother you, or just women who you happen to come in contact with?"

Cheetah flips? Sweeney wasn't having this conversation. "I ain't some kind of sugarpants, if that's what you mean. I don't like taking orders from a woman. That's all."

Rip nodded. "I can see that, bro."

Sweeney busied himself checking his ammo magazines for the third time that morning.

After a moment, Rip spoke up again. "Let me ask you another question."

Sweeney rolled his eyes. "Oh goody."

"I've been wondering about this for a while. When we were in that bunker in Panama, you said, 'It is appointed unto men once to die, but after this the judgment.'"

"So?" *Did I really say that?*

"So I was reading my Bible on the plane, and I found that exact quote. That's a Bible verse, bro."

"So?" *Guess some of that sixth-grade Sunday school stuff is still in there.*

"So where'd you learn it? I didn't know you read the Bible."

Sweeney was indignant. "That's what you get for assuming."

"Maybe so. I always thought you were an atheist since you never go to church."

Sweeney spun on Rip. "I'm no atheist."

Rip's hands shot up. "Dude, chill out. I'm not accusing you. Just wondering. How long did you go to church and stuff?"

Sweeney turned away, eyes clamped shut and wishing he were somewhere else. "Every Sunday morning. Every Sunday night. Visitation on Tuesdays. Prayer meeting on Wednesdays. Awana. Vacation Bible school. You name it." Just saying it brought back the dread he'd felt as a kid every time he'd been stuffed into the car to go to church. For a rambunctious kid like him, the services had been about as much fun as a spanking and a nap. *Sit still. No running in the Lord's house. No shouting in the Lord's house.*

"Wow," Rip said. "I had no idea. So why'd you quit going?"

Sweeney let out a humph. "In case you haven't noticed, I'm not very good at following rules."

Rip furrowed his brow. "Faith is not supposed to be about rules, bro."

"Try telling that to my mother."

"Ah." Rip tapped the side of his head and pointed at Sweeney. "Maybe that's why you have a problem with women in authority."

If Sweeney had been able to think of a snappy comeback, this would have been a good time to use it. Unfortunately, Rip was kind of making sense.

Rip continued. "Look, man, I understand. My mother hauled me off to church too. I didn't mind, though, because there were lots of pretty girls there. But I don't blame her for trying. You shouldn't blame your mom either."

"I don't blame my momma," Sweeney said quietly, without looking up. *There is more to it than that, isn't there?*

John came up on the radio. "Good news, gentlemen. Bring our rides up and I'll show you what we found."

Sweeney exhaled. Saved. He wasn't about to admit that Rip

might be on to something. "Thank you, Dr. Phil. Now can we get back to the mission?"

Rip winked at him before pulling on his helmet. "Don't worry, bro. Your secret is safe with me."

"I'm gonna punch you."

They climbed onto their respective ATVs and fired the engines. Sweeney kicked his into gear and sprayed Rip with mud as he hit the throttle.

His angry voice came over his headset. "Aw, man! Come on!"

Sweeney grinned. *Finally, something to smile about.*

John and Mary had taken a knee near a large pine tree whose branches almost overhung the new fence. As the four-wheelers pulled up to them, Sweeney saw that the trail turned hard left along the fence. Mary had gone to inspect the gap and was thirty yards away, trudging back toward them and carrying her AK-74 at the ready. Though it looked too big for her slender hands, Sweeney had no doubt she could use it. He'd seen her disassemble the firearm back at the safe house, and she clearly knew what she was doing.

John nodded toward a spot fifty yards down the fence line, where the tracks indicated another breach. "That barrier didn't stop them for long. They just went around it."

"Looters must be pretty determined, huh?" Sweeney said.

"Yep. Listen, Bobby, I want you to go easy on Phoenix. She and I talked about it, and I think she understands why I ought to make the tactical decisions out here. But it doesn't make it easier if you two are fighting like an old married couple."

I'd never enter that noose. Sweeney swallowed a snide retort and nodded. "You got it, boss. I'll play nice."

John slapped his helmet. "Attaboy. Let's go."

Mary was putting on her helmet as she covered the last fifteen feet to where the ATVs sat idling. "Bobby, why don't you drive for a while?" Apparently she wasn't still mad.

"Roger that." Sweeney revved the engine as she unslung her weapon and climbed on behind him. *Now this is more like it.*

As they edged through the gap in the fence, the sun crested the horizon and bathed the landscape in brilliant shades of coral. The fog immediately started to burn away, revealing immense pastures separated by stands of mixed hardwood and pine. Whatever Sweeney had imagined the dead zone would look like, this wasn't it. Except for the complete lack of civilization, he could have imagined he was trail riding around Grandpa's farm.

The readout on the radiation meter said 613. As Olenka had explained it, one thousand on the meter equaled one milli-whatever they weren't supposed to get too much of. He stole a look at his watch: 0653. With any luck, they'd be out of the dead zone by noon. He pushed the ATV as fast as he dared, noticing that John was hanging back a bit.

Eventually the trail turned to a heavily deteriorated paved road, which actually made their progress slower as the team had to dodge man-eating potholes. At one point Mary tapped his shoulder and pointed off to their right. A herd of what looked to be Shetland ponies was grazing on the far side of the field they were skirting. Several of the horses eyed the two four-wheelers intently as they passed, but other than that showed no interest in their presence.

Half an hour later, a lone fox darted across the road in front of them. Contrary to what his imagination had been expecting, none of the animals they saw had three heads or looked abnormal. The sun came out and warmed him as they rode along.

Sweeney had almost forgotten about the radiation when John's voice came over his headset. "The GPS shows we're within three miles of the reactor. Better slow up so nobody hears us."

Sweeney tapped his mike button twice to confirm the message and backed off the throttle.

He glanced down at the radiation meter on the handlebar and immediately wished he hadn't. The level was up to 1,100.

He pushed the ATV a little faster and wondered what radiation poisoning felt like.

9

SWEAT TRICKLED DOWN Alexi's back, soaking his shirt and jacket. It had been a long time since he'd exerted himself like this, and he was far too old to be doing so now.

But there was little choice. He had to help Mother.

He straightened up and listened, willing his breathing back to normal. There had been a flurry of activity outside the vestry, his cell, but sometime in the last hour the scuffling, scraping, and muffled commands had ceased. Now, over the sound of his own heartbeat, Alexi could discern no sound from beyond the door. Whether his captors had left temporarily or for good, he did not know.

What he did know was that they had no intention of ever allowing him to leave. Since being locked in the vestry, he'd been given neither food nor water, and though the stink emanating from the closet filled him with shame, it reminded him that these were merciless men.

He had to find a way out. After finding the door barricaded from the outside, as he'd suspected, he'd searched the room for another way. There was none, except for the tiny window high up the wall, through which Pasha had entered. Alexi was certainly no cat, but he was a farmer. He'd learned that there was always a way around a problem. A plan had hatched in his mind. *Bozhevillia*—crazy, perhaps— but not for a man who was desperate.

He put his shoulder to the wardrobe once again and shoved. His joints cracked and his neck bulged, but little by little, the heavy piece of furniture slid along the wall, every inch requiring more strength than Alexi thought he had. But finally it stood beneath the window.

Alexi collapsed on the floor, coughing the ancient dust from his lungs. *If they've hurt Mother…*

He stood on shaky legs and shuffled to the opposite corner of the vestry, where the two drawers had been tossed. They were built solid, which made them heavy. His back protested as he lifted the first one, then carried it across the small room. He took a deep breath and hefted the drawer over his head, pushing it up onto the top of the wardrobe. He rested a moment, and after another fit of coughing, he did the same with the second drawer, lifting it atop the wardrobe with shaky arms.

Satisfied to be doing something, he pulled open the wardrobe and found the two wire hangers that still dangled from the rod inside. These he carried over to the high-backed wooden chair. One of its back legs was missing, but he had a plan to make it usable.

He sat down next to it on the floor and pulled the hangers apart with some effort, then twisted the hook ends together like a chain. He created a loop in one of the other ends. Standing, he connected the remaining end around the back of the chair on the side that was missing its leg, twisting it around several times to make sure it was fastened securely.

He carried the chair to the wardrobe, trailing the length of stiff wire. He pulled open the wardrobe's door and then fished the wire through the gap, where it caught on the protruding hinge. When the door closed, the wire made it bounce back open. *No matter.*

Alexi tested the chair by sitting gingerly on it. The door pulled open more but stopped against the seat back. It held him.

Now for the hard part. Alexi placed a foot in the center of the seat. He stood, sucking in his breath as the old wood protested under his weight. This brought him to eye level with the top of the wardrobe, and he noticed that it was covered with a thick layer of dust. He blew the dust away and immediately regretted it, as the resulting cloud caused another fit of coughing.

He reached his left foot up and placed it on the back of the chair, then crossed himself and murmured, "Blessed Mother, give me the strength to do what I must, and the same for this old chair."

He grasped the top of the wardrobe and pushed. He couldn't see if it was his leg that was shaking or the chair, or both, but he slowly rose up so the top of the wardrobe was at his navel. He strained for the other side, lying over the top and pulling with his arms. He lost his footing on the chair. Another bout of hacking almost made him lose his grip, but with one last effort, he pulled himself onto the dusty top.

Panting, he turned over and sat trying to catch his breath. *Thank you, Blessed Mother.*

The window was still at least seven feet higher than Alexi's precarious perch. He stood carefully and stacked the two drawers atop each other, but this only brought him chin high to the opening. It was overcast outside, and the cool air coming in the window smelled wonderful. He tugged at the broken pane, and it came out easily. By wrapping his coat around his fist, he was able to push the rest of the window out, sending shards of glass skittering down the wooden shingles outside. Once he had the opening large enough to fit through, he stepped off the drawers and sat on the edge of the wardrobe.

With one foot, he hooked the wire made from the hangers and brought it within reach of his bony hands. Then, he pulled carefully, ignoring the pain as the wire bit deep into his flesh. With much difficulty, the chair scraped up the side of the wardrobe until he could get hold of it. Once he'd pulled it up onto his lap, he had to rest again.

When he'd caught his breath, Alexi pushed the chair onto the stacked drawers, leaning it carefully against the wall. This was quite precarious, but he saw no other way.

It occurred to him that he would have loved this when he was a boy. He and his best friend, Andrei, had climbed every tree in Parishev. Andrei was always getting him in trouble—like the time they had started the Drosnys' barn on fire trying to smoke a pipe like they'd seen their fathers do. They'd been caught and punished severely, but Andrei just grinned once they were allowed to play together again, as if that was part of the fun.

Alexi surprised himself by smiling, wishing Andrei were here now to help him. He'd left with his wife and two boys after the reactor fire, and Alexi had never heard from them again.

"Well, Andrei, you'd be proud of me now, you would. I'm going to get out of here."

He stepped once again on the creaky broken chair, holding tight to the window ledge. With a deep breath, he stood and started pulling himself through the opening, just as he'd seen Pasha do.

A moment of exertion…and he was through.

He crouched on the roof of the church, feeling more alive than he'd felt in ages. The clouds were being pushed along by gusts of wind that shook the spring leaves on the trees. There was no sign of life in the village. The only evidence of the foreigners who had locked him inside was an old gray cargo truck parked beside the church. Its bed was covered with a brown tarpaulin.

Whoever these men were, they were evil, *malenke*. Very bad. *I'm coming, Mother.*

The old wooden fence stopped against the side of the church, reaching to within a foot of the eaves. Alexi shuffled down to the edge of the roof on his rear end, ignoring the splintery wooden shingles.

Frantic to get home, he clambered down onto the top of the fence. But the wood was older than he was, and just as he put his full weight upon it, the planks groaned and gave way.

Alexi's heart nearly stopped as he toppled backward, arms windmilling behind him. He stifled a cry just before landing with a crunch in an overgrown shrub that broke his fall.

He was laughing again. "Ah, Andrei, if you could see me now." Still chuckling, he rolled several times and landed on the ground with a thud. He got to his feet and brushed the twigs and leaves from his clothes, noticing for the first time the trickle of blood from a cut on his hand.

Rather than risk being seen on the road, he took the path through the woods. When he arrived at his home, the front door was open.

Fear gripped him, only to be quickly replaced by anger. After all he'd been through, he was ready to fight for Mother if need be. She never wanted to leave this house. He would give his life before he would let them take her away.

He stepped inside. The house had been ransacked. Blood rose in his face when he saw that the icon of Saint Nicholas had been torn from its place on the wall and thrown on the floor. *Varvary!* He picked it up and clutched it to his chest. What men could be such barbarians?

Stepping farther inside, over the shards of his broken shaving mug, he spied the door to Mother's room—and froze. It was open. *Mother's door is never open. Mother likes her privacy.*

Suddenly timid, he moved to the doorway and peered inside, his heart beating as if it wanted to escape from his chest.

Tears welled up in his eyes when he saw her, there under her covers as she had been the last time he had peered into her room. It seemed like a lifetime ago. They hadn't taken her after all.

He let out a ragged sob. "I'm sorry, Mother. Foreigners came and made a mess of the house, and they locked me in the vestry. But I got out the window. Now everything will be all right. I won't let them take you. Don't worry. They won't take you away. I promise."

He sobbed again, the tears running down his face. He turned away and went to his room and yanked open the bottom drawer of the dresser he'd had since he was a child. With trembling hands, he dug through a pile of clothes until he felt the bottle of vodka. They hadn't taken that either. He snatched his father's old brass lighter off the floor and stomped out the door to the kitchen where he found a bag of sugar still in the cupboard.

"Don't worry," he called over his shoulder. "I'll make sure they don't bother us again!"

When he slammed the front door, the breeze carried into Mother's room, causing a wisp of white hair to fall down over her shriveled and lifeless eye sockets. Eyes that hadn't seen in over fifteen years.

Near the Reactor, the Dead Zone

A breeze rustled through the trees, and the noise it made was a good thing. Mary fretted, though, tapping her finger on the trigger guard of her assault rifle as she waited for John and Sweeney to finish covering the two ATVs with brush. What was making her impatient was the reading on the Geiger counter, which had been hovering around 1,100 millisieverts for the last twenty minutes.

They had decided to go on foot from here because of their proximity to the reactor and its garrison of Ukrainian soldiers. Besides, according to the GPS, they were within six hundred meters of the lab. But that put them only about three hundred meters from the ghost town of Pripyat, whose derelict high-rise apartment complexes were visible through the trees.

John and Sweeney finished their work quickly, communicating only with looks and hand gestures. Mary was amazed at how they did that. Amazed, and a little jealous. It was like a secret handshake that they shared with each other and not with her. She also felt silly for getting so upset at Sweeney before. John had been very diplomatic about pointing out that the Task Force Valor team had been attached to the CIA specifically for their tactical skills, and it would be counterproductive to hobble them now that they were in a tactical environment. She could see the logic in that.

But why does it bother you so much then?

She didn't have a problem conceding that these men had more tactical training, even though she herself had been through the CIA's special operators' course, which included weapons training and even parachuting. But what didn't sit well was the insinuation that she couldn't hack anything just because she was a girl. She'd spent her whole life disproving that notion, and it irked her to think she would never be rid of it.

A horn sounded in the distance. They all stopped what they were doing and looked up. Rip tapped his wristwatch and mouthed the words "Shift change." John nodded and motioned for them to move out.

Sweeney took point at a fast walk, carrying the GPS unit, and Rip brought up the rear carrying the sniper rifle. John motioned for Mary to fall in behind Sweeney. As she passed John, he whispered, "Keep an eye on the Geiger counter, okay?"

Mary nodded and jogged a few steps to catch up with Sweeney. Their path had once been a road, but now there were trees the size of her wrist growing up in places through the cracks in the asphalt. From the looks of the pushed-over and crushed underbrush, it was apparent that someone had driven through here recently.

The Geiger counter was pushing 1,300. *Not good.* The amount of time they could stay in an area this hot was measured in minutes, not hours.

They passed through what remained of a high chain-link fence, now rusted and almost invisible underfoot, barely hanging from what few metal fence posts remained standing on either side of the path. Mary was sweating, but was it more from exertion or worry?

Sweeney froze and raised a fist to signal a stop. He pointed to his eyes and then off to his left front in a gesture that said, *Look at that.*

Mary stepped forward and saw the concrete doorway built into the side of a mound of earth. The entrance to the lab? A shiver worked its way up her spine when she realized that the door looked almost the same as the bunker in Panama where she had almost died.

John was beside her. "You and Bobby go take a look inside," he whispered. "Rip and I will stand guard." He tapped the Geiger counter. "Don't stay long."

Gee, thanks. She certainly wouldn't have minded if he'd sent someone else, not that she would ever admit it. She hustled up to Sweeney, and together they approached the doorway.

Sweeney raised his weapon and hit the switch on the SureFire tactical light affixed to its side. "You got the camera?" he growled.

"Yep," she said, patting a pocket on her tactical vest, then turning on her own tac-light. "Let's hurry."

Sweeney stepped through the door, looking over the top of his weapon as he swept what had once been a guard room. Other than some unrecognizable metal debris and a length of thick rope, the room was empty. On one wall were the remnants of some sort of electrical mechanism, judging from the frayed wire ends protruding from the wall. Opposite that was a large, open double door.

Sweeney stepped deftly around the rubble, then whistled in surprise. "Long way down."

Mary went to his side and saw that it was an empty elevator shaft, descending into blackness. She couldn't gauge the depth of the hole.

"Over here," Sweeney said, motioning to a second door, which opened to a stairway leading down. He disappeared into it and she followed.

A cool draft of air hit her. It stank of mildew with a slight chemical tinge that made her nauseous and brought back a flood of unwel-come and very recent memories. She could again feel the cold, hard concrete of her cell in Panama and the rough hands of her kidnapper. She shivered at the thought of the handcuffs that he had used to chain her to a pipe. For a moment, she could even remember the smell of smoke and his cheap cologne.

Her heart was beating way too fast. She willed herself not to hyperventilate.

Sweeney stopped descending the stairs and turned around to look at her. "You okay?" he whispered.

That was all it took to snap her out of it. "I'm fine. Go!"

Sweeney descended the metal stairway. It spiraled down a verti-cal shaft like the inside of a lighthouse. There was no use in being quiet, as their footfalls echoed off the metal stairs, so they descended into the gloom as quickly as possible. This left Mary a little dizzy by the time they again stepped onto concrete.

Their tac-lights stabbed garish holes in the darkness, revealing a subterranean hallway made of block walls that had once been white, giving it the appearance of a hospital in a horror movie. She could see several doors set into the walls leading off in each direction, and a large open room directly to their front that looked like it might have been the main laboratory by the long tables that were still there.

Mary shivered. The reading on the Geiger counter had dropped to around 250. "Look," she said to Sweeney.

He glanced at it and shook his head. "I never thought I'd say this, but I can't wait to get back to where the radiation is."

Mary pulled a digital camera from her pocket and dropped the radiation meter into the pocket where it had been. "Me too. This place is creepy. Let's split up. You take that side and I'll go this way. Yell if you find any large metal canisters."

They moved in opposite directions down the hallway. Mary peered into each room she passed, finding most of them empty. Some had clearly been used for storage, but now, except for moldering wooden shelves, they were completely bare. Graffiti littered the walls in a few places.

Not much to take pictures of.

"Over here," Sweeney called from the other end of the hallway. "I've got something."

She hustled to where he was standing. He pointed to a solid metal door with a large shiny lock affixed to the outside.

She furrowed her brow. "This might be what we're looking for." She snapped a photo of the door and the lock.

"How are we going to get in?" Sweeney asked. "We can't shoot it, in case there are explosives left inside."

She thought for a moment. "Actually, we can. Remember, the chemical is diluted in its original state to make it nonexplosive. The lab in Panama was distilling it to its pure form, remember?"

Sweeney's eyes shot up. "Good point. In that case...stand back."

Mary took two steps back.

Sweeney pointed to the corner. "You probably want to go over there. This thing's liable to ricochet."

This time, she didn't argue. She crouched in the corner while Sweeney's assault rifle spat flame three times, the 7.62-millimeter rounds shattering the lock with a thunderous roar that echoed up and down the hallway long after the firing stopped. Sweeney kicked the door with his boot. Nothing happened. He fumbled with the latch for a moment, then pulled, grunting as the door scraped outward.

As soon as he got it open, Mary was past him, shining her light inside. It was a small storeroom the size of a walk-in closet. Concrete all around. But no bottles.

Empty.

"I guess the scientist sold it all," she said.

"Hope so. Let's git."

"All the way down here for nothing," Mary said, checking the corners of the room again.

"Come on," Sweeney said, already halfway down the hall. She followed.

When they reached the bottom of the stairwell and took their first steps up, she tried raising John on the radio. "Valor One, this is Phoenix, over."

The team sergeant came back immediately. "Phoenix, this is One. We heard shooting. What've you got? Over."

"It's empty. We're coming out."

"Roger that. Wait..." The transmission cut out.

Three seconds later, John's voice returned, more urgent than before. "Move! We're taking fire!"

Before she could blink, Sweeney sprinted past her up the stairs.

Chicago, Illinois

Clad in black from head to toe, Samael Berg's face was invisible in the moonless night as he paddled a small inflatable kayak along the smelly Calumet River. There was no time to waste. The news was already buzzing with stories of possible terror attacks taking place on the West Coast.

So the Panamanian is doing his job. Excellent.

But now it was time to fan the flames—to spread them across the country so that no American could feel safe.

Not three hours earlier, he had taken possession of the product from an independent freight man he had hired from a Web site. He declined a receipt, and the cash payment ensured his anonymity.

Then he'd gone to work.

The cheap inflatable raft wasn't durable, but it didn't need to be. It had been bright orange out of the box, so Samael had spray-painted it flat black. He'd then loaded it in his rented box van and driven to his preplanned parking spot in an abandoned lot in a run-down neighborhood in south Chicago. From there, it had been an easy trek across Torrence Avenue, some railroad tracks, and a garbage-strewn patch of woods to the river's edge.

His objective rose up ahead of him: the enormous train yard at Irondale.

As he passed beneath the bridge on 106th Street, he could see the vast coal storage yard, more than a hundred acres in size, piled with five-story-tall mountains of coal bound for iron smelters on the south shore of Lake Michigan.

Even though it was well after dark, the yard was being prowled by huge bucket loaders filling their maws with coal from one of the piles and then rumbling off to the other end of the yard to load a line of dump trucks. Long conveyor belts jutted above several of the piles, dropping steady streams of coal brought in by barge or by train.

Perfect. If he placed it correctly, it would take only one of the bottles of clear liquid he had stashed between his feet to set a blaze that would take weeks to put out.

But he had brought three bottles, just to be sure.

He paddled to shore and stashed the boat under some low-hanging trees. With great care, he extricated himself from the inflatable kayak. He wasn't worried about staying dry but about dropping one of the precious bottles into the slimy black water.

He secured the boat and hid in the shadows, watching as one of the bucket loaders approached, bouncing on its seven-foot balloon tires while its headlights stabbed erratic patterns in the dust kicked up from another machine's passing. Giant klieg lights overhead illuminated pools of gray in a sea of black. Dressed as he was, Samael would be all but invisible.

After watching their pattern for half an hour, he determined that he would have a little less than sixty seconds to do what he must. In that time, he would need to cross one hundred yards of open ground to the place where the machines were scooping coal from one of the piles, set his charges where they would be struck by one of the loaders, and get out of sight before another machine rounded the corner.

He looked at his watch as a machine gouged several tons of coal from the pile, pivoted, and drove off in a cloud of diesel smoke.

Now!

He ran at a low crouch, clutching the trio of bottles like a nuclear football. When he reached the pile, he put the bottles down and began digging with his hands to make a space for the bottle where the machines were digging. But the chunks of coal were larger than they'd looked, and every time he pulled one away, more cascaded down in its place.

Sweat dripped down his forehead, washing the black makeup into his eyes. He was getting nowhere. It was like trying to dig a hole in a pile of loose sand. He stole a glance at his watch.

Thirty seconds. He dug frantically at the pile, getting nowhere.

Forget it! He placed two bottles at his feet and scooped coal down over them, silently cursing himself for not thinking of it sooner.

There was no time to emplace the third bottle. Breathing heavily, he scooped it up and ran toward the wood line.

That was when he tripped.

Almost in slow motion, he pitched forward, involuntarily throwing his arms out and losing his grip on the third bottle. In that split second, his mind screamed, *No!* He wrapped his arms over his head as he plowed face first into the filthy, oil-soaked coal dust, knowing it would do nothing to shield him from the blast.

But the fireball didn't come. Samael lifted his head to see the bottle skittering away, unbroken. *It is a miracle!*

He heard the end loader returning.

He jumped to his feet and sprinted toward the tree line, not bothering to retrieve the third bottle.

When he reached the shadows once again, he felt like it was liquid explosive, not blood, coursing through his veins, threatening to detonate any second. He gasped for breath as he sloshed into the ice-cold, knee-deep current, then slid back into the kayak. Seconds later, he was paddling with all his remaining strength toward the place where he had left his van.

He felt for the folding knife in his pocket. It was still in place.

Good. As soon as he reached the shore, the cheap inflatable boat would be heading straight to the bottom of the Calumet.

A flash lit up the water behind him, followed by a thunderclap. Samael turned to see a small mushroom cloud of orange flame ascending above the trees from the direction of the coal yard. A surge of adrenaline shot through him at the sight.

Excellent. A hundred acres of burning coal will blacken the sky for miles around.

But that was someone else's problem now. Samael turned and paddled faster. He'd been lucky this time. He would not be so careless again.

Parishev, in the Dead Zone

ALEXI BABICHEV DIDN'T OWN a gun. He'd never needed one before. But whenever he didn't have the right tools, which was most of the time, he made do with those he did have. That was what he would do now.

He crouched behind a hedge near the church. There was no sign of the terrible men who had imprisoned him. But their truck was still there, the bed full of barrels of the foul-smelling drugs or whatever it was they had been making. He was sure they would be back for it, probably after searching nearby Pripyat for any treasures others might have missed.

But I will make sure their truck does not go far. He looked down at the bag of sugar in his hand and smiled at the thought of their breaking down halfway to their destination.

He took another pull on his flask of vodka, feeling the liquid warmth spread through his torso. *Mother will be proud.*

His old knees popped as he rose from his crouch. There was not much time. These *malenke* men might be back soon. He hurried to the side of the truck and put a hand on the gas cap.

Before he got it free, the warmth in his chest turned to ice.

Footsteps!

———

Sweeney could hear the explosions even before he'd reached the top of the metal stairs. By the time he and Mary reached the outer portico, his legs and lungs were on fire.

They burst out of the lab's guard room. Sweeney was surprised to see Rip and John not firing back. Instead, they were crouched on either side of the door, staring skyward.

What the—?

At that moment there was a pop from the direction of Pripyat, and a missile streaked over their heads. Several seconds later, a distant *crump* sounded as the rocket impacted on its target.

"They're not shooting at us?" Mary gasped, trying to regain her breath.

Rip was peering through the scope on his sniper rifle. "Nope. Someone is firing RPGs from that high-rise back in the ghost town."

Sweeney was doubled over, waiting for all his body parts to get back to their original shape. "Great. Let's get out of here."

"Not great!" Mary said, puffing. "They're shooting at the reactor! We have to stop them!"

Sweeney straightened. "No, that's the job of the company of ticked-off Ukrainian soldiers that'll be coming this way in a hot minute. And we'd better scoot before that happens."

"No," John said suddenly. "Olenka said the sarcophagus on the reactor is already shaky. Obviously, someone is trying to help it along.

If they succeed, we're talking a major radioactive catastrophe. Who knows how many could die—including all of us. The Ukrainians might not make it in time."

"Then what are we waiting for, bro?" Rip jumped up and started running toward Pripyat without waiting for an answer. John was right behind him.

Mary gave Sweeney a wide-eyed look and sucked in a ragged lungful of air, then jogged off after the others.

Sweeney groaned and fell in behind her. A siren wailed from the direction of the reactor.

I wasn't planning on dying today.

They covered the distance back to the ATVs in the time it took whoever was firing the RPGs to get off two more rounds toward the Chernobyl reactor. From here, Sweeney could clearly see the top of the abandoned apartment building—twelve stories high and only two hundred meters away. Just before the last shot, he had seen two figures silhouetted against the sky as one lifted the rocket launcher to his shoulder and fired.

What kind of suicidal idiots…

John Cooper pointed to the vehicles and shouted, "Rip, you and Phoenix stay here and engage them with the sniper rifle. Try to keep them from firing another round. Bobby and me will try to get up there. Be ready to come get us."

"Roger that!" Rip flipped out the bipod on the sniper rifle, while Mary started tearing the branches away from the four-wheelers.

Sweeney jumped on the nearest one and kicked it into gear just as John threw his leg over the seat behind him.

"Go!" John shouted.

They covered the two hundred yards to the high-rise in under thirty seconds. Sweeney careened around the side of the building and slid to a stop. The entrance was obscured by overgrown shrubs. He heard a shot ring out from Rip's Dragunov just as they made the stairs.

Inside, the building was completely trashed, as if a mini-tornado had swept through and created a tossed salad of broken furniture and appliances and had then garnished it with the stink of rot, rust, and mildew.

"There!" John said, pointing to a stairwell.

Sweeney had no energy for talking; he was saving it all for breathing. With a quick nod, he swept up the stairs two at a time.

I ought to start an elevator business. If I live long enough.

Chernobyl Guard Barracks, at the Reactor

Captain Mykola Kirichenko hated his job.

He sighed and adjusted the olive-green beret that covered his prematurely gray hair. He walked stiffly up the disintegrated concrete path that had once been a sidewalk, his ample bulk assuring that he was winded by the time he reached the door. It led into the gray steel box where he spent half of every month sitting on his backside.

Though intended to save their lives by shielding him and his men from the radiation that would plague Chernobyl for a dozen lifetimes, the soldiers in his command referred to it as "the tomb." To Mykola, that was an understatement. For him, the suffocating, windowless space was only one step from hell.

Mykola stopped before the door and turned to look at the massive concrete sarcophagus that had been hastily erected over the reactor more than twenty years ago. It looked like an industrial-gray cathedral, rising over thirty-five meters into a similarly colored sky and now encrusted in scaffolding. But it was more like a monument to the ineptitude of a broken system—Soviet Communism. He could still remember the lessons he'd learned as a ten-year-old schoolboy: The individual is nothing, society is everything. God is irrelevant.

But now, it was the Soviet system that had proven to be irrelevant. What that said about him and God, Mykola wasn't sure.

As bad as his job was, he felt sorry for the men who composed the work crews that labored in shifts around the clock to shore up the crumbling concrete case that was all that stood between eastern Europe and a total nuclear meltdown. Though some of the workers were allowed as little as two minutes a week at their jobs because of the intense exposure to radiation, most would likely die of lymphoma or some other horrible cancer long before becoming grandparents.

Mykola, on the other hand, would most likely die of boredom. The platoon of Ukrainian soldiers he commanded was assigned to guard the reactor. What that boiled down to was spending untold hours sequestered in the lead-lined dayroom, watching old movies and rereading tattered men's magazines until one could no longer stand to gaze at them.

He actually looked forward to the infrequent patrols through Pripyat and the surrounding area. The unseen, unfelt killer that radiated from every building, tree, and blade of grass no longer bothered him. After all, there were a few who actually lived in the area...like that crazy old farmer in Parishev. Mykola had once asked him his secret for staying healthy.

"Get plenty of sleep, pray every day, and drink only kvass," he'd said.

The old man may have had a point with that last one. Kvass was made from juice of the beech tree, whose roots went deep to find water. This made its sap less likely to be contaminated—a natural filtration system. Maybe the codger wasn't so crazy after all.

He sighed, then spit on the ground. "May you rot, Oleksandr Opanasovich."

It was a sort of ritual he practiced every day—curse the lieutenant whose incompetence was responsible for Mykola's assignment to this toxic wasteland.

The man had once been his subordinate, when he'd commanded an artillery battalion in Crimea. Mykola had enjoyed a promising career until a gang of Russian mafia had stolen a crate of 9K111 anti-tank missiles out from under Lieutenant Oleksandr Opanasovich during a field exercise. As his commander, then-Colonel Mykola Kirichenko had also taken the fall. He was demoted, humiliated, and relieved of his command.

And so here he was, biding his time for another three months before he would finally be eligible to retire.

Mykola swung the door open and was hit in the face by an acrid blast of stale cigarette smoke. The twelve men watching television in the room barely noticed their commander at the door. He sighed again and stepped inside.

No sooner had the door swung closed behind him when Mykola heard a crash outside.

One of the men looked up and said, "Oh God, someone fell off the scaffolding again." Nobody made a move to investigate the sound.

"Well, don't everyone jump at once," Kirichenko said, laying on the sarcasm. "I'll have a look."

He stepped back out into the fresh air but saw nothing. Then he noticed a wisp of smoke coming from the side of the reactor, partially obscured by the tall chain-link fence that separated his building from the plant.

Now he saw workers running—some toward the smoke and some away from it.

Oh no. Something has exploded!

Every nightmare he'd had for the last two years flooded into his mind. Everyone knew the sarcophagus was unstable, but the consequences of a collapse were too terrible to contemplate.

Before he could call to anyone, something streaked in from the east and detonated with a flash in the yard between him and the reactor. A fireball erupted skyward, accompanied by a blast that hit him like a sledgehammer to the chest, knocking him off his feet.

He fought for breath as his men poured from the building behind him. Unaware of what was going on, they crowded around their commander, looking down at him with half-amused smiles as if he'd slipped on a banana peel.

"What happened, *Capitan*?" one man inquired.

Mykola struggled to his knees, gasping for air. "A…ah…attack!"

he sputtered, gesturing to the wispy trail of smoke that traced the missile's path.

Bedlam descended on the platoon, and men went running in all directions.

Suddenly the thought of another boring day in the tomb sounded very appealing. But Mykola was not going to watch his retirement go up in smoke. He rose to his feet, feeling the muscles on his thick neck bulge in anger. "Sound the alarm!" he roared.

He could not fathom who would be trying to bring down the reactor, but Captain Mykola Kirichenko would stop the madmen, or die trying.

11

IT SEEMED STRANGE to Maxim that he should feel so alive on the day of his death.

A butterfly flitted past as he hurried along the path to the village. The mist had disappeared, and everything seemed more vivid. Even the sun peeked through the clouds, as if to entice him to delay his departure for the next life.

But Maxim wasn't to be swayed. A glorious death had been the focus of his life for decades. He had anticipated this day ever since he was a child, sitting together with the other youths at the mosque while the imam painted in their minds glorious pictures of martyrdom, Paradise, and virgins. And despite his having resisted the infidel bravely in three countries, Allah had not granted his wish until today.

The plan was working perfectly. He had gone with Kyr, Ayad, Omar, and Khamzad before dawn, each of them packing three rockets. They carried no delusions, however, that the Soviet-made weapons would actually cause the two-foot-thick concrete walls of the sarcophagus to collapse. The distance from the apartment building to the reactor was almost eleven hundred meters—the extreme edge of the shoulder-launched missile's range. It was unlikely they'd do much damage.

But once the firing started, that made little difference. As soon as the first rocket dropped inside the tall chain-link fence around the reactor, the view through Maxim's binoculars resembled an anthill that had just been kicked. It was obvious that the Ukrainian defenders were mobilizing almost every man to Pripyat to deal with the threat.

For a few moments, at least, the reactor would be virtually unguarded.

Smiling, Maxim broke into a run. His truck was loaded and waiting with almost two thousand pounds of homemade ammonium nitrate explosives that he and his men had cooked up in the last few days. He imagined what the blast would look like—knowing he would not see it, as he would already be stepping into Paradise. But those left behind would likely see a mushroom cloud of radioactive poison thrown high into the heavens, only to be carried across Europe and Russia by the wind.

The news of it would reach around the world within seconds. Those who shared his jihad would celebrate this day forever. There would be songs and poems written about him.

He reached the truck where it was parked by the church, and circled around to the driver's side, already rehearsing the route that would take him to the reactor. He jerked the door open and climbed inside.

The heavy gasoline engine coughed, then roared to life.

He smiled. It was a good day to die.

Eighth floor.

Sweeney's heart pounded like a high school drum section, but he was spurred upward by every clatter of automatic weapons fire echoing through the jagged holes that had once been windows.

Rip's voice sounded in his headset. "We've engaged shooters on the rooftop and are taking return fire!"

Sweeney never thought he'd be glad to hear that his buddies were under fire. But if the guys on the roof were shooting at Rip, maybe they wouldn't be shooting at the reactor. And that was definitely a good thing.

John responded curtly. "How many?"

"Two personnel that we can see."

"Roger," he gasped. "Keep shooting."

"No problem."

Tenth floor. Sweeney's lungs were going to explode.

As they had on each previous level, once they reached the top of a flight of stairs, they had to run down the hallway that traversed the building from front to back in order to reach the next flight. The floors were layered with plaster dust and large flecks of paint that had fallen from the crumbling concrete walls and ceilings like misshapen, man-made leaves. Light filtered in through long-destroyed windows and reflected off the dust thrown up by the men's passing.

Sweeney knew they ought to be progressing more carefully, since the enemy might well have booby-trapped the way up. But in this particular clash between speed and safety, speed took the upper hand.

Sweeney vaulted over the remains of an old bed frame and had almost reached the next stairwell when a finger of white smoke stabbed toward the reactor from the roof above. He slid to a stop, watching the RPG round streak toward its target, then explode with a puff of flame against the side of the reactor.

John skidded up next to him. "That thing is going to cave in with another round or two."

Sweeney's earpiece crackled. It was Mary. "Valor One, please hurry. We can see Ukrainian forces heading this way."

The two men stepped up to the window, panting.

John hit his transmitter. "Break contact, Phoenix. If you stop shooting and lie low, maybe they won't see you." He turned to Sweeney. "We don't have much time."

"Well, quit talking! Go!"

"God help us," John said as he pushed past Sweeney and charged up the stairs.

"You can say that again." Sweeney fell in behind him. It was the closest thing to a prayer he'd uttered in years.

Twenty seconds later they reached the top landing and heard another shot ring out from below. *Hopefully that's Rip keeping them occupied.* As they rounded the corner, Sweeney could see a large wardrobe lying across the hallway, blocking it.

John looked back at him and held a finger to his lips, then signaled for Sweeney to cover him while he navigated the obstacle.

But just as John turned his head, Sweeney saw a face peer out from the stairway at the end of the hall. "Down!" he shouted, bringing his weapon up.

Without hesitating, John dropped to a crouch just as Sweeney slapped the trigger on his assault rifle.

A round exploded from the barrel of his AK, followed by a cry of pain as the terrorist went down.

John jumped back up, weapon at the ready, just as Sweeney saw something drop from the wounded man's hand and roll across the floor.

"Grenade!" He tackled John and drove him back to the floor as his world erupted with a roar.

A stab of fiery pain shot through Sweeney's left shoulder. His head rang like a tin washtub rolling down a hill. He groaned and rolled off his team leader.

"You dead?" John asked, coughing.

Sweeney spit and got to his knees. "I think so."

John stuck his head over the top of the wardrobe. "Let's go, then." He vaulted over the cabinet.

Sweeney hauled himself to his feet in time to see John collide with a large bearded terrorist with an assault rifle who had just reached the bottom of the stairs. The swarthy man was fat, no match for the stocky and athletic Special-Ops warrior, but his momentum drove them both to the ground.

Sweeney dove clumsily over the cabinet and rolled onto the floor as John fought the terrorist. The man's rifle discharged, just missing Sweeney and punching a hole in the wooden barricade where he'd just been.

As he stumbled to his feet, John rolled on top of his opponent and delivered a vicious head butt to the bridge of the man's nose. By the time Sweeney reached them, the man appeared to be unconscious, with John astride him.

"Go!" John rasped.

Sweeney stepped through the haze lingering from the grenade and sighted his weapon up the stairs. They were empty. He stepped over the crumpled body of the first terrorist and took the stairs two at a time, keeping his weapon trained on the open metal door at the top.

Just as his head cleared the landing and he could see onto the roof, a loud *pop* accompanied by a *whoosh* kicked up more dust on the rooftop in front of him.

Sweeney threw himself out the door and emptied his magazine in the direction of the sound, and was rewarded by a clatter on the roof.

He landed hard on both elbows just as the *crump* of the RPG's impact reached up from below. This time the sound came from much closer than the others had. That one, at least, wasn't going to hit the reactor.

He turned over and saw the empty rocket launcher lying in the dust. The terrorist, however, was gone. *Must have fallen off the roof.*

Sweeney rolled to his feet and trotted over to the edge. He was just about to look over when a shriek sounded behind him.

"Allahu Akhbar!"

Sweeney turned to see a bloody figure rushing at him from behind a cooling pipe. Fighting the instinct to raise his weapon and fire, he threw his feet out from under himself and dropped to the rooftop like a stone.

The terrorist tripped over Sweeney and disappeared over the edge of the building with a feral scream.

Sweeney rolled to a crouch, scanned for additional threats, and found himself alone on the rooftop, which held only two remaining RPG rounds, the rocket launcher tube, an AK-47 assault rifle, and a black duffel bag.

"Clear!" he called down the stairs.

Mary's frantic voice exploded in his still-ringing ears. "Rip is down and we're taking fire!"

———

"Faster!" Captain Mykola Kirichenko screamed at his driver over the whine of the jeep's engine as they raced toward Pripyat.

Mykola braced his sagging bulk against the frame of the old Russian Volga 4x4 as it bounced along the potholed road, hoping the even older GAZ military truck carrying the rest of his men wouldn't break down before they got there.

Whatever madmen were using the vantage point of the tall apartment building on the edge of the radioactive ghost town to shoot at his reactor, Mykola would make sure they paid with their lives. Perhaps he might even garner a promotion out of it for saving the reactor.

Suddenly, there was an explosion in the field off to his right. He jerked his head around and saw a cloud of dust.

"They're shooting at us!" screamed his gunner, swiveling the mounted .50 caliber around.

"Fire!" Mykola roared, pointing his Yarygin MP-443 pistol at the spot. The machine gun opened up above his head, spitting flame—and nearly bursting his eardrums.

The truck stopped behind them, and his men added the chatter of their AK-74s to the din.

Mykola turned to his driver, a young private.

The driver's hands were clamped over the radio headset he wore. When he looked up, his eyes were full of barely controlled panic. "Sir," he shouted, "the gate guard just radioed that a large unidentified truck is approaching the reactor at high speed. What are your instructions?"

The news hit Mykola like an ice pick in the chest. "Oh no. They are behind us. We have been drawn away. A coordinated attack!"

12

MAXIM SAW THE GATE approaching and pushed the accelerator to the floor. With nothing to slow him down, the truck would smash through the chain-link fence as if it were made of ice. From there it was a short trip to Paradise. He had only to cross a hundred yards of pavement and detonate his cargo against the side of the reactor, which would obliterate much of the sarcophagus and cause a vapor cloud that would spread millions of gallons of radioactive waste across the globe.

"Allahu Akhbar," Maxim began chanting, relishing the adrenaline that was coursing through his veins.

A sentry emerged from a guard shack and began waving frantically for him to stop. Maxim only chanted louder and gripped the steering wheel as tight as he could. Even if the guard shot him, his course was set.

Then Maxim's eye caught movement in the side mirror. Jerking his head around, he looked out the side window, and time stood still.

It cannot be...

The old man from the church! He was clinging to the bed of the truck as he reached over the side toward the gas tank. Somehow he'd escaped the room, though Maxim had himself nailed the door shut.

Maxim convulsed in shock and horror as the man looked up at him. It wasn't the spiteful look on the old farmer's face that stopped Maxim's chanting—it was the ancient brass lighter he held in his hand, its top open and wick alight.

Before he could react, the old man dropped the lighter into the truck's gas tank and looked up at him, their eyes meeting one last time.

The last thing Maxim heard was the *whoosh* of flame meeting fuel, and in that instant he knew that he had failed. He opened his mouth to scream, but it was too late.

His soul was torn from his body and swallowed by darkness.

———

Mary clawed her way through the cloud thrown up by the RPG's impact less than fifteen feet away. She reached for Rip's limp form. Flames licked up the trees and smoldered in the grass covering the berm they'd taken cover behind. Her ears weren't working right. Her vision was blurred and slow, like the world was drenched in corn syrup. Every movement required herculean effort.

Oh please, no! "Rip! Wake up! Rip!"

She reached the spot where his body had been thrown by the blast. She started to feel for a pulse, but then a fusillade of bullets cracked over her, causing her to bury her head in his chest. The heavy *thuk-thuk-thuk* sound of the gun followed, echoing off the deserted buildings in Pripyat. She felt a strange buzzing in her chest.

Is this what it's like to die?

The headset screeched in her ear. It was John. "Phoenix, this is Valor One. How bad is Rubio? Over." He sounded far too calm under the circumstances.

She could feel Rip breathing. She keyed her mike. "He's alive but unconscious."

"Roger. Can you move him?"

"I...I don't know. We've got the whole Ukrainian army headed this way!"

Peering over the berm, she could see a dark green military jeep followed by a large truck with its bed full of soldiers moving parallel to her position only a hundred meters away. They must have been heading into Pripyat. She'd seen them coming before.

But now they were stopped, and the jeep's mounted machine gun was hammering away at her, kicking up geysers of dirt and cutting off leaves and small branches over her head. The buzzing continued in her chest.

John's voice was still cool as ice, and it was making her mad. "Listen, Bobby and I will draw their fire to the rooftop. You get Rip on the four-wheeler and meet us at the rear of this building. We'll break contact and meet you there."

That did not sound like a very good plan. *What have we gotten ourselves into?*

"Phoenix, are you ready?"

Some small arms fire added to the din of advancing troops, and she knew there was no other way. She hit the Transmit button. "Okay. But hurry."

"All right. Ten seconds and we're going to make some noise. Out."

Mary was doing her best not to hyperventilate. This was not what she'd expected combat to be like. She never knew she could be so afraid.

She slithered around to get a better grip on Rip's battle harness. "I can do this," she breathed. *Mind over matter, isn't that what Dad always used to say?*

A few seconds later, she heard John and Sweeney open up on full automatic from the rooftop. Almost immediately, the ground fire shifted away from her and toward the high-rise as the Ukrainians responded. Bullets began exploding up the side of the building, stabbing dimples in the already-crumbling concrete.

Go! Now! Mary jumped to her feet, grabbed Rip's web gear, and pulled as hard as she could. He was heavier than she expected. His body barely budged.

She heaved again. Veins throbbed on her neck as she pulled until she thought her arms would break. An involuntary cry escaped her lips. For all her effort, though, she had managed to drag him only halfway to the ATV. It was clear she'd never be able to lift him onto the vehicle's rack.

"No, I can do this!" she shouted to herself. "Come on, Rip!" She pulled again with all her strength, but his dead weight was just too much. The battle raged on across the field, and she knew time was running out. The buzzing in her chest started again. She sat down hard, blinking back tears. "I can't do it."

She touched the trickle of blood on Rip's head. It didn't seem to be bleeding too bad. What was it he'd said that morning? *God will get us through.*

Maybe God was busy. But just maybe…

Her prayer was almost indignant. "Pay attention, God. Rip needs Your help right now." Then she hesitated, choking on the words. "I need Your help too. I can't do this alone."

Her radio crackled. "How you doing down there? We're almost out of ammo."

She pushed the Talk button. "He's too heavy, John. I can't get him on the ATV. I don't know what else to do, over." She stifled a sob. *What am I doing here?*

Rip groaned.

Mary pounced on him. "Rip! Wake up! Can you hear me?"

John came back over the radio. "Okay, listen, stay where you are, we'll try and fight our way to you."

Rip's eyes fluttered open. "Ohhh…am I dead?"

"You're going to be if you don't get up," Mary said. "Rip, you've got to help me get you on the back of the ATV."

"Ugh…okay." Rip rolled over slowly. "Who's shooting?"

"The Ukrainians." She keyed her mike. "Wait, John, I think we can make it. Rip woke up."

Rip groaned and got to his knees.

"Roger," John said. "Make it quick. Out."

Mary jumped up and grabbed Rip's arm. "Help me, Rubio!"

The groggy Latino struggled to his feet, leaning heavily on Mary's shoulder. Then he hesitated. "Wait, let me get the sniper rifle."

"Leave it! Get on that four-wheeler, Staff Sergeant!"

"Ugh…uh…I'm going." He let her guide him the last few steps to the ATV and then climbed aboard.

She jumped on in front of him. "Hold on to me, Rip!"

When Mary felt Rip wrap his arms around her waist, the buzzing started up again in her chest. That was when she realized it was her satellite phone vibrating. Someone was calling from headquarters.

They'll just have to call back. She started the motor and slammed the vehicle into gear. The back tires spun in the dirt, and they sped off toward the building where John and Sweeney were. She cast a glance across the field and could see that the army vehicles were moving that way again as well.

The ATV bounced hard as she pushed it up and over the berm, causing Rip to moan again. Mary hunched over the handlebars and mashed the throttle with her thumb, then hit the Transmit button on her chest with her other hand. "Valor One, we're headed your way!"

"Roger, we're coming down."

She abandoned all hope of being able to keep her voice calm on the radio and screamed into her mike. "Make it fast, Sergeant, or you won't make it at all!"

Mary's arms burned with exertion as she tried to coax more speed out of the all-terrain vehicle, slashing through the low branches that reached out like adoring fans to grab at their clothes as they ripped past. The apartment complex loomed up ahead, but she could feel the Ukrainians racing to beat her there. She slid around the corner and saw the other ATV parked by the stairs leading to a crumbling entrance.

But the men weren't on it.

She reached up to call them on the radio, but before she could hit the Transmit button, an olive-drab army jeep fishtailed around the other end of the building and bore down on them. Protruding from the roll cage was the large-caliber machine gun that had been firing at her moments earlier. And this time, the soldier manning the gun couldn't miss.

Mary shot her hands skyward in surrender

Rip did the same. "What now?" Rip whispered in her ear.

"Keep your mouth shut." Mary instructed, eyes locked onto the machine gun. "Whatever you do, don't let them know you're an American."

Mykola Kirichenko was sweating, despite the cool morning air. He'd almost forgotten what adrenaline felt like.

He swung his flabby bulk out of the jeep, keeping his pistol aimed squarely at the two terrorists on the all-terrain vehicle. With his other hand, he raised the radio transmitter to his lips. "Give me a situation report! Now!"

Even through the static of the old radio, he could sense the panic in the voice of the sergeant who was guarding the gate. "A truck just exploded in the road sixty meters from us!"

"Is the gate intact?"

"Affirmative, Capitan."

"Lock down the area, and alert headquarters in Kiev that there has been an attack."

The truck with the rest of his soldiers skidded up behind the jeep. Men exited the bed with their rifles even before it had come to a stop.

His blood was at full boil. He shouted up at the machine gunner in the jeep. "Keep those two covered. If they so much as sneeze, you shoot to wound only. Headquarters will want to interrogate them."

The gunner nodded, deadly serious. Even a young soldier like that one probably understood how close they were teetering on the edge of apocalypse. Mykola turned to his men. "First squad! Clear this building! Go! Go!"

Six men immediately turned and charged up the steps and into the building.

Mykola turned his attention to the other men. "The rest of you, set up a security perimeter. There may be more of them. And you two—" he jabbed a fat finger at two privates—"handcuff these terrorists and put them in the back of the truck. If they resist, shoot their kneecaps. I want them alive."

As the men heeded his instructions, he turned back to the two captives, who sat unmoving on the tiny sport vehicle, hands held high. He suddenly realized that neither of them carried weapons, and wondered why. No matter, he would soon find out the reasons for their plan. A warm feeling of well-being was seeping into his consciousness. By thwarting an attack on the reactor, not only could he retire in dignity, he would do so as a national hero.

His thick lips parted into a smile. This was turning out to be a very good day after all.

13

Las Vegas, Nevada

EDGAR OSWARDO LERIDA, a.k.a. Gustavo Soto, spread a new copy of *USA Today* over the table and smiled. He'd made the front page, again.

He sipped his *mojito,* peering over the wedge of lime at the grainy black-and-white security camera image on the page. Printed next to a full-color blowup of smoke billowing in front of the Los Angeles skyline, the image showed him scaling the fence between Lincoln Avenue and the railroad bed where it crossed above the infamous I-5 freeway.

The head scarf had been a stroke of genius. Even before the police found the stolen car—abandoned in a residential neighborhood where he'd left his SUV—they were suspecting a "middle-aged man of possibly Middle Eastern descent." The copy of the Qur'an he'd left under the seat had completed the ruse, leaving no doubt in the average American's mind that a coordinated attack by one or more Islamic terrorists was underway.

He looked around the Rubalcabas Taco Shop in east Las Vegas where he sat. The place was almost deserted at this time of night. He was surprised they were still open. He'd discerned from speaking with the diminutive waitress that both she and most of the kitchen help were in this country illegally. Which was good, since that meant the food would be authentic and they probably didn't read the paper.

Edgar scooped up some salsa with a tortilla chip and leaned over the table so he could read the article. Its headline blared, "Deadly Explosions: Possible Links to Terror Group."

Six people are dead and thirty-seven wounded after a large explosion derailed a train in Santa Ana last night.

Authorities responding to the resulting blaze say they believe a powerful firebomb was placed on the tracks where they cross Interstate 5, which caused the freight train to derail and fall onto the busy freeway. The busy interstate remains closed, causing major traffic jams that have affected the entire city.

Federal agents from several government agencies arrived on the scene within hours and have taken over the investigation. An FBI spokesman told *USA Today* that the rail line was a backbone of interstate commerce and will also be disrupted for the foreseeable future. No one yet knows whether this will affect prices of basic commodities across western and southern states.

Law enforcement officials are concentrating their efforts on finding a man security cameras captured climbing the fence around 11 p.m. A suspect thought to be the same man was seen driving away from the area in a car that later was found to be stolen.

The man is described as being between five feet ten and

six feet, one hundred ninety-five pounds, with black hair and
dark skin. At first, authorities were hesitant to label the man
as Middle Eastern, but when the stolen car, recovered six
hours after the tragedy, was found to contain materials written
in Arabic, Orange County Police Chief George Thompson
says they are "virtually certain" the suspect is of Arab descent.

The most troubling aspect of the tragedy, Thompson
said, is that "certain elements of the crime are very similar to
the devastating fire that caused a widespread Internet outage
on the West Coast a day earlier."

He was referring to a fire in an underground storm drain
in San Jose, California, that caused an evacuation of the building that houses a data center known as the Metropolitan
Access Exchange–West. The intense heat from the fire report-
edly caused major damage to the switching center and some
of the fiberoptic cable that carries data to and from the center.
The resulting Internet blackout has caused an uproar across
the heavily Internet–dependent Silicon Valley.

So far, no group or organization has claimed responsibility, but talk-show callers and even some politicians are specu-
lating that a radical terrorist group based in Lebanon may be
behind the firebombings.

Chief Thompson, for his part, refused to assign blame,
but said, "At this point we are pulling out all the stops to find
the killer or killers responsible, but we're not calling it 'terrorism' just yet."

Whether or not the authorities are calling it terrorism,
local residents say they hope the perpetrators are caught soon.

Fifty-eight-year-old John MacElroy, a native of Anaheim, told the *Los Angeles Times,* "It's like September 11 all over again. Except this is worse, because it's not icons that are being struck, it's the places everyone goes—freeways and the Internet. If we can't travel, we can't stay home either. We've got to put a stop to this, and fast."

The governor of California has been briefed on the situation and is asking the president to declare a state of emergency, which would make federal financial assistance available.

In the meantime, state and federal legislators are calling for action to better protect our nation's commerce from terrorist attack.

Gustavo folded the paper with a sigh and placed it in the seat next to him. The demure waitress sidled over with his food. He smiled up at her. *"Amor,* could I trouble you for another mojito, *por favor?"*

"Claro," the girl replied. *"Buen provecho."* She retreated toward the bar.

Edgar watched her go with a lustful grin. With the money he would make on this job, he could finally afford to have all the mojitos he wanted, and for that matter, all the young ladies too. But he did not care to spend a single day longer in the United States than absolutely necessary. The risks of discovery were just too great.

America calls itself a free country—bah! He had much more freedom in any country in Latin America than he had here. There, it was still very simple to be anonymous. The United States was far too computerized, too littered with security cameras, and too liability conscious to afford its citizens real freedom. But from what he had seen, Americans wanted it that way. They were like cattle who mistakenly thought that the slaughterhouse corral was intended to keep them safe.

Being the shrewd businessman that he was, and since he was being forced to work in such a restrictive environment, he had thought of a way to outsource part of the job and thereby finish it more quickly. Doing so would cut into his profits, to be sure, but every business had overhead, and this was no different. If it threw the authorities off of his trail, it would be worth every penny.

He pulled a map from his briefcase and studied the areas circled in red. The trick would be to hit as many of the targets as possible before authorities could coordinate a response. The first targets had been easy, but once a pattern emerged, he expected security to become much more of an issue.

There was very little difference between this and running a company, he reflected. There were logistics concerns, accounting, and human resources to manage. Edgar's experience in his former life—running his late brother's coffee business in Panama—had made him an expert at all of them.

And deadlines. He smiled at that. This job would make the term much more literal.

That's where his contacts with MS-13 would prove invaluable. The huge Central American gang had chapters in every major city in the United States and maintained an enormous network that trafficked in everything from cocaine to bullets to bodies. They would be the perfect subcontractors to finish the job and ensure that he could minimize his risk.

Ah, the beauty of outsourcing.

His watch told him it was nearly midnight. His contacts were already thirty minutes late. But he wasn't surprised. In his culture, late was a relative thing.

He'd almost finished his meal when three men entered the cantina dressed in blue jeans and white tank tops that exposed home-grown tattoos that Edgar could read like a book. The lead man was an MS-13 lieutenant and, by the looks of his body art, had already spent considerable time in "gang finishing school"—the U.S. prison system. Edgar flashed them a grin and the ring and pinkie fingers of his right hand, extended like the horns of a bull. The three men returned the salute and strode over to his table.

Any misgivings he'd had about recruiting such a brutal gang of thugs had disappeared with his third mojito.

To their credit, the men were all business, and their leader, a square-jawed, bald Mexican named Cholo, listened carefully as Edgar—"Gustavo" to them—launched into his proposal. An hour later, they had agreed to terms and set a price he could live with. Edgar stood and the three followed him outside.

As they split off to get their car, Edgar went to the forest green Ford Expedition that had become his home in the United States. He lifted the gate at the rear of the vehicle and reached into his pocket. Inside were two tiny black plastic objects, each no larger than a raisin: leftovers from his former life. He surreptitiously dropped them inside one of the cardboard boxes full of bottles, where they would easily go unnoticed.

A businessman always needs insurance.

A moment later a large 1959 Chrysler Imperial, painted blood red, rolled to a stop in front of his vehicle. He hefted the case of bottles and walked to the gang members' car.

Cholo opened the car's trunk, which was large enough to sleep in.

Edgar set the case inside. "You will want to secure this box somehow. I can't stress enough that these bottles are fragile. If you take a corner too fast, hit a bump, or do anything that breaks one of these bottles, the last thing you will remember will be the hair burning off of your head before you die. Claro?"

The gangbanger scratched himself. "Claro, *caballero*. Don't worry. We'll take good care of the boom juice."

"Okay. Do the job just like I described it and I'll be back to pay you the other half of your payment." He handed over a wad of hundred-dollar bills.

As the Imperial drove away, blasting Tejano music, Edgar wondered if he'd made a mistake.

———

The scene unfolding at the foot of the high-rise was uglier than a bucket of mud. Bobby Sweeney lay on his stomach, peering over the edge of the rooftop. "Bad news, boss. Rip and Phoenix just ran right into the Ukrainians. Looks like they're surrendering."

"Wonderful," John replied. He was busy dumping out the black duffel bag that had belonged to the terrorists.

Sweeney looked back at him. "Maybe if we had some grenades we could create a diversion down there."

"We'd probably just get Rip and Phoenix killed. Besides, we can't start whacking Ukrainian soldiers. They're not the enemy."

"Well, what do you suggest?"

"I'm working on it."

Sweeney looked back at the scene below him. "Work faster, Coop. I count six men coming this way."

"Got it! Check this out." John held up a thick coil of black assault line. "The bad guys must have planned their own fast getaway. Help me rig up a rappel, quick."

Sweeney hurried over, and in sixty seconds he had secured one end of the rope to a sturdy metal cooling pipe while John had dropped the other end over the side of the building opposite the soldiers. The duffel bag left by the terrorists contained harnesses and gloves as well, but the men wore their own second-chance emergency rappel belts and assault gloves.

"All right, boss," Sweeney commented as he clipped a locking carabiner through his belt at the small of his back. "I'll go Australian style so I can cover what's below on the way down."

John's face was grim as he looped the line through Sweeney's carabiner. "When's the last time you rappelled headfirst?"

Sweeney's reply was sardonic. "No worries, boss. Gravity does all the work."

"Okay, Spider-Man. Make for the tree line when you hit the ground. And don't use the radio. If Rip and Mary are compromised, we don't want the Ukrainians to know there are more of us still out here."

"Roger. I'm on rappel."

Sweeney turned away from the sun and peered at the one hundred fifty feet of air between the soles of his boots and the ground. He gripped the AK-74 in his right hand. Then he routed the rope around his left hip and through his left fist, which was clamped securely against his chest.

He sucked in a deep breath, threw his left arm out to the side, and let himself fall forward into space, ignoring the pain in his wounded shoulder.

A second later he was running down the side of the building as if it were a vertical sidewalk. The farther he got from the top, the longer his strides became until he was bounding away from the wall with every step.

The ground rushed up at him with frightening speed, but he refrained from braking until the end of the very last bound. When the tops of the unkempt shrubs around the building brushed against his head, he slapped his brake hand across his chest.

The force of the maneuver jerked his body upright and slowed his descent with a force that popped his spine better than any chiropractor could. His boots impacted earth, and he continued away from the building until the end of the rope slipped through the carabiner and he was free. John would see the rope go slack and know to follow.

He took cover next to a large tree, where he made a grisly discovery.

Splayed unnaturally on the ground was the body of the terrorist who had tripped over him. His torso was twisted, and unseeing eyes stared from a pallid face that registered shock and fear.

That last step was a doozie.

Sweeney stepped past the corpse and wondered what hell those eyes were seeing now. But there was no time to dwell on it. The Ukrainians would surely send someone to search this side of the building any second.

Come on, Coop!

As if on cue, the assault line jerked, and John burst through the treetops, braking hard before landing with a soft thud. He quickly ran off the end of the rope and headed for his partner. He sidestepped the body of the terrorist and ran past Sweeney with a hushed, "Let's move."

They ran about a hundred yards into the woods before John paused in a slight depression.

"What's up?" Sweeney said, panting.

"Give me a sec. My satphone has been buzzing for ten minutes, and I haven't had time to answer it." He pulled the sleek black and gray Iridium phone from a pocket on his vest and punched the button, then put it to his ear, speaking in a whisper. "Cooper here… Olenka, listen. Rip and Mary just got captured by the Ukrainians. There— What?" There was a long pause and the team sergeant's face went pale. "God help us."

Sweeney poked him. "What?"

John put a hand over the receiver and fixed him with a look that chilled the sweat on the back of Sweeney's neck. "ITEB has made it to the States. People are dying."

14

AYAD SHISHANI OPENED his eyes and wondered why they wouldn't focus, trying to remember where he was. He'd been expecting Paradise, but this certainly wasn't it.

At first he thought it was his run-down flat in Grozny, judging by the chipped plaster on the ceiling above him. But why did it feel like someone was inside his head, beating his way out with a hammer? He reached up and ran a hand over his stubbly face.

The sticky blood coming from his nose brought it all back in an instant. The apartment building in Pripyat. The rockets streaking toward the Chernobyl reactor. The explosion in the stairwell. Fighting with the ferocious soldier whose forehead had destroyed his nose.

Ayad rolled to his side and groaned when he saw Kyr's mangled body at the foot of the stairs. How had the soldiers responded so quickly? Had Maxim's attack been successful? A wave of revulsion and hate swept through him. Though they'd all been ready to die, seeing the young man's torn and bloodied corpse brought regret like a rifle butt in the stomach.

He shook his head to try to bring his surroundings into better focus. Ayad could hear voices approaching from below. He felt around him in the dust and debris until his hands fell on his rifle. Struggling to his feet, he staggered back up the stairs to the rooftop, where he blinked painfully as he took in the empty asphalt-covered space, the discarded RPG tube, and scattered remaining rockets. Nobody was in sight.

What happened to Omar?

His gaze shifted to the oily black cloud rising in the distance. It was very near the reactor, but if Maxim's truck bomb had succeeded, the reactor itself should be belching toxic smoke. From what he could see, it was still intact.

Rage seeped into the edges of his still-fuzzy vision. They could not have failed. Allah was, after all, on their side!

Perhaps you have been spared for this moment. It is up to you to give the final blow to the infidels.

Yes, that had to be it. With the voices behind him getting louder by the second, there was no time to spare. Ayad dropped his rifle and hurriedly scooped up one of the remaining rockets and slammed it home in its launcher. He hefted the tube to his shoulder and sighted down the barrel, lining up the reactor beyond the tip of the warhead.

Just as his finger began to squeeze the heavy trigger, a crack sounded behind him, accompanied by a painful, hollow sensation in his gut that drained all his strength in the space of a half second.

He could no longer hold the heavy launcher, and it slid from his grasp. In a red-tinged daze, he turned to see two green-suited soldiers, very different from the first two, emerge from the stairwell, pointing rifles at him and shouting in a language very similar to the Russian that he hated so much. Then his knees gave out, and he crumpled to the ground.

Ayad knew what he should be saying at this moment. Allahu Akhbar. But if God was so great, how could their plan have failed so miserably?

The darkness returned before he could think of an answer.

———

"Come on, kids! Junior, get off the railing!" Monique Jordan snapped her fingers to show she meant business. "The tour is going to leave without us if you don't get it moving!" Her other hand clutched four just-purchased Hoover Dam tour tickets like they were a week's pay, which, unfortunately, was just about the truth.

The day was near perfect—sunny, cool, and not a hint of wind. And it was dry. But of course, Las Vegas was always dry.

Monique adjusted her oversized sunglasses and let her gaze sweep along the white concrete expanse of the dam and the deep blue of Lake Mead behind it. The scale of it all fascinated her, and she kicked herself for not having taken the tour sooner. *After all, we've lived in Vegas for four years now.*

Her seven-year-old son, Junior, raced ahead of his two older sisters to catch up to Monique and grab her outstretched hand. "Momma, Keisha says we have to call it the 'Hoover Dang.'"

Monique laughed, and it felt good. "No, honey. You don't have to call it that. But we better run. I don't want you kids to miss this." She giggled as her two daughters caught up, and she had to trot to keep up with them.

Their lives since moving away from New Orleans had held precious little of what she would consider "family fun time." She thought of Marvin, her husband, who had left them not long after their home was destroyed by the flooding caused by Hurricane Katrina. Back then, she had wondered if they would ever be happy again. But after four years of working at the Tropicana as a keno girl during the day, then moonlighting as a waitress at Denny's, she was finally starting to see light at the end of the tunnel.

She looked down at her three children—twelve-year-old Keisha was now a budding young woman who was growing up all too fast. The gangly ten-year-old, Savonne, was her pensive, introverted one. And then there was Junior, the kind of boy who could make you want a shot of whiskey one minute and make you spew milk through your nose the next. The three of them were her whole life now.

A knot of people had formed on the sidewalk overlooking the incredible canyon that spread out below the dam. The unfinished bypass bridge yawned out into space directly in front of it. Which according to the recent papers had fallen behind schedule.

A uniformed man with a nametag labeled "Ken" stood at the top of a staircase that led down into the bowels of the mammoth concrete structure. He held up a hand to quiet the dozen or so others who were waiting for the tour to begin. "Howdy, folks. I'm your guide for the dam tour this afternoon. Now for security reasons, I'm gonna ask you to put your cameras away once we go inside. Before we do that, though, here's a little history about the dam." Ken started spouting a list of trivia about the structure and its construction back in the 1930s.

While he was talking, Monique sidled over to the three-foot concrete barrier that rimmed the top of the structure. She peered over the edge, then pulled back immediately when the sheer drop below made her head swim. She squeezed Junior's arm more tightly.

"What, Momma?" he said, looking up at her.

"Nothing, baby. It's just a long way down, that's all."

"…seven hundred and twenty-six feet to the bottom." Ken continued addressing the group. "And enough concrete to pave a road from San Francisco to New York City. Now you all follow me and we'll take the elevator down to the hydroelectric plant."

The tour progressed for the better part of an hour, leading through the gleaming power generation facility where spinning turbines harnessed the waters of Lake Mead to generate electricity for millions on the West Coast. The kids ate it up, and Monique found something very encouraging about the fact that men could create something so big and so *positive* out of concrete and steel—taming a raging river and putting it to work for the good of mankind. It was just the kind of "anything is possible" attitude she hoped to instill in her children.

Ken opened a side door, letting in sunlight and a thunderous roar. He waved for the group to follow him outside. When Monique stepped through the doorway, she saw the source of the noise. They were at the bottom of the dam. Tens of thousands of gallons of water shot out of enormous gates at the sides of the canyon. A fine mist floated in the air and raised goose flesh on her arms.

Junior tugged at her hand and shouted, "Momma! Look!" He pointed at the sky that was visible between the canyon walls towering above them.

Monique looked up and saw a rainbow floating on the mist. "Yes, isn't the rainbow pretty?"

"No, not that! Look!" His stubby finger stabbed at the sky. "What is it?"

She looked beyond the rainbow and finally saw it. A white zeppelin was descending toward the base of the dam. *That's strange...* "It's a blimp, honey."

"Like the one they have at the Super Bowl?"

"Well, yes. Only I don't think it's very big." She really couldn't tell how large the thing was, only that it couldn't be anywhere near as large as the Goodyear blimp. She squinted into the late afternoon sun. The craft bore no markings and was descending rapidly toward the power plant. The hair on the back of Monique's neck suddenly stood at attention. *Something isn't right.*

By now some of the other tour-goers had noticed the blimp. "Hey, Ken," one of them shouted. "What's that thing doing down here?"

Ken peered up at the zeppelin. Monique could now see twin propellers set on either side of a small boxy-looking compartment beneath the sausage-shaped balloon. They seemed to be steering it toward the roof of the building that housed the turbines. Only at the rate it was descending, it was coming in for a crash landing.

This can't be good. Monique grabbed for her children. "Kids, get back inside, hurry!"

From behind her, a voice yelled, "It's gonna crash!"

Somebody screamed. Before she knew it, there was a mad rush as everyone on the terrace scrambled for the door.

She stumbled across the threshold, and a thunderclap threw her to the ground on top of her children.

A piercing alarm horn sounded, mixing with shrieks of confusion and pain. When she looked up, panic washed over her like a tsunami.

Junior wasn't there.

The scream tore itself from her lungs as smoke filled the air. "No!" Monique clawed her way to her knees, suddenly realizing that man's awesome creativity wasn't always used for good.

In the chaos, nobody noticed the men high above, watching the scene unfold from an overlook at the rim of the canyon. Before the smoke from the inferno below reached them, they got into their low-rider Imperial and drove away.

Washington DC

"Ladies and gentlemen, our government is failing us."

Michael Lafontaine paused for dramatic effect, looking over the packed-out National Press Club banquet hall on Fourteenth Street Northwest, only two blocks from the White House and three from his own office.

It had taken some doing to get an audience with this group on such short notice. His perfectly tailored navy blue suit, taut frame, and close-cropped gray hair complemented his hard features and intense blue eyes as he stepped up to the wide oak dais and stared down the crowd. State flags adorned the walls beneath a soaring tongue-and-groove ceiling.

The room was full of people he loathed—arrogant journo-snobs who had their collective finger on the jugular of public opinion, and knew it. That these caviar-sniffing stuffed shirts shaped the American consciousness qualified as a crime against humanity in his book. Normally, he did everything in his considerable power to stay well outside the realm of their attention.

But it was time to use their agenda for his own purposes.

He cleared his throat. "After the tragedies of September 11, America ran to its politicians, demanding increased security. The politicians responded by punishing the very people they had pledged to protect—curtailing our freedoms and creating more bureaucracy at a cost to taxpayers that is almost inconceivable. When the economy fell apart, these same senators and congressmen made grand speeches about economic security while mortgaging the futures of our children and grandchildren.

"But as the tragic events of this week have clearly shown, we are still vulnerable to attack within our own borders. If the reports coming out of Silicon Valley and Los Angeles are correct, the explosive being used in this new wave of attacks has been traced to an Islamic terror organization in Lebanon with alleged ties to Iran."

He straightened and thumped the podium with his fist. "This is happening on American soil, people. The war has come to our shores again."

Michael could tell by the way the assembled journalists were shifting in their seats and exchanging glances with one another that he'd hit a nerve. Whether they agreed or disagreed, he didn't care, so long as they reported what he had to say.

"Make no mistake, the Islamic radicals working to destroy us are cowards—they ply their trade of death and destruction against peaceloving noncombatants. They aren't attacking military bases, they're attacking our infrastructure—the very rails that carry our products to market and the roads we use to take our children to school. But cowards though they may be, they're committed and clever. And they won't stop as long as they draw breath.

"The solution, however, won't be found in giving up more of our freedoms. Turning America into a police state will only hand a greater victory to those bent on destroying the American ideal. It's time to stop half-stepping in this war. It's time to force our government to do what our former president committed after 9/11. I quote from his speech before Congress on September 14, 2001."

Michael looked down at his notes. "'Our grief has turned to anger, and anger to resolution. Whether we bring our enemies to justice, or bring justice to our enemies, justice will be done.... Al Qaeda is to terror what the mafia is to crime. But its goal is not making money; its goal is remaking the world—and imposing its radical beliefs on people everywhere.... Our war on terror begins with al Qaeda, but it does not end there.'"

Michael leaned over the podium, punctuating his words. "It will not end until every terrorist group of global reach has been found, stopped, and defeated." The intensity in his voice had the effect of a laser beam on butter, and the audience of skeptics melted, offering up a smattering of applause.

Good, that's very good.

"Ladies and gentlemen, it's time to put our money where our mouth is. We can win this war if we set our collective will to victory. The ideals we aspire to as Americans will evolve into something very different if we do not confront this problem at its source and fully prosecute the war on terror. We must, as President Bush declared, 'destroy it where it grows.'

"In the years since this long struggle began, we as Americans have become tired of war, because we are not a warlike people. But it's time to renew our commitment to take this war to the enemy and put an end to it once and for all."

A few of the journalists present appeared to be in hearty agreement, and their enthusiastic applause made up for those who remained silent. Michael waited for the din to settle before continuing.

"I spent twelve years as a soldier. I left the military as a colonel because I realized that I could have a greater impact on the world if I were outside the military framework. This country has been good to me—as you no doubt are aware. I feel a deep responsibility now to leverage that success and do my part to stiffen the resolve of our elected officials to live up to their commitments to all of us and finish this fight.

"To that end, I am embarking on a speaking campaign in the coming weeks to raise awareness for this cause. I appreciate your generosity in allowing me to begin this effort with you here at the National Press Club. In addition, I will be establishing a scholarship fund for the children of families affected by this disaster. I encourage all of you to put your money where your mouths are by supporting a similar charity. Thank you."

Michael stepped away from the podium as the applause returned. When he sat down at his table, he realized his hands were shaking. Not from having to speak in front of several hundred people or even from the passion he felt about his topic.

He was shaking from fear.

Michael Lafontaine had decided on a course of action and was going to see it through, even though he was now sure that doing so would forever change the course of his life.

The motor of the Ukrainian army truck whined as the vehicle ground its way along the barely improved road leading away from Pripyat.

Mary sat in the back, chafing at her bonds, staring defiantly at the dozen Ukrainian soldiers who surrounded her.

The men gazed back with unadulterated malice at the two "terrorists" now in their possession. None more so than a bald sergeant wearing a green bandanna, who stared at her from hate-filled slits carved in a pumpkin-shaped head. He saw her looking at him and said, *"Rosiiska? Nimetska? Angliiska?"*

When she didn't answer, he spat on the floor of the truck at her feet.

Mary dropped her gaze. *I can't believe this is happening again.* She fought back the depressing ramifications of their situation and tried to focus on her options. Unfortunately at this point, escape wasn't one of them.

The Ukrainians had stripped her and Rip of their combat gear before putting them in handcuffs and shoving them unceremoniously into the back of the army truck. She'd heard nothing from John or Sweeney since before their capture. If they'd escaped, they weren't in a much better position than she and Rip were, since she could see both ATVs behind them, being ridden by two soldiers probably having the time of their lives.

On foot, Sweeney and John had little chance of escaping the dead zone, especially cross country, without absorbing a horrific amount of radiation. Giving themselves up might actually be a better option. And if they hadn't escaped… She wouldn't allow herself to follow that train of thought any further.

Either way, there was no way she and Rip could count on them for a rescue.

The truck braked hard, sending Mary sliding forward into Rip and causing him to grunt in pain. She twisted to look at him and could see he needed medical attention. The side of his head was caked with blood, and his usual olive complexion was closer to maroon on that side. But his eyes locked on hers for a moment, and he gave a barely perceptible wink.

The pumpkin-headed sergeant grunted and dug the toe of his boot in Mary's side, causing her to gasp in pain. She leveled her gaze at him, eyes daring him to kick her again.

He was about to oblige when the tailgate of the truck slammed open. An overweight officer shouted a command, and the soldiers rose and hopped one by one onto the pavement. A staccato discussion ensued out of her view.

"Where do you think they're taking us?" Rip said.

She shrugged. "I hope John and Bobby are all right."

"Don't hope," Rip whispered. "Pray."

She nodded, wondering if her previous cry for help would qualify as a prayer. It seemed like hours ago. "I'll try," she said quietly.

Two soldiers hoisted themselves back into the truck. A moment later, the engine revved, and they began moving again.

The truck navigated around a large crater, which Mary could see once they'd gotten past it. The frame of an unrecognizable vehicle sat at the bottom of it, smoldering. Only then did Mary recall hearing a large thunderclap in the distance during the firefight with the same soldiers by whom she was now being guarded.

The truck turned, and Mary saw that they were only a few hundred meters from the reactor, which looked like a giant concrete aircraft hangar surrounded by a high chain-link fence. As far as she could tell, it was undamaged in the attack. The fence was guarded by a phalanx of soldiers, each with his AK-74 at the ready.

The truck rolled through the gate, and the soldiers disappeared into the dust thrown up as the truck growled away from the reactor. Her hopes of escape or rescue faded with every passing kilometer.

Ten minutes later, when the truck stopped again, her shoulders were burning from being shackled, and her legs had fallen asleep.

The fat Ukrainian officer appeared again at the back of the truck and ordered them out. She slid to the tailgate and was helped down by the two young soldiers who had ridden along with them. Then they did the same for Rip.

The overweight officer's jowly, pockmarked face and pronounced underbite made him look like an unhappy bulldog. "You speak English?" The man's voice sounded like gravel in a blender.

She regarded him for a moment before answering, weighing the wisdom of speaking Russian. If they thought she couldn't understand it, they might speak more freely with each other in her hearing, something that could be to her advantage. She decided on English.

"Yes," she said evenly.

"You are from America?" His accent was as thick as cold peanut butter.

"Ireland," she lied, giving him a defiant look.

The officer was faster than he looked. Before she saw it coming, his huge open hand crashed against her jaw.

"Hey!" Rip took one step forward but was dropped to his knees by a rifle butt in the midsection. Two soldiers hauled him, retching, back to his feet.

"I think you lie," said the fat man.

Though her face burned from the blow, Mary forced herself to hold his gaze.

They were in a parking lot next to a two-story block building. There were no cars in view, but based on the fresh paint and recently cut grass around the base of it, the building appeared occupied. Mary guessed it was a military headquarters of some sort.

Two more guards arrived, and the prisoners were prodded along a well-kept sidewalk and into the building, then down a set of wide concrete stairs into the basement. At the end of a brightly lit hallway, they turned into a dank-smelling room covered in cheap tile. At one end were a row of toilets. The other end held a row of dripping shower heads.

The officer in charge squeezed into the room, holding his pistol in one hand like a forgotten cigar. "You take your clothes."

Not comprehending what they were being told, Mary looked at Rip, who shrugged.

Frustrated, the officer repeated the command, adding hand motions as if he were engaged in a game of charades.

Suddenly she understood, though her mind refused to believe what he was saying. *Strip, he's saying. He wants us to strip!* She stared at him, wide eyed. "I will not!"

"Contamination. Must wash."

She gaped at the officer and the four soldiers, who now had their guns leveled at her. *They are serious!*

"Hey," Rip said quietly. "They're right. We've been rolling around in radioactive stuff all morning. We've got to shower this stuff off."

Mary's head was swimming. She could tell by the serious looks the Ukrainians wore that she was going to do this whether she wanted to or not.

Rip was already peeling off his clothes with his back turned to her. "If it makes you feel any better," he said, "I promise not to look."

15

THE RISING SUN was reflecting off the Rio Grande behind Edgar as he pulled off of what the map told him had once been the celebrated Route 66 south of Albuquerque, New Mexico. But the historic significance of the road meant nothing to him. He sped southward, glancing at the map occasionally as he honed in on the next red circle. He'd plotted them himself from the grid coordinates that had accompanied his final instructions.

He did not appreciate having to drive through the night. But the objective would be an easy one, so he had chosen it for himself.

A few minutes later he turned right again and wound his way through a neighborhood of ridiculously large houses, which, in his country, would have been the domain of the very few super-rich. But in America, everyone was rich, it seemed.

The Albuquerque neighborhood soon gave way to scattered farms that took their irrigation off the river. A stray chicken scurried across the road in front of him, but he didn't slow down. When the road turned to gravel, he knew he was getting close.

Edgar edged along the dirt road slowly, not wanting to risk hitting a pothole with the morning sun in his eyes. Eventually he came to a bluff overlooking the river where the road again turned south. Five minutes later, he spied his target.

The bridge that stretched across the river was far too narrow for vehicles, but that wasn't its purpose. Girders rose from a concrete base that surrounded a twenty-four-inch metal pipe as it emerged from underground like a silver snake from its hole. The pipeline then crossed the wide muddy river on its way back to California, carrying millions of cubic meters of compressed natural gas.

The area was deserted. Edgar put his Ford SUV in park and stepped out, stretching his legs after the eight-hour drive. The heat of the day wouldn't arrive for several hours yet.

He smiled. The day was predicted to be a scorcher.

Walking around to the back of the vehicle, he lifted the tailgate and flipped open one of the four giant Coleman ice chests he'd purchased at an outdoor store. He removed the thin leather gloves that he wore as a matter of habit, then fished around in the ice that was packed carefully around the glass bottles within. He found what he was looking for—a can of Budweiser—and cracked the top open to down a long, satisfying gulp. He sighed and wiped his mouth with the back of his hand.

The desert air was cool and fresh. He imagined sitting on the patio of a home like those he'd just passed, enjoying the good life. Before long that dream would be a reality. He downed the beer in another gulp and tossed the can into the weeds.

He checked his phone. No text messages. He considered calling the leader of the gangbangers he'd hired at the restaurant but finally decided against it. *Give them just enough rope to hang themselves.*

Despite their attempts at professionalism during the meeting—making careful notes of his instructions and studying the map he'd given them—Edgar knew how their minds worked. MS-13 was a well-organized criminal gang, but it was still a gang, and its members rarely thought about much more than their own petty turf wars. If they succeeded at the mission he'd given them—hitting the power station at the base of Hoover Dam—it would be a miracle.

Edgar thought the plan was insane. ITEB was powerful, but not that powerful. He knew two bottles wouldn't do much damage to the dam or the power plant. But now that the press had gotten wind of the attack, he realized it didn't matter. People *believed* that it could have knocked out a significant percentage of the electricity to power-starved California. And in fact, the news was reporting that the plant was being taken off-line while federal investigators inspected the damage.

If they found anything, his use of MS-13 would serve his purposes well. It would confuse the authorities as to the source of the attacks. If the gangbangers were caught, they knew only the name Gustavo Soto and the number of his anonymous VoIP phone number in Jordan, which was set to forward his messages to his prepaid cell phone purchased in Cartagena. If discovered, this information would serve only to add to the illusion that Islamic jihadists had joined forces with MS-13—a nightmare scenario for the United States.

Edgar returned to the back of the vehicle and removed one of the tall, clear, ice-cold bottles. Turning it over in his hands, he watched the sparkling liquid inside catch the rising light. It mesmerized him. How could such a small, innocent-looking package wreak such incredible destruction simply by having its bottle broken? He and his friends had constructed Molotov cocktails as teenagers and had used them with devastating effect against rival gangs. But the bottle in his hand would burn hotter than ten of their rudimentary firebombs—and it had the shattering power of a stick of TNT as well. *Amazing.*

Carrying the bottle, he put his gloves back on and opened the door behind the passenger seat. He rummaged through a plastic bag from a local hardware store, producing a set of wire cutters, a roll of tape, and a three-dollar magnifying glass. These he carried to the base of the pipeline.

The concrete base was surrounded by a rusty eight-foot chain-link fence topped with barbed wire. Edgar was delighted to find that someone—probably local kids—had already cut a hole in the fence, making his job that much easier. He dropped the cutters in his pocket and squeezed through the sagging wire.

Once inside the fence, he clambered up the metal bridge supports until he could reach the top of the pipe. Bracing himself, he tore several narrow strips of the silver tape and secured the magnifying glass to the widest part of the glass bottle. Next, he cut longer strips and hung them from a support beam by one sticky end. Standing carefully, he reached up and placed the bottle on top of the pipeline with one hand, then taped it in place with the other.

Two minutes later he was fishing two large cans of Rockstar energy drink from one of the coolers and climbing back into the

Expedition. He would have preferred to recline the seat and catch a few hours of sleep, but there was more driving to do.

Edgar put the SUV in gear and wheeled a quick U-turn. By the time the sun rose high in the sky over the New Mexico desert later that day, he would have to be far from here. Because once the sun began heating the metal pipe that was now receding in his rearview mirror, the day would get very hot indeed.

Pripyat, in the Dead Zone

A rusted Ferris wheel towered over the edge of the parade ground that had once occupied the center of the city. Its rusty spars stood like a silent memorial to the community of people who had once lived there. Sweeney shook his head. Tragedy had sneaked up on those people in the middle of the night, an unfathomable horror that had chased them from their beds, forcing them to leave behind all the things from which people construct their lives.

Sweeney wiped sweat from his eyes and checked his handheld GPS. They were a third of a mile away from the apartment building and exactly one mile from the reactor. They'd been inside the dead zone for nearly six hours. He was following John Cooper, moving as quietly as possible while they skirted the edge of the parade ground past a crumbling concrete pavilion filled with the rusting hulks of bumper cars.

"You have any idea where we're goin'?" Sweeney asked.

John answered over his shoulder. "For now we're just putting some distance between us and the reactor. Hopefully the Ukrainians aren't out looking for us."

"Think we can make it out of here? I've had enough radiation for one day."

John's answer was quiet. "Let's just take it one thing at a time. Olenka should be calling back any minute. Hopefully she'll have worked out some way to locate Rip and Mary."

"I know." Sweeney's tone was dry as he surveyed the faded yellow bumper cars scattered about the cracked and weed-infested pavement. "Let's hot-wire a couple of these babies and drive out."

The smile was evident in John's voice, though Sweeney couldn't see it. "That's what I like about you, Bobby. Always thinking!" The satellite phone in his left hand buzzed. He flipped the antenna skyward and punched a button. "Tell me you've got something for us."

They took a knee while John listened to Olenka. Besides an occasional "Uh-huh," John said little to give Sweeney an indication whether the news was good or bad.

He looked up at the Ferris wheel, whose gondolas had somehow retained their bright yellow color. *How many children once played here? And where are they now?* The place didn't *feel* radioactive, and that only made it creepier. The whole town didn't look that much different from the area around the safe house they'd visited in Kiev. Except that that place had been run down from overuse, and this one was run down from neglect.

John snapped his fingers to get Sweeney's attention and pointed to the GPS Sweeney held. He passed it to John, who began rapidly entering coordinates.

Sweeney spied what looked to be a withered demon's face staring up at him from the pavement off to his right. Looking closer, the realization of what it was caused a sudden revulsion in him like nothing he'd ever felt before.

It was a tiny gas mask made of some sort of green rubber bleached almost white by the sun. Twin eyepieces, situated above a trunklike nose that led to a small green canister, stared at him. What made it so horrible was that it was obviously made for a child.

For some reason, it had never occurred to him that there might be a need for children's gas masks, and for a moment, the horror of that night in 1986 stared back at him through sightless glass eyes. Suddenly Mrs. Sweeney's boy was very, very glad to be an American.

A shudder ran up his spine when he remembered that his homeland might soon become a place where kids *would* need such things if the terrorists weren't stopped.

John ended his call and put away the satphone. "We've got an objective."

"What'd she say?"

John's face was grim. "There's the good, the bad, and the ugly."

Sweeney rolled his eyes. "I hate it when you do that. Just tell me, for Pete's sake."

John shrugged. "The good news is, Phoenix's personal locator beacon is working. The bad news is they're eight kilometers south of here."

"We can hump that in a coupla hours."

"Sure, but they could be moved again anytime. We've got to hurry."

"What's the ugly?"

"Olenka says there have been at least three explosions in the U.S.

so far, all traced to ITEB. Eight people dead, but it looks like whoever's behind this isn't looking to cause mass casualties. Rather, they're
out to disrupt the economy by hitting major arteries of commerce."

"Wasn't that one of the tactics al Qaeda had in mind on 9/11?"

"Exactly. Bringing down the Twin Towers was more than a sym-
bolic gesture. Osama bin Laden made millions by shorting the U.S.
stock market just before the attacks."

"Shorting?" Sweeney's idea of an investment was season tickets to
the Atlanta Braves.

"Shorting is how investors make money when prices fall."

"You can do that?"

John shrugged. "Dad is always talking to me about that stuff.
And my godfather."

"Well, I'd listen to him, Coop. Colonel Lafontaine probably has
more money than Dale Earnhardt Jr. and Jeff Gordon put together."
Sweeney grinned. "My dad plays the stock market too...at the cattle
auction."

John's eyebrows twitched. "Probably more profitable than buying
blue chips lately. Anyway, the speculation is that someone is trying to
shut down the American economy and make money in the process."

Sweeney became deadly serious. "We gotta get back to the States,
and fast."

John nodded. "Olenka's working on that. In the meantime, we've
got to find a way to get Mary and Rip free."

Sweeney stood. "Well, boss, let's quit talking and start walking."

Fifteen minutes later they found themselves on the outskirts of
Pripyat, where the land again melted into open pastureland sur-

rounded by thick rows of pine trees. They were just coming through one such tree line when John froze in his tracks.

Sweeney hurried to close the gap between them. "What you got?"

"Check it out." John pointed across the field in front of them. "I think we might have found some transportation."

Sweeney squinted across the field and saw a large animal slowly grazing along the edge of the pasture. "It's a horse. What's that it's tied to?"

John turned and grinned at him. "Looks like a wagon to me."

———

Rob Denny had just sat down in his easy chair when the lights went out. Again.

"Stupid rolling blackouts! I wish somebody would string up the son-of-a-guns who are setting bombs off all over the country!" He was more frustrated with the lack of television than he was with the lack of lights and air conditioning. They hadn't even been able to record their shows on TiVo.

Doreen called from the kitchen. "Honey, where'd this glass bottle come from?"

Rob groaned, dropping the footrest on his La-Z-Boy and struggling to his feet. "Aw, shoot. That was supposed to be a surprise!" He had totally forgotten about the fancy water bottle in his lunch pail. He sauntered into the cream and teal kitchen.

Doreen was wearing curlers and a frustrated expression. She had the bottle on the counter, struggling with the cap. "I can't get it open."

"Well, why do you want to open it?"

"Because." She gave him that special look that he always interpreted to mean *you're a buffoon.* "I want to use it to put some flowers in."

"But it's expensive bottled water! I figured we could share it while we watch our show tonight."

She rolled her eyes. "It's water, Robbie. Not Cabernet Sauvignon. Now help me get this open."

He sighed. "Geez, Doreen. Give a guy a little credit for trying to be romantic." He snatched the bottle from her and wrapped his thick hand around the cap. Maybe his impressive display of grip strength would get him some man-points. Especially since the fancy-water idea had been a flop.

Just then the doorbell rang.

"Oh, you get that!" Doreen cried, running for the bedroom. "I'm in my curlers and pajamas!"

"So? You wear them grocery shopping, for Pete's sake!" Rob chuckled and carried the bottle with him to the front door. Outside were his neighbors, Scot and Terri Estep, both holding flashlights.

"Hey," Scot said, holding up a wooden box. "We got some new dominoes. Y'all up for a game of Mexican Train?"

Terri smiled, her eyes crinkling behind wire-rimmed glasses. "Scot's been at a conference the last few days, so I made him promise we'd do something together tonight. This is what I get."

"Just a sec," Rob said. "Gotta check with the social coordinator." He turned from the door and shouted. "Hey, Doreen! The neighbors want to play Mexican Train!"

"Might as well," came the muffled reply. "Can't watch TV."

Rob stepped back and waved his friends inside. "Right this way, Doctor."

Scot wasn't a medical doctor but something called a veterinary pathologist. As far as Rob could tell, it had something to do with looking at dead animals all day. He shuddered at the thought. They'd have to pay pretty big bucks to get him to do that sort of thing.

"Where'd you get the bottle?" Scot said.

Rob looked at the container in his hand. "Oh, uh…it's some kind of expensive bottled water. I got it for Doreen, but all she wants to do is make a bud vase out of it."

Doreen came hustling into the room, now dressed and minus the curlers, carrying a box of candles. "Are you still on about that bottle? I told you, it's just water. I mean, how good can water get?"

Scot smiled. "The bottle is pretty. My boss at work collects them. He could probably tell you exactly where that one was made."

Rob grinned. "Tell you what. You beat us at Mexican Train, you can have it."

"Honey! I was going to put flowers in it!" Doreen slapped him on the arm.

"Come on, Doreen, I'll get you a nice vase to put your flowers in," Rob said. "Give us guys something to compete over."

She rolled her eyes again, which was something Doreen was very good at. "Oh, all right. Let's play."

An hour later, Scot and Terri left with their dominoes and the bottle of water. Though Scot would rib him about losing—on Saturday, when they would compete to see who could mow their lawn the fastest—Rob was actually glad to be rid of the thing. It had caused him nothing but grief.

———

When Scot Estep went to work the next day, he parked in front of the laboratory sciences section of the UCLA Medical Center. He'd intended to take the bottle inside to show his boss but ended up forgetting it in his car.

The day was a hot one, and before long the temperature inside his locked Honda Accord soared to over a hundred twenty degrees.

Scot was eating lunch in his office, looking over some slides of a guinea pig with intracytoplasmic protozoal amastigotes when his car erupted like a volcano, spewing flames and shrapnel in all directions and shattering every window in the front of the building.

A SMALL, NEARLY OPAQUE window high up on the wall was the only source of light for the tiny basement room that held Rip and Mary. Mary sat against the outside wall with her knees pulled up to her chest, and fought back tears, hiding her face in the sleeve of the white one-piece jumpsuit they'd given her to wear. Rip sat across from her, head leaned into the corner and saying nothing.

So far, it had been the most horrifying, humiliating day of her life. And judging from the light coming through the window, it was only early afternoon.

If being forced to undress and shower in front of a squad of leering soldiers hadn't been bad enough, she was now forced to contemplate the final words of the Ukrainian commander before the solid steel door of their cell had slammed shut.

"You are the only survivors of this despicable plot. Your fellow terrorists were all killed resisting our fine security forces. But don't worry. Once you are convicted, you will certainly see them again—in hell."

What was worse was the crushing dread she bore, knowing that it was probably her fault for not having been strong enough to get Rip on the ATV and escape fast enough.

Rip sat up and looked at her. "I think John and Sweeney got away. I bet the fat guy thinks the other terrorists are our compadres."

Mary shook her head and stared at her bare feet on the cold concrete floor. "How? I mean, there was only one way to the roof of the building as far as I could tell."

Rip shrugged and leaned back against the wall. "If anyone could figure out a way, those two could."

"I hope you're right." She looked up at Rip, their lanky staff sergeant, and smiled. "Thank you, by the way."

Rip gave a quizzical look. "For what?"

"For not looking."

He broke into a smile. "You're welcome. And thank you for not looking back." He gave her a playful wink.

"You won't…tell anyone, will you?" She choked on the words.

He huffed and spread his hands, encompassing the dank-smelling room. "Who am I gonna tell?"

Anxiety and grief overcame her, and she again dropped her head into the crook of her arm.

Rip was quiet for a long moment. Then he murmured, "Well, you're the *jefa* on this mission. What happens now?"

She sniffed and wiped her eyes. "I don't know, Rip."

"Do you really think they'll execute us?"

She sniffed. "I'm afraid they'll ship us off to some prison and we'll never be heard from again." Now that she thought about it, she wasn't sure which would be worse.

"Even if they find out we weren't with the terrorists?"

The weight of despair pressing on her made it a chore to even shrug. "Especially if they find out who we are."

Rip made a face like he was trying to figure out a math problem. "But what about, you know, due process?"

Mary gave a little snort and threw her hands in the air. "All I know is, they did everything they could to cover up the Chernobyl disaster the first time—to keep it from the world press. I can't imagine they would want news of a security threat to the reactor advertised around the world."

"But won't our embassy try to get us out?"

"Maybe through back channels. But that could take months, even years."

Rip sat back against the wall, his face impassive. After a moment he said, almost to himself, "*Pues,* if that's the way it has to be."

Mary sat up and shot him a hard look. "What's that supposed to mean?"

Rip shrugged. "Nothing. I guess this is where we're supposed to be right now. So we just need to roll with it."

"What kind of philosophical gibberish is that?"

Rip fixed her with his dark eyes. "What makes you feel like you have to control everything in your world?"

Mary had to fight to keep from unloading all the frustration she was feeling. "Control! I'll tell you why I have to control my world." She punctuated her statement by jabbing a pointed index finger in his direction. "Because if I don't control my world, nothing will."

Rip's eyebrows shot up, but there was no trace of anger or resentment in his face. "That's where you're wrong, *amiga.* That's where you're wrong."

"Yeah? How so? Am I supposed to just not care what happens to us?"

"Of course you should care. But if you hold on to things too tightly, you're sure to lose them."

"Well, excuse me if I hold on too tight to my life. It's the only one I have."

Rip chewed his lip for a moment. "Look, forgive me. I didn't mean to upset you. A lot of things have changed for me recently, and I don't have them all worked out in my head yet."

Mary wiped her eyes, angry at herself for being so weepy. "You sit here without a care in the world when we're about to spend the rest of our lives in the gulag. I'm sorry, I just can't do that."

The edges of Rip's mouth turned up into the slightest hint of a smile. "That's because I'm already dead."

"Is that more of your psychobabble?"

Rip gave her a full grin. "Yeah, kinda. I mean, I'm a Christian now. I'm still learning all I can about it, but I know that one of the things Jesus said is that unless I'm willing to die, I can't really live."

Mary was surprised at his words. They weren't what she expected to hear from a tough-as-nails former gang member. She sniffed. "Did you say John and Sweeney are Christians too?"

"John is—though he doesn't make a big deal about it all the time. I don't know about Sweeney."

Mary shook her head. It felt like it was half full of water. "Well, that's fine for you and John, but—"

"But what? If it's fine for me, why wouldn't it be fine for you?"

The sound of footsteps in the hall kept her from answering. Mary looked up to see the enormous head of the Ukrainian officer appear in the window. She and Rip struggled to their feet as the door ground open on rusty hinges. Two soldiers, weapons ready, flanked the rotund man.

"You will come with me," the officer commanded. "We have an appointment with my superiors in Kiev."

In fifteen years as a broadcast journalist, Demi Rouseau had interviewed plenty of famous people. She had no expectation that this one would be any different.

She gave herself a once-over in the mirrored elevator on the way up to retired Colonel Michael Lafontaine's office in downtown Washington DC. She kept her coffee-colored hair cut to shoulder length to make it easier to manage. It offset an open, unblemished face the color of rice paper. But today her high cheeks were tinged a bit pink from covering the antiwar demonstration at the White House a day earlier—one of the few assignments she didn't like that came with working in DC.

Demi checked her purse, making sure the digital recorder was in its place. The cameramen would, of course, be recording audio during the interview, but she always liked to have a backup she could listen to in her car or at home as she mulled over angles for the stories she produced.

In her current job as a reporter for the Christian Broadcasting Network, she had to constantly battle the perception that CBN wasn't a "real" news network. As if having *Christian* in the name guaranteed the reporting would be biased. Which was a joke, since she'd hardly ever met a reporter for any of the major networks who didn't have an agenda. She recalled the time when she'd sat next to two CNN hacks at a press conference and listened to them openly mock the vice president under their breath like a couple of junior high schoolers.

If anything, her network was less biased simply because it didn't insist on only reporting the bad news. In her mind, the one thing missing from most news reporting was context—the good as well as the bad. But since good news was rarely as sensational as bad, it usually got buried.

And that was what kept Demi working at CBN, even when she could have gone elsewhere and made more money. But on days like today, finding a positive story in Washington DC was more difficult than finding a taxi at rush hour.

The elevator slid open, and she stepped into a sumptuously decorated hallway. At the end of the corridor, she came to a solid wooden door with a brass nameplate that said simply, M. LAFONTAINE.

Understated. Nice.

She tried the door. Locked. Before she could knock, a buzzer sounded at the latch, so she pushed her way inside.

The bright reception area had a blond hardwood floor with an expensive Oriental rug in the center. A matronly woman in a Burberry suit rose from behind a contemporary metal desk that was empty except for a flat-panel computer monitor on one corner. Her smile was graceful, but her blue eyes had a certain hardness that told Demi the woman was not the kind to cede access to her boss easily.

"Welcome, Ms. Rouseau," the woman said. "Your camera crew is in the colonel's office setting up. Would you like something to drink? Chamomile tea, perhaps?"

"I'll pass, thank you. Is Mr. Lafontaine here yet?"

The woman shook her head. "He is on his way. I'm afraid his testimony before the Senate Intelligence Committee took longer than expected."

Demi wasn't the least bit surprised. Important people never got anywhere on time. "That's fine. We appreciate the colonel's giving us an interview. I'll just see how the crew is coming along."

The double doors to the left of the secretary's desk were ajar. When she stepped through them, she spotted Robert Norman and Tim Tupper, cameraman and audio engineer, both from CBN's Nashville bureau. They'd been on loan to DC since the bombs had started going off around the country. She smiled. Besides being experienced and efficient, Tupper and Norman were always fun to work with.

"Hey, guys. How's it going?"

The two men looked up from adjusting a monitor. Tupper's mustache and goatee split in a goofy grin. "Hi, Demi. You look nice today."

Norman groaned. "You're such a suck up, Tim."

Tim Tupper, the audio tech, feigned offense. "Easy for you to say. You're already married!"

Demi laughed. "Stop it, you two. We've only got half an hour to nail this interview. I want to be sure everything's ready."

"Who is this guy, anyway?" Norman asked.

Demi took a seat in one of two expensive Moroccan leather chairs the crew had moved to the center of the room to make way for their lights. "Michael Lafontaine is the billionaire son of a former North Carolina senator. He retired from the Army as a colonel and now spends his time lobbying politicians for various causes."

"Old southern money," Tupper said.

"Kind of. He inherited a large fortune, but from what I've been told, he's doubled it through investments in pharmaceuticals and technology companies."

Tupper shook his head in amazement. "Some people make it look so easy."

"What I don't get is why he lives in DC," Norman said. "If I had that much money, I'd be scuba-diving in the Caymans for a living."

Demi shrugged. "I wanted to ask him that in the interview. Officially, he oversees the philanthropic arm of Lafontaine Enterprises."

Tupper's eyebrows shot up. "Hey, great. Ask him if he wants to donate to the Starving Tupper Fund. The STF."

She rolled her eyes. "Oh, I'm sure he'd jump at that."

Lafontaine's secretary pushed the door open. "The colonel is on his way up."

"Thank you." Demi stood and turned to her crew. "Are we ready?"

Norman scoffed. "I was born ready."

"You weren't born, you were hatched," Tupper shot back.

Two minutes later Michael Lafontaine strode through the door in a custom-tailored pinstriped suit that revealed an almost six-foot frame and a trim waistline. He was much younger than Demi had imagined, with just a touch of gray around his temples and eyes like polished blue granite.

He extended a hand that gripped hers softly. "Ms. Rouseau, it's a pleasure to meet you."

"Thank you, Colonel. But please, call me Demi."

"Demi, yes. And I'm Michael. I'm sorry to have kept you waiting."

"No problem. We're happy to be here. And we're ready to begin whenever you are."

Normally at this point, politicians would ask for a moment to freshen up. When Demi had first started in Washington, she'd been amazed at how image-conscious senators and congressmen could be. Some needed to don a fresh suit. Others even used makeup.

Lafontaine simply looked her in the eye and gave a disarming smile. "Let's do it."

She liked him already. After introducing the crew, who slid microphones onto both Lafontaine's and Demi's lapels, Demi removed the digital recorder from her purse and turned it on. She sat down and looked up at Norman. "Are we rolling?"

Norman nodded without looking up from the camera monitor. Tupper, wearing his headphones, gave her a thumbs-up and mouthed the words "Starving Tupper Fund."

She ignored him and looked into the camera. "I'm here with retired Army Colonel Michael Lafontaine, now a philanthropist in Washington DC." She turned to look at Lafontaine and continued. "Michael, until recently you've never granted interviews. But in the last few days, you've done at least a dozen on all the major networks. Why the sudden change?"

The intensity of the billionaire's gaze could have melted plastic. "Demi, I've stepped to the forefront because I'm concerned about the future of this country. I've been working behind the scenes for more than five years to get our politicians to understand the scope of the threat that radical Islamic terrorism poses to this nation. And for years, I've been saying that if we didn't take a harder line against the terrorists, they would eventually be back on our shores, killing our people and crippling our freedoms."

Lafontaine crossed his legs. "That's exactly what we see happening now. As you're probably aware, another explosive device went off this morning in New Mexico, severing an important gas pipeline and causing havoc in the energy markets. Last night in Nevada a major explosion at the Hoover Dam knocked out electricity to over two million Americans, and California is predicting more rolling brownouts today.

"My sources indicate that these attacks are a concerted effort by radical Islamic groups to disrupt our economy. Some believe that the explosives being used were smuggled across our very porous border with Mexico, and that South American gangs may even be working with the jihadis in coordinating these attacks."

Demi was furiously taking notes on her legal pad without actually looking at it. It was a skill she'd perfected years ago. She was uncomfortable with his use of terms like "some believe." She made a note to ask him to confirm his sources but knew enough to save those kinds of questions until the end of the interview.

She looked up at him. "So you believe these attacks are all being perpetrated by the same group of people? If that's the case, what can our government do to stop the attacks?"

Lafontaine spread his hands. "Do you remember General Jerry Boykin?"

Demi nodded. "The Special Forces commander who got in trouble for speaking to church groups a few years ago. We interviewed him on our show."

"Right. Boykin got flambéed in the press for telling it like it is. He said this war is against radical Islam, and the press tried to crucify him for it. The point I've been making all along is that you can't fight a war without calling your enemy the enemy. And you can't win if you hobble your military and make them try to defeat the enemy without actually offending him."

Lafontaine sat forward, punctuating his points with a knife-edged hand. "Listen, Americans are peaceful people. But when that peace is threatened, we must have the guts to send in our forces to root out the evil and destroy it. The jihadis are a cancer on the planet, and unless our limp-wristed politicians can grow backbones and do something substantive about it, I believe the American people have a duty to throw them out and vote in folks who will get the job done.

"And I think we *would* do that, except that our people are so divided over things like the environment and the economy that we fail to see the freight train bearing down on us."

Demi shifted uncomfortably. Though it was hard to deny what Lafontaine was saying, she wasn't used to anyone in Washington being so direct. *Enough of the softball questions. Now for the good stuff.* She cleared her throat. "What about the peaceful Muslims in this country? Aren't you painting with too broad a brush?"

Lafontaine sat back. "If the Muslims in this country truly are peace loving, shouldn't they be leading the call to hunt down and rid the world of those who kill and destroy in the name of Allah? So where are they? Let me make something crystal clear—and please promise me this will be in the interview, Demi—I am not condemning Islam. I'm condemning our government for a half-baked response to the threat against us.

"I'm calling on Americans to demand that our military forces be given the latitude and resources to do the job right. Not only that, but Homeland Security needs to stop wasting its time frisking elderly nuns at the airport. We need to throw our weight behind border enforcement like never before. And I'm going to keep yelling about it until something gets done."

Demi tapped her pen on the edge of her legal pad. "So tell me this, Michael: what if you fail?"

He looked genuinely surprised by the question, and for the first time, a flicker of some darker emotion passed across his face like a cloud. Demi couldn't tell if it was fear, sadness, or something else, but it was surprising from this man who had been all over town in the last week, captivating rooms full of people with his very presence.

"If I fail?" He hesitated. "It's not about me. I didn't quit defending this country when I took off my uniform twelve years ago, Ms. Rouseau. I love America, but the country I swore to defend years ago is being lost. Lost through cowardice, inaction, and self-centeredness." When he looked back up at her, his stare was back, so laser focused that it almost made her shiver. "And now, Ms. Rouseau, I'm going to do something about that."

South of Chernobyl, Leaving the Dead Zone

Captain Mykola Kirichenko was happier than a sailor on shore leave as he stood watching the two surviving terrorists, in handcuffs and over-sized white jumpsuits, climbing awkwardly into the canvas-covered bed of the two-and-a-half-ton army truck.

Attached to a hitch on its rear bumper was an old flatbed trailer they had rushed over from the motor pool, upon which were loaded the two small four-wheeled motorcycles that had been captured. As the detailed report in his hand explained, his men had responded with characteristic speed and discipline, clearing the entire area in a matter of minutes, and had bravely fought and killed the remaining three terrorists on the roof of the apartment complex.

He grinned. The failure of their diabolical plan to blow up the reactor would become his finest hour when this truck arrived in Kiev.

Already headquarters was in an uproar over the event and was mobilizing an entire army brigade to form a defensive perimeter around the reactor and to search the dead zone for any more signs of terrorist activity. They might even ask him to command the effort.

It was an offer he looked forward to refusing. Captain Kirichenko—or, more likely, *Colonel* Kirichenko—would be far too busy attending parties with the power elite and giving speaking engagements all over Europe once he received his decorations and retired. Perhaps he could even run for elected office. Who wouldn't vote for the man who had literally saved the world?

A burly sergeant wearing a green bandanna on his head hustled over to him. "The prisoners are loaded and ready, Capitan."

"Thank you, Yuri. Did you remember their gear as well? Our intelligence people will want to examine it."

"Tak," Yuri said.

"Very well. You and Private Os will guard the criminals in the rear of the truck. I trust the two of you can handle a woman and a skinny, wounded man?"

Yuri gave a sideways sneer. "Yes, Capitan."

"Good."

Mykola sauntered over to the vehicle and made a show of kicking tires and checking tie-downs. When he was satisfied that all was in order, he stepped to the cab of the truck and hefted his oversized body into the passenger seat. He was too large to reach the seat belt, so he slammed the door and turned to the fresh-faced private who was driving. "What's your name, son?"

"Stepan, sir."

Mykola was pleased to see his men had once again remembered military courtesy. "Stepan, I want to get to Kiev as quickly as possible. We have very important cargo to deliver to headquarters. So do not delay. Understand?"

The young man nodded, Adam's apple bobbing as he put the truck in gear and pulled away from the barracks.

Once they passed the sign announcing that they had left the town of Chernobyl, the truck picked up speed on the empty road—the only one still in use that led toward Kiev. Mykola found it hard to contain his excitement, humming quietly to himself and enjoying the breeze on his face with his arm out the window.

Stepan interrupted his thoughts, shouting over the roar of the truck's motor. "They call it the dead zone, but really, it's not, you know?"

Mykola looked at him. "What do you mean?"

The young man indicated where the road disappeared around the bend into a forested area up ahead. "Those pine trees have all grown up since the accident. See how thick they are? They don't look dead."

Mykola nodded. The boy had a point. If anything, the nature

they were speeding past was fuller and greener than ever, despite the invisible radiation in the soil. As the truck sped around a bend in the road, he dreamed of returning to Crimea, where—

"Hold on!"

The driver slammed on the brakes, sending Mykola headfirst into the windshield. The glass spidered out from the point where his head collided, leaving him stunned.

He cried out as the truck skidded to a halt. His vision swam, but he could make out what appeared to be a horse and cart stopped in the middle of the road. Groaning, he put one hand to his head, feeling warm, sticky blood between his fingers. He turned to look at the driver. "How did—"

But Stepan was staring past him out the open window, eyes wide with horror. "Capitan! We're—"

Mykola jerked his head around just in time to see the butt of a rifle coming toward his face.

Pain exploded like a grenade inside his head. But one fleeting thought invaded just before unconsciousness came.

Retirement was going to be nothing like he had hoped.

17

SWEENEY WAS SPRINTING for the back of the truck even before it and the trailer slewed to a stop at awkward angles in the road. Every muscle strained to go faster, harder, because something in him knew that he had only seconds before it was too late to rescue Rip and Mary.

It had been a suicidal plan to begin with—hatched in desperation by men who had no other options. But if they were going down, Sweeney was determined to die knowing he hadn't held anything back.

He ran up to the truck, hoping against hope that the poorly trained Ukrainians would surrender without resistance. He didn't want to shoot any of them, but if they put up a fight, he would do what he must and deal with the regret later.

Just before he reached the rear of the vehicle, however, a brawny soldier came flying headfirst through the canvas covering the truck bed. He landed with a grunt and a thud on the pavement just to Sweeney's left. The impact of the fall sent the man's assault rifle skittering across the road.

Cursing, the bullish man sprang to his feet but went right back down as Sweeney sucker-punched him from behind with the metal stock of his AK-74.

No slack in this game, buddy.

Sweeney swung his own weapon up and pointed it through the hole the man's exit had torn in the canvas, just in time to see Mary, clad in some sort of white jumpsuit, do a little hop-kick that caught a second soldier right underneath his nose. The force of the blow caused the man to crumple to the floorboards like an empty set of clothes—right next to a surprised-looking Rip Rubio.

They're alive! Hot dog!

Since Mary looked to have already given every soldier within kicking distance an epic shellacking, Sweeney jumped to the driver's door and yanked it open with one hand, training his rifle on the soldier inside.

The freckle-faced kid that stared wide eyed back at him couldn't have been more than eighteen. His hands left the steering wheel and hit the roof.

"Out!" Sweeney shouted, grabbing the young soldier's lapel and yanking him from the truck. He pushed the Ukrainian to the ground and put a knee in the center of his back. Then he yelled, "Clear!" loud enough for John to hear him on the other side of the vehicle.

Mary and Rip leaped from the back of the vehicle. The burly soldier was still conscious, so Rip wrapped his shackled arms around the burly man's neck from behind and squeezed with a ferocity that made it clear the soldier hadn't treated them well. In a matter of seconds the man blacked out from lack of blood flow to the brain.

Sweeney jerked a ten-inch combat knife free from the holster on his chest harness and tossed it underhand to Mary. "Quick! Cut the ATVs loose."

She caught the knife in both hands. "You got it. Are we glad to see you!"

Sweeney produced a set of flex-cuffs and secured the hands of the soldier he was sitting on. "Sorry, buddy. Nothing personal. You were just in the wrong place at the wrong time."

John came around the front of the truck and took in the scene. "Wow, Bobby. Great job."

Sweeney jerked a thumb at Mary, who was busy sawing away at the straps that had been used to tie down the four-wheelers. "Miss Kickboxer took care of two of 'em." He looked behind John. "What happened to the passenger?"

John smirked. "He'll be sleeping for a while."

Rip fished around in the pockets of his unconscious soldier. "Got 'em!" He held up a set of keys, one of which would hopefully unlock their handcuffs.

John smiled and gave Rip the standard Ranger greeting: "Great to see you, Rubio. How come you're not dead yet?"

The lanky Latino beamed. "Guess the Lord still has plans for me today."

"Hallelujah," Sweeney said sarcastically. He strode over to Rip. "Let's get movin' before the Lord changes His mind. Here, gimme those keys. We'll put your handcuffs on Rambo here, and then we'll let the dude in the back of the truck try Phoenix's on for size."

Within three minutes Sweeney and the two former captives had handcuffed the other soldier, freed the ATVs of their moorings on the flatbed, and secured Rip's and Mary's combat gear from the back of the truck. John was making a quick call to Olenka on the satphone to let her know the rescue had been successful.

"Leave the clothes, bro," Rip said as John waited for the call to connect. "They're contaminated. Yours are too," he said to Sweeney. "You're going to want to get out of those things as soon as you can."

"Let's worry about getting back to the safe house first," John replied, then spoke into the phone. "Olenka, we got them. We're—" He listened for a full thirty seconds while Sweeney worried that someone else would come along the road at any moment. "Roger that. We'll meet you there. Okay. Out."

He slapped the phone closed. "Olenka's coming with the SUV to meet us. She says we'll hit an old road about four klicks west of here, that will lead us to the hole in the fence we snuck through this morning. There, we'll ditch the ATVs and our gear. Olenka says she has a plan that will get us out of the country just after midnight."

"Whatever we're paying that *muchacha,* it isn't enough," Rip said.

"No question." John climbed aboard the trailer and slid onto one of the ATVs. "Rubio, you're with me."

Sweeney retrieved his knife from Mary. "Gimme one sec. There's one more thing I've gotta do."

He ran to the front of the truck where the horse was still standing, connected to the cart they'd ridden in. He and John had placed two big rocks under each wheel to keep the horse from bolting when the truck came around the corner. He quickly cut the leather bindings that held the horse to the cart, then whispered in its ear. "Sorry for the trouble, big guy. We owe you one." He slapped the animal's hindquarters and sent it charging into the woods.

Sweeney ran back and jumped onto the trailer and then got on the other ATV.

"Where's the ramps for unloading these things from the trailer?" Mary said before climbing on behind him.

"Aw," Sweeney drawled, "we don't need ramps. Get on."

She did so, and Sweeney gunned the engine, letting out a *whoop* as the Polaris shot off the end of the flatbed, catching air before bouncing to the ground, with John and Rip right behind. Sweeney grinned, not so much at the rush of adrenaline it gave him, but at the way Mary was holding on to him for dear life.

Metro Red Line, Washington DC

The United States Capitol Police had been good to Steve Strettmater. But after nineteen years, eleven months, and twenty-two days, he was looking forward to retiring.

The Metro Red Line train rocked gently as it thundered toward the nation's capital. Though it was early enough not to be packed with morning commuters, those few passengers on the train with him sat lost in their own thoughts. Except for the swish of the car over the rails and a few passengers who murmured to one another, the car was as quiet as a church sanctuary during a prayer meeting.

Steve closed the newspaper he'd been reading and let his mind ponder his own future. Despite the alimony payments to his ex-wife, he had managed to hoard away enough cash to buy five acres of good land in North Carolina's Appalachian foothills. He planned to build a cabin with his bare hands and live out the rest of his days with a beer in one hand and a fishing rod in the other.

In his career he'd protected five sitting and former presidents and scores of diplomats, and he'd met more foreign dignitaries than Jimmy Carter had. But he'd long since gotten over the idea that anybody in Washington would miss him once he exited the scene. That was okay—the feeling was mutual.

The Metro train slowed, and its driver said something unintelligible over the loudspeaker. It sounded strangely like the voice at the drive-through where he stopped every morning to order a large coffee on his way to the Shady Grove Metro station. But Steve, a graying ex-Marine, didn't need to comprehend the driver's thick inner-city accent to know this was his stop. He picked up the faded Adidas duffel bag from between his polished Corcoran shoes and joined the short line of people exiting the train.

Seven minutes later, Steve was walking up Seventeenth Street toward the White House, trying not to sweat too much in the DC humidity. He looked at his watch and noted with satisfaction that he was twelve minutes early for his shift. Nineteen years and he'd never once been late for work, even though that had sometimes meant staying the night there when snow or when other acts of God had nearly shut down the city.

After September 11, he'd stayed at his post for three weeks straight, sleeping on a cot in the break room. But he was glad to do it, especially then. If he had been any younger, he would have rejoined the Marine Corps and volunteered to personally hunt down every camel-loving radical remotely tied to al Qaeda.

A short black limousine pulled to the curb just ahead of him. A man about his age threw open the back door and stepped out without waiting for the driver. Steve would have recognized Michael Lafontaine at once even if the man hadn't been on just about every television program except *Oprah* in the last week.

Lafontaine was highly respected by everyone Steve knew on the Capitol Police force, if for no other reason than so many politicians despised him. Plus, he probably had more money than some of those other billionaires who were always in the news, most of whom were just one step to the left of Ho Chi Minh on the political spectrum. Lafontaine used his money more wisely, from what Steve had heard. The billionaire's office was somewhere high up in the building directly across from his guard post, he knew that much. And it didn't surprise him that the man was at work before everyone else—he was known to keep odd hours.

Steve came up even with the limousine and tossed the former colonel a friendly salute. "Morning, Colonel Lafontaine. Good to see you."

Lafontaine turned and took in Steve's Capitol Police uniform with a glance. "Why, thank you, Officer. And thanks for the work you do guarding our city. You boys don't get enough recognition for the job you do."

Steve nodded, feeling that strange tension in the air that always surrounded very important people. "Thank you, sir. My buddies and I have been following you on the tube. Everyone's real happy to see these politicians finally getting their feet held to the fire a little bit. Don't let the bureaucrats get you down—you are right on the money about us needing to get tougher with the terrorists."

Lafontaine smiled, but it was the kind of smile that betrayed the heavy burden the man must be carrying. "I appreciate that more than you know." He patted Steve on the shoulder and turned to go. "You have a good day, Officer. Thanks again."

Steve watched Lafontaine push through the revolving door of his building. Then he turned and crossed the street to the guard shack at the west entrance to the White House.

Earl Parvin, a longtime friend and one of the only officers who had been on the force longer than he had, grinned at him through the window.

Steve scanned his plastic ID badge and smiled through the four-inch Plexiglas. The gate buzzed and he pushed through, then repeated the process to enter the guardhouse itself.

"Sell your house yet?" Earl asked.

Steve made a disgusted sound and dropped his newspaper on the desk. "Nah. Had a coupla nibbles, but nobody has come up with cash."

"I'm telling you," Earl said, shaking his head, "you're asking too much. The market's still in the dumper."

"Maybe so. But I can afford to wait it out. I'm planning to live in my travel trailer while I build my cabin anyway."

"Well, when you get it done, lemme know. Me and the missis will come for a visit."

"You do that, Earl." Steve picked up a ceramic mug and filled it from the coffee maker near the door. But as he reached for the bottle of nondairy creamer, a thunderclap nearly knocked him off his feet.

A fireball erupted from the building across from the guard shack, causing both of them to throw themselves to the floor as glass and flame rained down on the street.

Steve was on his feet in an instant, staring wide eyed at the inferno outside the window.

The colonel!

"Sound the alarm, Earl!" He sprinted out the door, hoping against hope that there was anyone left alive at Seventeenth and G.

———

When the two Polaris ATVs made it back to the hole in the fence through which they'd entered the dead zone, Mary's watch told her they'd spent nearly twelve hours inside the radioactive wasteland. She wondered if that might have something to do with the nausea she was feeling.

Of course it could have been simple motion sickness caused by racing through overgrown fields and disused farm tracks on the four-wheeler, arms reluctantly clamped around Sweeney's taut midsection to keep from flying off the back. Or it could have been lingering humiliation from being made to shower in full view of a half-dozen Ukrainian soldiers. She hadn't eaten all day, either, which only added to the discomfort.

If Sweeney was feeling any ill effects from the radiation, he wasn't showing it. He piloted the Polaris like a pro, skillfully navigating even the roughest terrain while keeping his eye on the GPS unit strapped to the handlebar. He seemed to take no notice of the saucer-sized area of dried blood on his left shoulder, either. She made a mental note to send him to a doctor as soon as they made it somewhere where there was one they could trust.

Twice they'd been forced into dense thickets when the sound of low-flying jet airplanes had made them run for cover. She assumed the Ukrainians were out searching for them, though the aging MiG fighters that flashed by overhead couldn't be too well suited for spotting concealed targets on the ground.

Sweeney slowed to a crawl as he navigated the gap in the fence line.

Mary searched the path ahead for any sign of Olenka's blue SUV. At first she saw nothing, but when they made it back up onto the trail, she spotted the vehicle tucked beneath some pine trees and covered with branches. She tapped Sweeney's good shoulder and pointed. "Over there."

Sweeney turned that direction and gunned the engine. The door of the SUV swung open as they pulled up next to it, and their Ukrainian operative stepped out wearing jeans, hiking boots, and a brown hooded sweatshirt. Her expression was all business. John and Rip arrived on the second Polaris and killed the engine.

"We must hurry," Olenka said, her voice urgent. "The army will be scouring the area soon with helicopters, if they aren't already. And they are setting roadblocks. We will return to the safe house long enough for you to shower and change clothes, but we only have a few hours to get you out of the country."

The team hopped off the ATVs, and John and Sweeney peeled off their combat gear.

"What are we going to do with the ATVs?" Rip asked.

"Leave them," Mary answered. "Leave everything. It's all contaminated."

Sweeney let out a low whistle. "It's a good thing Buzz isn't here.

He would never throw away a perfectly good Polaris, even if it did glow in the dark from radiation."

"Desperate times, desperate measures," John said, stripping off his web gear.

"What about our weapons?" Rip asked.

Sweeney picked up his AK-74 and began disassembling it. "Take the bolt out, John. We'll leave the rest here and toss the bolts somewhere down the road."

"Good idea." John reached for his rifle. "That'll keep anyone else from using them."

"Please," Olenka said quickly, "we must go."

Leaving everything except the GPS unit and their clothes, the team piled into the SUV. John got in the passenger seat, and Mary sat between Rip and Sweeney in the back. Olenka brushed the leaves and branches off the vehicle and hopped into the driver's seat. The four-cylinder engine whined as she piloted the SUV south toward the safe house, retracing the route they had taken on the four-wheelers early that same morning.

To Mary, it had been the most treacherous and terrifying twelve hours of her life. It seemed like they'd been in the dead zone for a year.

"I have much to tell you," Olenka said. "First, there have now been seven attacks in your country attributed to this liquid explosive you have been seeking."

Mary's eyes went wide. "*What?* ITEB is exploding in the United States?"

John turned to look at her. "Oh, I forgot to tell you about that."

"Yeah," Sweeney said. "Things were a little crazy."

"*Dios mio,*" Rip breathed.

Mary leaned forward and dropped her face into both hands. "We've failed, haven't we?"

Nobody offered an answer.

Sweeney's tone was dark. "We've got to get home, boys."

John turned to Olenka. "How are you planning to get us out?"

Olenka kept her eyes on the road as she spoke. "Flying is no longer an option. The news in Kyiv is reporting that a large group of Islamic radicals made a concerted attack on the reactor this morning, but that the brave and well-trained Ukrainian army repelled the attack and killed or captured all the terrorists. They have photos of Rip and Mary and will undoubtedly be scrutinizing every passenger at the airport."

Sweeney huffed. "So what do we do, walk home?"

"There is an overnight train to Kovel that I think is your best option."

"Kovel? Where's that?" Sweeney said.

"It's near the Polish border. They are supposed to check passports when you board the train, but it makes stops in small villages along the way, and the enforcement there will be low since it will be the middle of the night. We'll meet the train in one of these villages, and you should be able to cross the border with no problems."

Rip spoke up. "Hey, did you say it's a sleeper train?"

"That's right."

"Sweet. Maybe we can rest a little. I feel like I got shot out of a cannon, you know?"

"Rip," John said, "you got shot *by* a cannon, remember?"

"Yeah. That too."

"We need to get you looked at before long."

"I'm all right, bro. Just got knocked on the coconut, you know?"

"Hey," Mary said, "I want to know more about the bombings. What are they saying about the explosions in the States?"

Olenka glanced at her in the rearview mirror. "Whoever is behind the attacks is targeting pipelines and the power network, things like that. They seem to be trying to cause panic and chaos across the country—and from the news coverage, the terrorists' plan seems to be working."

Mary shook her head. "Any deaths?"

"Some in the first two explosions in Los Angeles, and the last bomb killed a billionaire in his office in Washington DC."

John's head jerked up. "What did you say?"

Olenka shrugged. "Right before I came to pick you up, the American news was reporting that a billionaire philanthropist was killed in his office near the White House. That caused quite a stir with your president's security detail. Most of the politicians in Washington DC are being evacuated."

John's face had lost all its color. "What was the billionaire's name?"

"I'm sorry, I don't recall. Fountain? Something like that."

"Michael Lafontaine?" John's voice was a whisper.

"Yes, I think that's it."

Mary couldn't figure out why the tall, über-confident team sergeant suddenly looked like a slowly deflating balloon. Not only that, but Rip and Sweeney were looking at each other as if the air had been sucked out of the car. "What's the matter, John? Do you know him?"

But he didn't answer. Instead, he buried his face in his hands. If she hadn't known better, she would have said he was sobbing.

Then Sweeney spoke in a quiet, almost reverent tone. "Michael Lafontaine was John's godfather. And a very, very good man."

Now she understood. "Oh, how terrible! John, I'm so sorry." She stared out the front window in a daze. *Can this day get any more horrible?*

Just then, it did.

Olenka braked hard, skidding to a stop.

Fortunately, everyone was wearing a seat belt, but that didn't prevent a chorus of surprised voices.

"What was that about?" John asked.

Olenka pointed out the front window through a stand of trees. "Do you see it?"

"What?" Mary asked.

"Police, or maybe Ukrainian army. They've found the safe house." Olenka threw the vehicle in reverse and hit the gas.

Mary braced herself against the front seats. Through the front windshield she saw where the road took a hard right turn. She knew the safe house was only two hundred meters or so beyond that. Peering through the tree line at the edge of a field to her right, she saw them: flashing red lights.

"This is bad," Olenka said, executing a quick three-point turn.

John turned and gave Sweeney a grim look, not bothering to wipe away the tears that streaked his stubbly face. "Maybe we shouldn't have dumped our weapons."

"What difference would that have made?" Sweeney said, almost growling. "We can't shoot 'em."

"How did they find the safe house?" Rip asked.

"Maybe a farmer was up early and saw us pass by on the four-wheelers," Mary said.

John craned his neck to look out the back window as they sped away. "Hope nobody noticed us just now."

Tension hung like chains on everyone in the vehicle. Mary could tell the team was taking the loss of Michael Lafontaine hard. For a long while nobody spoke.

At length, Rip said, "Our clothes were at that safe house. What are we going to do about changing? Mary and I need shoes, and none of us exactly blends in."

Olenka was chewing her lip. "We should not go to Kiev—they will certainly be stopping traffic between here and there. But I have an idea. My grandmother's village is about an hour to the west. If we stick to farm roads, we could still be there just after dark."

"Can we buy clothes there?" John said.

She shook her head. "The village is very small. But my grandfather died last June, and I think she still has all his things. They aren't fancy but would certainly help you look more like Ukrainians. And I'm sure she could find something for Mary."

John nodded. "I don't guess we have much choice. Let's go for it."

By the time they turned off the paved road and onto a double-track dirt path, the sun had set, and Mary and Olenka were the only ones still awake. Mary spent the time telling her Ukrainian friend about everything that had transpired at Chernobyl. Somehow doing so made her feel much better.

"I just can't believe they made me shower without giving me any privacy," Mary finished.

Olenka cocked her head. "Why? Does that bother you?"

"Of course it does. Wouldn't it bother you?"

"I suppose it would, though I don't think Ukrainians are as concerned with public nudity as Americans seem to be. They probably didn't think anything of it."

Mary sighed. The cultural differences might help explain what had happened, but it didn't exactly make her feel better.

"Did they let you keep anything?" Olenka asked.

Mary nodded. "They did return my...my underthings."

"Well, that's good. Those are expensive!"

Mary couldn't help but smile. Olenka had a point.

The track wound across a huge pasture dotted by black and white cows munching on scrubby grass. What looked to be a cluster of small homes lay silhouetted in the waning light.

"Is this the way to the village?" Mary asked.

"Yes. It's called Peremyshl." Olenka eased her foot off the gas and rolled to a stop.

Even in the dim cab, Mary noticed the contorted lines of her face in the rearview mirror. "What?"

"I...I don't know if this is a good idea."

John sat up, blinking away sleep. "Are we there?"

"Yes," Mary said, "but it sounds like we might have a problem."

John looked at Olenka. "What's up?"

She hesitated. "It's just that *Baba* won't be happy about you coming to the village. She's not unfriendly, but...well...she's very superstitious."

John's expression softened. "We have that superstition in the States too. It's called 'aiding and abetting known fugitives.'"

Olenka sputtered. "Oh, it's not that. Actually, I don't think there have ever been westerners in Peremyshl. She'd be very excited to meet some. But because you've been in the dead zone…" Her voice trailed off.

John thought for a moment. "You know, I hadn't thought of that. Actually, it wouldn't be right for Sweeney and me to drag our contaminated selves into that village and maybe jeopardize the safety of everyone there. How about you drop us in that wood line over there and we'll wait for you to bring some new clothes? Then we'll bury ours and get going."

Olenka considered his proposition. "That's a good plan. There's a small pond through those woods where you could wash off. Mary could come with me since she's already been decontaminated, and we could bring back some clothes and food and pick you up here."

"Works for me," Sweeney said.

Rip slapped Sweeney's shoulder. "I'll guard your clothes while you go skinny-dipping, *ese*."

John frowned. "Okay, Olenka, we'll do it. But try not to stay long. If someone finds the three of us out here, they're liable to have seen on TV that there are fugitives on the loose and call us in."

Olenka gave a short laugh. "Except that nobody here has a television or a phone."

Outside Peremyshl

John, Rip, and Sweeney watched the taillights of Olenka's SUV bounce down the dirt track leading to the village. Open fields lay between them and the cluster of dark homes they could see a quarter mile distant. Aside from several dozen cows standing or lying down in the pasture, there was no other life visible around them. The cool air felt colder when the breeze gusted in their faces.

"All right," John said, "let's find that pond and get out of these clothes." The three men struck out into the gathering darkness, a gloom made deeper by the cover of the closely spaced pine forest.

Sweeney took point, pushing pine boughs aside. "She said it was only a few hundred meters. Let's hope we can find it in the dark."

As they walked along, Rip spoke up. "Hey, Coop, I'm real sorry to hear about Mr. Lafontaine."

"Yeah, thanks," John said quietly.

"Do you know if he was a believer?"

For some reason the question really bothered Sweeney. "Oh, come on," he hissed. "Leave the guy in peace, will you?"

John pushed a branch away from his face. "It's okay, Bobby. That's a valid question. The truth is, I don't know. Michael went to a Catholic church in DC sometimes, but I never heard him talk about following Christ."

Sweeney was still perturbed. "So what? If he didn't quote Scripture to everyone he met, that makes him a heathen?"

John's retort was matter of fact, but not confrontational. "Not necessarily, but the Bible makes it clear that all you have to do to see heaven is believe in your heart that God raised Jesus from the dead *and* confess with your mouth that Jesus is Lord."

"Michael Lafontaine was one of the most generous men I've ever met," Sweeney said. "If he can't make it to heaven, nobody can."

John nodded. "You're right, he was generous. But nobody can make it by being good or following all the rules, because heaven is perfect and even Michael Lafontaine couldn't make that standard.

Personally, I've done all kinds of horrible things in my past. If I have to make it by being a good person, I'm sunk from the get-go."

That sounds familiar, Sweeney thought. Coop must have heard one of Pastor Lawrence Sweeney's sermons.

"Me too, bro," Rip said.

It was completely dark by the time they found the half-acre pond a few hundred meters into the wood line. The water was as black and calm as a pool of molasses. The whirring crickets and frogs along its banks masked the involuntary gasp Sweeney made after he stripped off his contaminated clothes and stepped into the frigid water.

John sucked in a lungful of air as he entered. "Man, this night just keeps getting worse. Rip, get busy burying our stuff."

"Roger that."

Sweeney just grunted, unable to speak. Twigs on the muddy bottom of the pond poked his bare feet as he knelt in the shallow water and began furiously scrubbing himself from head to toe. *I'd trade my Harley for a hot shower right about now.*

Rip knelt on shore, scraping an indentation in the earth with a big stick. "Hey, what are you two gonna wear until Mary gets back?"

"How about I beat you up and take your jumpsuit?" Sweeney grumbled.

Rip chuckled. "You'd look pretty funny trying to catch me, bro."

"Let's just hurry up and get washed off before we die of hypothermia," John said.

Sweeney couldn't agree more. The thought of a slow death by some nasty form of cancer, however, was good incentive to be thorough.

By the time the two men sloshed out of the water, a sliver of moon had risen on the horizon, making their white skin appear to glow in the dark.

"Hey, check it out," Rip said with a laugh. "Two full moons in one night!"

"Rubio," Sweeney said through chattering teeth, "as soon as I can feel my arms, I'm gonna punch you."

The darkened village consisted of little more than two well-kept rows of thatch-roofed white cottages, situated on either side of a tidy dirt road. Mary rolled down her window and inhaled the cool smell of hay and tilled earth. No lights were visible inside the windows. Apparently the villagers went to bed early.

"Do they have electricity?" Mary wondered aloud.

"Oh yes," Olenka said. "But they don't like it much."

"Expensive?"

"Yes, but also they are superstitious about it." She waved her hand. "They are superstitious about many things."

"Like what?"

Olenka shrugged. "They would never ride in a car with the window down, like you are doing now. They believe drafts bring evil spirits. Sometimes they wear mirrors under their clothing to ward off the evil eye. Things like that."

Mary shook her head. "That's fascinating."

"Here we are." Olenka turned in next to a tiny white house. "You're going to love *Babusya*."

They got out, and Mary winced as small stones on the driveway pricked her bare feet. They climbed wooden steps to a door on the side of the house and knocked. A moment later, a light came on inside. There was some shuffling, then the door swung inward, revealing the cutest old woman Mary had ever seen.

Olenka's grandmother stood just over four feet tall. She wore a faded blue housedress with a flowered print. Her crystal blue eyes were set into a face that looked like a dried apple. They went wide in surprise, then became sparkling gems as the creases on her face split into a wide smile. "Aaaahhhh!" the babusya cried, throwing her arms wide and wrapping them around her granddaughter. Then she pulled back and began chattering excitedly.

Olenka held the small woman by the shoulders and explained the situation in rapid-fire Ukrainian. Mary stood to the side, smiling and feeling somewhat self-conscious in her white jumpsuit. After a moment, Olenka straightened and wrapped one arm around her grandmother, turning her toward Mary.

"This is my friend," she said in Ukrainian. She put a hand on Mary's arm and spoke in English: "Mary, this is my babusya."

The old woman's eyes sparkled as she reached up and cupped Mary's face in both hands, then proceeded to smother it with kisses.

Mary was surprised by this, but it was so sweet that she immediately felt at ease. She felt herself flush. "Oh, Olenka, she's so *cute!*"

The younger woman laughed. "Yes, she is, isn't she? She says you can call her Millya."

Still chattering, Millya led Mary by the hand into a tiny kitchen lit by a single bare bulb. She sat Mary down at a sturdy wooden table next to a small brick fireplace, then went to the sink in one corner. It had no faucets, and it drained into a bucket. Millya poured some water from a pitcher into a basin and brought it over, placing it on the plaited rug at Mary's feet.

"She says for you to wash your feet in this while she finds you some clothes to wear," Olenka said.

Millya straightened and stepped back, sizing Mary up, then clucked her tongue. *"Malenke, malenke,"* she said, crossing herself several times before disappearing into the back room.

Mary blushed. "I guess I do look pretty bad."

"You stay here while I go help her gather clothes." Olenka followed her grandmother down the hall.

Mary slipped one foot into the foot bath. But even as she enjoyed the feeling of the cool water on her feet, she couldn't help but agree with the babusya's assessment.

A few minutes later, Millya and Olenka returned from the back bedroom with their arms full of clothes. "I think these will work for the guys," Olenka said, holding up some faded overalls. "Grandpa was a little shorter than they are, but I don't think anything will be too small. Plus, he had big feet. Mama Millya has some of his old work boots we can take.

Mary smiled. "Please tell her how grateful they will be. And we can send you some money later to pay her back."

Olenka shook her head. "No, she wouldn't accept it."

Then Millya took Mary by the hand and led her into the tiny back bedroom. From an aged wardrobe, she produced several worn work dresses and held them up to Mary's frame, finding all of them were far too short. The old woman continued clucking her tongue and keeping up a nonstop, albeit one-sided conversation. Finally she found a blue denim dress that was longer than the others.

"She says this belonged to her sister, and she never got around to altering it," Olenka explained. "Try it on."

Mary would have preferred to do so in private, but it wasn't worth making an issue over. It wasn't the most humiliated she'd been lately. She quickly peeled off the jumpsuit and pulled the dress on over her head.

"It's a little snug," she said, tugging at the waistline, "but it will do."

Mary could feel the time ticking away. She knew the men would be anxious to get going. Even still, it took them another fifteen minutes to break away from Millya, as the woman kept coming up with more and more food to send along with them for the trip, most of which was canned or pickled.

"It's a Ukrainian custom," Olenka explained, balancing the quart-sized glass jars full of food. "We always give food when someone is going on a journey."

"Thank you," Mary said again. "But we do have a long way to go."

When they finally made it back to the vehicle, Millya stood on the stoop and waved at them as they drove away.

"What a sweet lady," Mary said.

"Yes, Mama Millya is a wonderful Christian woman. She loves to help people."

Mary dug a small loaf of bread out of a paper sack at her feet and took a bite. "Oh, this is fantastic." She savored the tart sourdough. "I bet the guys are hungry too. Wait until they see all this food."

The satphone started ringing on the dashboard. Mary scooped it up, pressed a button, and put it to her ear.

"Phoenix."

It was Major Williams. "You kids making progress?"

"Yes sir. We all have clothes now."

"What?"

She realized how that sounded. "Uh…I'll tell you later."

"Listen. You folks need to get out of that country ASAP. We're getting all kinds of chatter from the Ukrainians. They're setting up a full-court press to find you and bring you in."

"Right. We're doing the best we can."

The major's tone turned sour. "We've had another explosion. A gas pipeline in New Mexico. They're having to evacuate a couple hundred thousand folks. This is getting serious."

Mary's stomach did a slow flip. "Oh no."

When Mary and Olenka pulled up to the wood line where they had left the rest of the team, only Rip emerged from the underbrush.

He was sporting a wide grin. "Hey," he said, sticking his head in the window. "Coop and Sweeney said to send some clothes quick." He snickered. "I think we should make the two jaybirds come get them."

Mary handed two paper bags out the window. "That would be humorous, but we don't have time. Tell them to get dressed. And hurry."

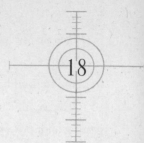

18

Washington DC

THE CHESAPEAKE AND OHIO Canal was lightly traveled in the fading heat of the afternoon. Samael Berg was perspiring as he pedaled a recently purchased mountain bike northwest along the age-old path. A bronze placard he passed announced this trail was once trod by teams of donkeys towing barges between Washington DC and Great Falls, Maryland.

So far, checking off the items on his list had gone very smoothly, and the great United States was in a tailspin to absolute chaos. Who would have believed that America was so vulnerable? That without even causing much irreparable damage, the media coverage elevated the perceived threat until the entire country was ablaze in conjecture. Hitting the billionaire's office had created a dramatic effect in the press, almost as frenetic as if he'd hit the White House itself. And now the president and Congress were almost apoplectic in their hysterical calls for action.

Yes, the objectives had been well planned. It showed the strength of this country to be little more than a facade.

This last objective would directly affect those same politicians, many of whom lived in the immediate area. Samael smiled, reassured by the weight of the last four bottles in his backpack, well cushioned by his fleece jacket.

He pedaled on, giving a friendly nod to two Lycra-clad women who were jogging the other direction. He hoped that the helmet and sunglasses he wore would make him harder to identify in case anyone he passed might actually remember seeing him. That wasn't likely, since he looked like every other outdoor enthusiast out for an afternoon ride along the canal.

Here and there he caught glimpses of homes perched along the forested rim overlooking the Potomac River. Actually, *castles* was more like it. America was so profanely wealthy. He was glad to be making them pay for their smug materialism. The radio news he had listened to while driving had told of the chaos his actions were sowing across the country. The Americans were being shown just how fragile their economy was, how easily its vaunted Homeland Security Administration could be sent scurrying around like chickens when a fox comes calling.

He rounded a bend in the trail and saw the American Legion Bridge up ahead.

The fox is about to strike again.

Samael took one look at the massive concrete span that vaulted the border between Maryland and Virginia, and wondered if four bottles would be enough. The structure was huge. But at least it was far enough out of Washington DC so as to not be under constant scrutiny. The eight-lane viaduct carried hundreds of thousands of the capital's most important commuters every day. And there was no easy alternative for them. Without the bridge, rush-hour traffic around the capital beltway would go from hectic to a real-life nightmare.

He decided that four bottles would be enough after all. The bridge didn't have to actually come down for the plan to be effective. Simply striking the gargantuan highway—wounding it—would have the über-safety-conscious denizens of diplomacy begging for committees of safety engineers to measure the damage, as they were now doing at the Hoover Dam. That process could see the bridge closed for weeks, at a cost of untold millions, even if it was found to be structurally sound.

It was the perfect picture of how Samael was using this corrupt nation's greatness against itself. The advantage was his. He had only to be clever, careful, and thorough to succeed. But to prevent him, they had to be omnipresent. If they weren't, he was sure to win.

The trail was deserted in both directions when he pedaled into the shade of the overpass. The noise of thousands of cars racing by overhead was almost deafening. He parked his bike against one of the support columns and shrugged the daypack off his shoulders. He pretended to stretch while carefully inspecting all around to make sure no jogger, bird-watcher, or homeless vagrant was in the area, anyone who might see what he was about to do. Then, satisfied that he was alone, he climbed the concrete embankment to the base of the bridge.

Scattered clothing and debris, along with the smell of urine, told him that people used the low space between the bridge supports as a bathroom and possibly a place to sleep, though he couldn't imagine the latter because of the incredible traffic noise that echoed through the cramped space.

He grimaced at the smell but hunkered down and crawled into the darkest corner of the recess, dragging the daypack behind him. Here, the roadway was only three feet above the concrete surface under him, and the vibrations of the vehicles overhead felt like a constant barrage of artillery.

Samael yanked open the pack and produced the four one-liter bottles. He looked at the liquid explosive in one of the bottles. The news was calling it "neo-napalm." The glass was cool to his touch and even now made him thirsty.

He arranged the bottles in front of him and then produced four pairs of nine-volt batteries he'd purchased at a gas station that morning. Opening the battery packages was difficult with the gloves he wore, but he didn't want to risk getting his fingerprints on anything, just in case something went wrong and everything around him wasn't incinerated.

He connected two of the batteries together, a short circuit that he'd determined earlier would allow him at least fifteen minutes before the batteries got hot enough to set off the explosive. He set the first bottle on the girder and placed the connected batteries next to it. Then he went to emplace the others.

Two minutes later, with his knees scuffed and muddy, he crawled out into the open and hurried back to his bicycle. A quick look up and down the path showed a silver-haired man in a tank top and running shorts advancing toward him at a slow trot. But the man's head was down, watching the trail, and he didn't appear to have seen Samael.

After hopping on the bike, he rode back the way he had come, exhaling the foul smell of the overpass from his lungs and replacing it with the fine Maryland springtime air. The ride back to his car left him winded, but he made it in under ten minutes.

He wiped down the bicycle and hid it in the bushes near the overlook where his rental car was parked. Checking his watch brought a smile to his face. *Almost the height of rush hour.* Striking the nation's capital would be the perfect way to finish the tapestry of chaos he'd woven across the United States.

So long as that fat Panamanian had done his job correctly.

Samael got in the car and set his rented Garmin Nüvi GPS to take him via back roads to Washington's Dulles airport. There, he would turn in his rental car and purchase his ticket out of the country. He could then wait for word that the Panamanian had finished his part of the job.

When he started the car, the radio blared to life as well. He started to turn it down but stopped with his hand on the dial.

"…as many as a hundred people feared dead in Nevada after a bomb went off in a crowded Las Vegas casino only an hour ago. Details are still sketchy, but it appears to have been the work of the same group of terrorists who have been setting off firebombs across the country. Only this time…"

Samael stared at the radio in shock. Something had gone wrong. Nowhere on the list he'd given Edgar Lerida had there been any mention of a casino. And his instructions had been very specific—any mishaps would cost him dearly.

He scrambled for his cell phone and punched in Edgar's number. As he was doing so, however, another call came in. The caller ID

showed simply, "International." When he answered the call, the angry
voice on the other end made his blood run cold.

———

North of Seligman, Arizona

The stars hung like Christmas lights, winking on one by one as the
desert sky above Blue Mountain, Arizona, began to darken.

Edgar Lerida filled the first of twenty-four balloons, one each for
his last twenty-four bottles of ITEB. It looked like his final assignment would be his easiest—and that suited him fine. He'd already
taken far more risk than he was accustomed to.

The three-foot balloons he'd purchased at a party store held just
enough helium to lift one bottle apiece. After he'd filled all twenty-
four from a helium tank purchased at the same store, and once it got
completely dark, he would attach a bottle to each one and send them
skyward from this remote desert location.

He couldn't be sure, but Edgar imagined that whoever had
planned this objective had analyzed the wind currents and knew that
the balloons would rise to an altitude where either the pressure or the
cold would cause them to burst, which meant that some area along
the West Coast would soon see a rain of fire. The winds aloft were
heading west, which meant Las Vegas or perhaps L.A. Even if they
missed the populated areas, the combined effect of twenty-four bottles of the most highly flammable liquid he'd ever encountered would
surely start a forest fire that would decimate much of the Southwest.

He had always been fascinated by fire, though, and so the mental image of bottles of liquid flame falling from the sky actually

brought a smile to his lips. He was still smiling when his phone rang. He knew who the caller would be before he answered it.

"I am just about to complete the final objective," he said, not bothering with pleasantries.

The voice on the other end was like a blowtorch erupting from the phone. "Forget it, you idiot. Have you heard the news?"

"*Dígame.*"

"You seem to have a problem following directions."

Edgar's eyes widened. "What makes you say—"

"Where are you?"

"Arizona. Why?"

"A casino in Las Vegas was just bombed. Scores dead."

Edgar closed his eyes and fought to keep from cursing aloud. "I can explain—"

The man's deep voice was flat, emotionless. "I'm not interested in explanations. There was nothing in your instructions that mentioned bringing in a third party. You were to accomplish these objectives yourself, in order, as given. Hiring a gang of Latin criminals was not part of the bargain. Neither was murdering scores of innocent people."

Edgar's adrenaline surged as if he were in a car sliding out of control. *How does the gringo know I hired MS-13?* "Wait, it was an accident! I…I simply thought—"

"You did not think!" The gringo's voice grew harsher, separating each word with cleaver-like precision. "If you had been thinking, you would have maintained control of the product. If you still hope to collect the rest of your payment, you will ensure that the remaining merchandise is disposed of. All of it."

Relief flooded through his body. He might still have a chance to redeem himself and get paid. "You have my word. But what about the remaining target?"

"Forget about it."

"Yes sir. How will you contact me once I have destroyed the remaining ITEB?"

"Idiot!" The line abruptly went dead.

Two minutes later, a server installed at the offices of Enterprise Satellite Systems in San Marcos, California, sent a highly encoded message to another server deep in the bowels of the National Security Agency's headquarters at Fort Meade, Maryland. The message was forwarded to an analyst and included a transcript of Edgar's phone call.

On the transcript, a single word was highlighted in yellow.

Slavuta, Ukraine

A throaty air-horn blast signaled the train's approach long before it was visible. The blanket of thick fog had rolled in over the small town a half hour before.

Olenka's blue SUV was one of only three cars parked in the gravel lot next to a bare concrete platform on the edge of the town. A single streetlight bathed the platform in pale yellow, and the drivers from the other two vehicles stood under it, smoking and beating their sides to ward off the midnight chill.

Task Force Valor sat in uneasy silence, crammed into Olenka's car, which was parked just outside the lamp's wan circle of light.

The train engine came into view, a single powerful headlamp pushing a white cone of light through the fog. As it got closer, Sweeney decided the locomotive looked like the box that the train had come in. It was almost perfectly rectangular and had smooth metal sides painted a rusty shade of red. The aging monstrosity huffed smoke onto the grimy tracks as it pulled even with the platform. Its three high-set windows in the front emitted a pale reddish glow, which only made the train look more menacing.

A shiver went down Sweeney's spine. That was partially due to the fact that he was still cold from his dip in the pond. But at least he had gotten rid of whatever radioactive debris had been plastered to his body in the dead zone. The shiver returned, and Sweeney wondered if he'd ever have children.

"Put this on, Bobby." John Cooper shoved a newsboy hat at him. He'd pulled it out of the paper bag that Olenka had brought. It was full of her grandfather's clothes.

"Shoot, this hat's a total chick magnet." *As if the dungarees and suspenders don't make me look like enough of an idiot.*

"Hey, don't complain," John said. "Grandpa's pants are too big on Rip and too short on me. You're like the little bear whose bed was juuust right."

Sweeney snatched the hat. "Just because you and Rip already have girlfriends doesn't mean nobody else wants to impress the ladies."

"Oh, good grief," Mary said. "Look at me! Anybody else want to try an ankle-length peasant dress and work boots?"

Sweeney flopped the hat onto his head and pulled the brim down, masking his grin. Getting her riled up was kind of fun.

John nodded. "Olenka, the train is a few minutes late. Does that change anything?"

As far as Sweeney was concerned, Olenka had already earned hero status and was well on her way to sainthood.

Olenka shook her head. "No. As I said before, normally you must already have a ticket to board the train. But in these small villages, people often get around this by paying the *provodnistas* a little bribe. If there are empty berths on the train, they will usually let you on." She produced a stack of Ukrainian hryvni from her purse and held them up. "I'm going to take this and go get you on the train. It will take you to the city of Kovel, near the Polish border. There, one of our agents will be waiting with a van. He will drive you to the border."

"What about Customs?" Mary asked.

"You cannot pass through at the entry control point. There will certainly be security forces there. But I will coordinate with the driver to take you to a point where you can easily get across the Bug River in an unpopulated area."

"The *what* river?" Rip said.

Olenka didn't flinch. "Bug. You must swim. I will coordinate with your Major Williams to have your people waiting for you on the other side as soon as you cross into Poland. If everything goes well, you should be on your way home within a few hours."

"I don't like this," Sweeney muttered.

John gave him a hard look. "You got any better ideas?"

Sweeney winked at him. "No, I meant the hat. I don't like the hat."

Most of the team groaned, and John's look changed to a wry grin. "Quit your whining, Bobby."

Sweeney didn't like the plan, either, but since the CIA seemed to have a thing for leaving them stranded in hostile countries, there was no use complaining about it.

"The train is stopping now," Olenka said. "I will go arrange your passage with the provodnista—there's one in charge of each train car. I'll wave at you when it's okay. Stay here until you see my signal."

The team watched as Olenka got out and hurried to the platform. A uniformed train employee appeared at the door of each car and stepped to the platform as soon as the train stopped moving. Olenka approached a squat woman in a garrison cap and spoke briefly. Sixty seconds later she turned and beckoned at the team with an urgent wave.

"Let's go," John said.

"I got the food, bro!" Rip replied, scooping up the paper sack off the floor. "Here, help me with these jars."

Olenka met them at the foot of the stairs leading to the platform. "You must hurry. The provodnista only has four berths left, and unfortunately they're not in the same cabin." The blonde handed them each a small packet of currency. "The provodnista will have bedding for you, but you will have to pay for it. It's not much."

John nodded, looking around the huddle. "It would be best if nobody hears you speaking English. Mary can use her Russian if you need anything. But if you need to communicate, whisper."

"What time does the train get into Lviv?" Mary said.

"About seven in the morning," Olenka said. "Your driver's name is Slev. I will text you with details on how to contact him. Now you must go."

Mary took Olenka's hands in her own. "I can't tell you how much we appreciate all you are doing. You've done a fantastic job, Olenka, and I'll make sure the right people know about it."

Olenka's eyes sparkled as she turned to leave. "Thank you. I hope to see you again someday. *Do pobachennya.*"

The team hurried up the stairs and nodded at the short but thick car mistress standing next to the door. John mounted the stairs into the train car, and Rip followed behind. But before Mary could mount the first step, the provodnista put a hand across the door and barked a command at them.

Sweeney tensed as he stared at the woman, trying to decipher what the problem was. Then she pointed to the next car and repeated the command. Recognition dawned in his head. "Ah!" Sweeney gave his best impression of a meek smile. "Tak!" It was the only Ukrainian word he'd learned. He pulled Mary's arm toward the trailing car and whispered in her ear. "I think we're back here."

"Wow, train Nazi," Mary whispered back.

"You got that right." Sweeney pushed Mary gently up the stairs and followed behind, giving the train Nazi a friendly wave.

The inside of the train car consisted of a long paneled hallway with windows looking out onto the platform. On the other side was a row of flimsy doorways, all of which were closed. A moment later the provodnista reappeared and directed them to the first doorway, which she pulled open with a bang, apparently not caring that doing so might awaken half the train.

Sweeney peered inside. A set of bunk beds adorned both walls, leaving less than three feet of space in between. Two of the four bunks were already taken by what looked to be a boy and his grandmother. Incredibly, neither seemed to have awakened at their noisy entrance.

Remembering that they had to pay for bedding, Sweeney handed the provodnista a ten-hryvnia note, and she stalked off down the hall. Once she was gone, he turned to Mary and grinned. "Spacious, no?"

"Shhhh!" Mary said, stifling a grin.

Sweeney clicked on the light overhead and lowered his voice to a stage whisper. "Wait until word gets out that you and I shared a cabin for the night."

She said nothing but tilted her head to give him a wide-eyed *don't even think it* look.

Sweeney chuckled. "Nothing to worry about, ma'am. Mrs. Sweeney taught me how to be a gentleman."

The train started up again with a lurch, and in a moment the intermittent *clack-clack* of the wheels gliding over the tracks took up a rhythmic beat offset by the snores of the babusya in the bottom bunk.

The train Nazi returned with two sets of linen sealed inside clear plastic. She handed them to Sweeney without a word, then slid the door to the cabin shut. Sweeney tossed his sheets on his bunk, then levered himself onto it with one swift move. Mary also seemed too tired to fully make her bed. She simply climbed up onto her bunk and sat down with her back to the wall.

Sweeney sat against the opposite wall and stared at her. Even with the unflattering dress and no makeup, she was still prettier than most women would be even after a professional makeover. Her almost pouty lips and soft blue eyes gave her face an open, vulnerable look that any red-blooded male would find mesmerizing. Until she kicked him in the face. What made a girl like this want to face possible death and certain misery by becoming an operative?

"What?" She was staring back now, the faintest hint of a smile on her face.

He held her gaze. "Nothin'. I was just wondering how you got into this line of work."

She shrugged. "I like to travel. I grew up around the military. It seemed like a good job."

"You're a military brat?"

She nodded. "Yep, Dad was an Army drill sergeant."

"So do you like the job?" He made sure not to mention the CIA, on the off chance that the babusya was a Russian secret agent. Using English at all was taking a risk as it was.

She huffed and rolled her eyes.

"What?"

She frowned. "Why don't we talk about you?"

He was surprised at her sudden turnaround. "Okay, sure. I was born in Alabama, I've got two brothers, and my dad is a Baptist minister. What else you want to know?"

"You? A preacher's son? I never would have guessed."

"Why, thank you. I'll take that as a compliment."

"So why'd you join the Army?"

He sighed. "Well, I'd say I joined the Army to get away from my mother."

"Really? Why?"

"If you met her, you wouldn't have to ask."

"But I haven't met her, so tell me. Is she an ogre or what?"

Aw geez. How did I get roped into this? Sweeney sighed. "No, she's not an ogre. She just ruled the house. I mean everything… She ran the place like—"

"Like a drill sergeant?" Mary's grin was priceless.

"Exactly. The Army was like a vacation after spending eighteen years in my house."

"Is that why you have a problem with women in authority?"

"Why does everyone keep saying that?"

"Maybe because it's true?" She nudged him with her toe.

"Why are we talking about this?"

"You started it."

"What? No, I didn't! I just asked how you got the job of master head-kicker."

She stifled a laugh. "What did you call me?"

He grinned, glad they were talking about her now. "That was pretty amazing the way you took care of those two soldiers in the back of that truck. Where'd you learn to fight like that?"

She shrugged. "Like I said, Dad was a drill sergeant. He used to make me spar with him in the sawdust pits at Fort Jackson." A look crept into the edges of her face that told him it hadn't been fun.

"Wanted you to be able to protect yourself, huh?"

She shook her head. "No, I think he just wanted me to be a boy."

He grinned. "Well, you'll never make a very good one, if you ask me."

Fire flashed in her face. "Tell that to those soldiers I took out back there."

Sweeney chuckled. "You mean the ones we had to rescue you from?"

Mary didn't answer. Instead, she turned away from him toward the window.

He thought he saw her lip tremble a little. Sweeney was no mind reader, but he could tell he'd hit a sore spot. He tried to back-pedal. "Look, uh, I didn't mean—"

"You're a real jerk, Bobby, you know that?" She said it almost to herself.

Sweeney raised his eyebrows. *Wow. What's that about?* He tried to retrace the conversation in his head and figure out exactly where it had blown a tire and sailed over the edge of a cliff.

"Listen, Mary, I wasn't trying to insult you. I didn't mean you weren't capable. I just meant you wouldn't make a very good man. But why would you want to? What are you trying to prove?" He shook his head. "It was supposed to be a compliment."

She stared out the window, her blue eyes suddenly brimming with tears. "You're right, Sweeney. I can't hack it with the men. I mean, I've pretty much proven that over the last month, haven't I? I've put the team in danger just by being here."

Way to go, bonehead. Now you've gone and made her cry. If there was anything he hated more than seeing a woman cry, he hadn't found it yet. Everything in him was screaming *fix this,* but he didn't know how.

He tilted his head. "I don't buy that. We would have never gotten out of Lebanon alive if it wasn't for you. Come to think of it, we probably would have all died in that bunker in Panama if you hadn't been there, because you told us about the explosives."

She rolled her eyes. "Come on, Bobby. You've had to rescue me twice. We probably wouldn't have gotten captured in the first place if it weren't for me. And when we were being shot at…I was so scared!"

He sat back a bit. "So? We're all scared."

"Oh, come on. I've heard you and Coop on the radio. Bullets flying everywhere and you two sound like you're ordering french fries."

"That doesn't mean we're not scared. Mary, it's just the way we've been trained. And unfortunately, we've had plenty of experience in the getting-shot-at department."

She just dropped her head into her hands.

He lifted himself across the space between the two bunks to sit next to her. He wanted to put an arm around her, comfort her, but thought better of it. "Look, Mary. I didn't mean to upset you. Please forgive me."

She sniffed. "Why are you being so nice all of a sudden? You never wanted me on this mission in the first place. You have a problem with strong women, remember?"

He sighed and looked away. Was it really that he was afraid of strong women? Or was it weak men? His father had kowtowed to his mother all those years, and if Sweeney thought really hard about it, he'd have to admit that his resentment was directed more at his dad.

He shrugged. "I don't know, Mary. Maybe that's not why I joined the Army after all."

"What was it, then?"

"Maybe...maybe it was to prove that I wasn't my dad. He was so into 'ministry' that he never did anything...well, manly."

"Like hunting and fishing, or what?" Mary seemed genuinely interested, and she wasn't crying anymore, so he forged ahead.

"Like taking responsibility for anything. He couldn't make the smallest decision without Mom's approval. I guess I just needed to prove I could be my own man, and maybe that meant not allowing any woman to run me."

She wiped her eyes. "I can understand that. For me, it was sort of the same. I wanted so badly to earn my dad's love, and I knew the only way was to be as tough or tougher than the boys."

"So you had to prove you were."

Mary nodded, looking away. "I guess I failed at that."

Sweeney shrugged. "Maybe. But you succeeded at being human."

Her laugh was laced with bitterness. "I don't think simply being human would be acceptable to Dad."

"Well, it's acceptable to me, if that's worth anything." He smiled softly when her eyes met his.

"Thanks, Bobby. That's sweet." She reached up and hugged him, and even though there wasn't anything sensual about it, it had been a long time since Sweeney had felt that good. He hugged her back, lingering for a moment.

The sound of a throat clearing at the door pulled them apart like a piece of paper being torn in half. John was standing there with an amused smirk that made Sweeney's face catch fire in an instant.

Washington DC

SAMAEL BERG CHECKED his watch as he hurried toward the front doors of Washington Dulles International Airport. Its soaring architectural curves made no impression on him at all. He wanted only to leave the country by the quickest means possible.

He'd dropped off his rental car and was now only an hour and a half from the departure of his flight to Frankfurt. Normally, that would have been cutting it close. But since the great "neo-napalm" scare, air travel had dropped off considerably. Besides, he carried only his briefcase, and with no bags to check, ticketing should go smoothly.

Samael now regretted having brought in the Panamanian. Still, he knew he'd had to hire someone, otherwise the project wouldn't have had the desired effect. It had been imperative that he hit multiple sites around this huge country in a short period of time. He couldn't have done them all himself. Surely his employer would understand that.

What worried him more was his last phone call with Edgar Lerida. The idiot had spoken the name of the explosive. On the phone. Samael knew from his own experience in the intelligence community that the government had very sophisticated listening programs that could cull out a conversation based on a single word.

He couldn't get out of this country fast enough.

Security officers patrolled the area on heightened alert for any suspicious activity. But Samael tried to just look like every other business traveler. Since he carried nothing that could tie him to the crimes, he had nothing to worry about.

He breezed through the business class check-in and then made for the security line. There, he removed his shoes and belt and set his laptop in the tray, then passed through the detector. The TSA employee running the machine was actually inspecting the bags now. On his flight in they had barely appeared awake.

Samael smiled. *America should thank me. They have been shocked from their stupor.*

His briefcase reappeared, along with his belt and shoes. He re-dressed and went searching for his gate, stopping for coffee on the way.

An hour later, he was sitting at the gate reading the newspaper and waiting for the flight to begin boarding. Suddenly two men, one black and one white, stood in front of him wearing identical midnight blue suits and very serious expressions. He looked up at them. "May I help you?"

"Are you Samael Berg?"

Alarm bells were going off in his head. "Who wants to know?"

One of the men opened his coat to reveal a badge and gun tucked in his waistband. "We're federal agents, Mr. Berg. FBI. We'd like to ask you a few questions."

Samael looked at the gate. "But my flight is about to leave."

The black man leaned toward him and spoke quietly. "Let me make this crystal clear. You are going to come with us for questioning. You can catch a later flight."

Samael was a former intelligence operative. He could tell this man wasn't bluffing. He racked his brain for anything that could have given him away but came up empty. He put his newspaper down and slowly stood. "What's this all about?"

The FBI agents each grabbed one of his arms in a vise grip and began moving toward a door opposite the gate area.

The white one muttered an answer in his ear that turned his insides to cold oatmeal. "Someone happened to look at the saved route information on the GPS that came with your rental car. We need to talk to you about the places you've been visiting during your stay in our country."

───────

The muscular soldier towered over Mary Walker, sneering at her as she bounced on the balls of her feet, fists at the ready. She tried to read his body language, looking for any opening that might give her a chance to take him down.

"You gonna dance around all day, or what?" he taunted.

His weight shifted slightly forward as he prepared to grab for her. It was the best chance she was going to get. With a shriek that she hoped sounded larger than her skinny body was, she charged at him, intending to knock him off balance.

But he pivoted at the last second and brought his forearm down like a guillotine, sweeping her off her feet. She landed with a thud that knocked the wind out of her.

Through tears caused more by her failure than the blow, she saw the soldier standing over her, shaking his head.

"When you gonna learn not to charge like that, Mary? You know better!"

She fought back the tears, gasping for breath. "Dad, I—"

"Come on, get up, girl!"

She rolled over and got to her feet, her fourteen-year-old body shaking and covered with itchy sawdust. "Can't we go home now?"

Her father's frown turned into a scowl. "What, you want to quit?"

"No sir. I…" Her eyes pleaded with him. How could she tell him how badly she needed his approval? His granite features said it all—that wasn't going to happen. She dropped her gaze to her shoes. "Yes. I want to go home."

"Now, listen here!" he bellowed, grabbing her by the shoulders. "I'm not raisin' no pansy girl, you understand?" He shook her, causing the tears to return. "Do you hear me?"

"Do you hear me? Mary, do you hear me?"

"Mary? Mary, do you hear me? Mary, get up!" Her father's voice faded into one that was quieter but just as insistent.

She itched all over from the sawdust. She blinked the tears away again, but this time it was Sweeney leaning over her, shaking her gently by the shoulders.

"Get up, Mary. The train's pulling into the station."

Groggy, she sat up and blinked, trying to get her bearings. "Oh,

I was dreaming." She looked down at the rough wool blanket pooling in her lap and pushed it away.

Sweeney smiled. "Those blankets have gotta be some kind of Cold War rejects. Mine itched like crazy."

"Blech. Yes." Mary combed her hair away from her face with her hand. "Where's the bathroom?"

Sweeney sat on his bunk in the white T-shirt Olenka had given him. His massive biceps rippled as he stretched and yawned. "It's at the end of the hall. But you might want to wait until we get off the train—this one's pretty nasty. Just a hole in the floor so you can watch the tracks racing by underneath you."

Mary wrinkled her nose. "Eww." She could wait.

The door to their berth slid open with a *bang,* and the train Nazi poked her head in. "Kovel!"

Immediately, the babusya in the bottom bunk sat up and roused her young grandson. The boy's sleepy eyes went wide when he saw the muscle-bound American sitting across from and above him.

Seeing that everyone was awake, the provodnista gave a satisfied nod and moved on to roust the other compartments.

"'Sup?" Sweeney grunted, flashing the kid a grin. Mary slapped his leg and gave him a look to remind him he wasn't supposed to let anyone know he spoke English.

When Mary and Sweeney stepped off the train a few minutes later, Rip and John were waiting for them on the cavernous platform. Both men looked well rested, if somewhat rumpled in their ill-fitting clothes.

Mary inhaled deeply of the cool morning air. Something about last night had been cathartic, like throwing open the door of an old garden shed after a long winter.

Before their talk, she'd known Sweeney only as a younger version of her father—a broad-shouldered, unfeeling warrior who, if he thought of her at all, it was only to want her to be more like the other guys. But last night Sweeney had done something her father had never done. He'd told her she was okay. He'd made her feel valued. And then he had opened up to her and given her a peek underneath the tough-as-nails exterior.

That was a Bobby Sweeney she'd like to get to know better.

Though she'd been terribly embarrassed when John had showed up at their door and seen her hugging Sweeney—he'd come with some of Olenka's grandmother's food—Mary decided it was probably for the best. She didn't need romance complicating her life at this point. And, to his credit, Sweeney had made no indication that he expected anything more than the hug she'd willingly given.

Rip was chuckling as they approached. "You two look like Little Red Riding Hood and the hunter."

Sweeney clapped an arm around Rip's shoulders. "Glad you're reading the classics, Rip. And you look like Tiny Tim."

"Maybe so, bro. But if I have to walk very far in these farmer boots, I'm going to need crutches."

As they walked toward the terminal, John hung back with Mary. "You two seem to be getting along a little better."

Mary looked up at him. "Don't get the wrong idea, John. We—"

John cut her off with a grin and a wave. "Hey, no need to explain anything. You're both adults. I don't need to know."

"You're never going to let me live this down, are you?"

John laughed. "I'll never let Bobby live it down. You, I'll give some slack."

She punched him in the arm. "Gee, thanks."

"So where do we find our ride?"

Mary had almost forgotten. "Oh, Olenka said she'd text me the instructions." She produced her cell phone from the pocket on her dress and checked her messages. There was one SMS. "Driver Slev. Yellow van. 035861 plate. 6695-2896."

John was reading over her shoulder. "So we're looking for some guy named Slev?"

Mary snapped her phone shut. "Let me go freshen up first, then we'll find our buddy."

When she emerged from the washroom she felt ten times better, despite the rumpled denim dress and the fact that she would have killed for a toothbrush. The men were standing by the exit doors.

Sweeney jerked his head in that direction when she approached. "We may have found our guy."

As they walked out of the terminal, Mary saw what they were talking about. A potbellied unshaven man stood munching on some sort of pastry as he leaned against the grille of a rusty yellow Volkswagen van. No license plate was visible from where they stood.

"Hang on, guys. Let's see if he's our man. Watch this." Mary produced her phone and quickly dialed the number Olenka had sent in her text message. She put the phone to her ear, and then everyone turned to watch the driver.

Sure enough, ten seconds later he started frantically patting his pockets for his phone. Satisfied, Mary ended the call and led the way across the cobblestone parking lot toward their man. He was still giving the phone a frustrated stare when they walked up on him. The man looked up, and Mary smiled, showing him her own phone. Recognition dawned on his face.

"Hi," Mary said.

"Phoenix?" the man replied, jabbing a greasy finger at John.

Mary just nodded. "Da." It wasn't worth trying to explain. She turned to the rest of the group. "Get in."

Fifteen minutes later, rain began to fall. They zipped through the outskirts of the city of Kovel in the rattletrap Volkswagen. The rundown old town gave way to rolling farmland abruptly as the jarring cobblestone streets changed to a long straight road heading northwest toward the Polish border. But even though the road ran in a near-perfect straight line, its surface was more potholes than pavement.

Situated in the passenger seat, Mary gripped the dashboard as Slev barely slowed, even for the biggest fissures. He didn't seem to be driving the decrepit vehicle so much as simply aiming it.

Sweeney sat directly behind her, holding the GPS out the window. "This thing says we're twenty-six kilometers from the border. You think this heap will hold together long enough to get us there?"

"I don't know," Rip replied through clenched teeth. "But dang, I need some shock absorbers for my back, bro."

John reached up and handed Mary the satellite phone. "Why don't you try raising Major Williams?"

"Great idea."

She took the handset and extended the telescoping antenna, then rolled down her window and powered on the unit, looking for a signal. It took ten minutes before the set locked on to the satellite, then five frustrating tries to get a call through to the command center. Thankfully, someone picked up on the second ring, even though by Mary's calculations it was just after three in the morning on the East Coast of the United States. Some clicks told her she was being transferred.

A moment later Major Williams's gruff voice came over the line, along with a lot of background noise. "Hey, kid, where are ya?"

"Hi. Justa sec." She covered the handset and yelled back at Sweeney. "How far?"

"Maybe ten kilometers."

She spoke back into the phone. "Sweeney says ten klicks."

"You all better get a move on. The Poles have given us very tentative approval to put a plane on the ground at an airstrip twenty miles inside their border. We've got a helicopter headed your direction now, but he won't be able to stick around long. If you don't get through in time, things will get a lot more complicated."

She didn't want to know what that meant. "How much time do we have?"

"Hard to say. We weren't able to run all this past Polish border security, and if they pick you up, people in the Polish security service are going to look bad for it. So the trick is going to be getting you guys off the ground as quick as possible once you cross the river. You got me?"

This didn't sound very well thought out. Mary wondered if missions like this ever were. "Okay, we'll try you again when we get through." She tried to sound confident but wasn't sure she succeeded.

"Don't worry," the major concluded. "I'm praying for you. Bye."

"Okay…thanks." But the line was dead.

Five minutes later, Slev shouted, looking in the rearview mirror.

Mary whirled around to see what was the matter. In the distance, she spotted two cars traveling the same direction they were, only faster. Her heart nearly seized when she spied the flashing red lights on top.

Suddenly everyone wanted to go faster, despite the potholes. Rip gripped the edges of both front seats and shouted at Slev as if volume alone would surmount the language barrier. "Go, man! It's the cops!"

Sweeney's eyes were glued to the GPS. "Two klicks out."

Mary kept her mouth shut and held on tight. If this was God's way of answering the major's prayers, He had a sick sense of humor. She silently willed the aged van to go faster, even when they hit a pothole so deep she hit her head on the ceiling.

"One klick. Almost there," Sweeney said. "The road turns left soon."

Mary saw it coming and braced. The van almost lost traction on the wet pavement as they rounded the bend. Without warning Slev slammed on the brakes, fishtailing to a stop. Startled cries erupted from the rest of the team, but Mary was almost strangled as her body was thrown against the seat belt harness.

"Get out!" Slev shouted in Russian.

Mary looked at him. "What are you doing?"

"Out! Hurry!" Slev reached across and opened her door, gesturing for them to get out.

Mary's eyes went wide. "You can't just kick us out in the rain!"

"Go! Go!" John shouted. "We'll go on foot from here."

Sweeney practically ripped the side door of the van from its track, and everyone vacated the Volkswagen like it was on fire. No sooner had John cleared the door than Slev ground the gears and the van tore off in a spray of mud.

The rain poured down in sheets as Sweeney consulted the GPS. "The river should be that way!" He pointed with a knifed hand.

Nobody had to tell Mary twice. She gathered up her long dress and ran for it as the wail of sirens reached her ears. Sweeney, John, and Rip were right beside her.

Crossing the freshly plowed field that separated them from the border was like running through ten inches of molasses. Wearing fifteen pounds of sodden cotton didn't help. Clumps of mud stuck to her boots, and several times she fell down between the rows. By the time they reached the tree line at the far side of the field, the two black police cars had reached the bend in the road and skidded to a halt.

Covered in mud, Mary clawed her way out of the field onto solid ground, feeling like her lungs had burst and she would cough them up any second. Rip knelt near her, puffing hard and looking like he'd gone swimming in milk chocolate. Dropping to her hands and knees, Mary looked back, heaving, as Sweeney and John came panting up behind her. A bullhorn sounded in the distance. Through the deluge she could vaguely see uniformed officers exiting both vehicles.

John stumbled up the bank, gasping for breath. "Holy cow." He bent over double, gulping mouthfuls of air.

Sweeney arrived, practically blue in the face. "Mud...evil..."

Mary could only nod in agreement.

Rip held out a trembling hand, pointing past them toward the border. "How...how're we going to cross that, man?"

Mary turned to see what he was pointing at, and her feet suddenly felt like cast iron. Which was bad, because the brown river they were looking at was at least a hundred yards wide.

"Aw," John panted. "We can swim that, no problem."

"Us, maybe," Sweeney grunted. "But try swimming in one of these." He picked up the hem of Mary's soaked peasant dress. "She won't make it ten feet."

Something snapped inside her. "Aww…crud. I've already been naked once this trip. One more time won't hurt."

The guys all stared wide eyed at one another. "Don't look at me!" Sweeney protested. Rip gave her a smile and a wink but said nothing.

Mary was just glad she'd gotten her sports bra and boy shorts back from the soldiers in Chernobyl. She stole another glance across the muddy field and wondered why the policemen weren't already halfway across.

Then she heard the shots and knew why. A bullet clipped a branch directly overhead, sending it down on top of them.

"Go! Go!" Sweeney pushed all of them over the bank as pine branches started exploding all around.

Mary pulled the wet dress over her head and threw it on the bank. She kept her boots on.

What was it her dad used to say? *If you're going to play with the big boys, you can't expect them to change the rules of the game just because you're a girl."*

She tossed the soggy mess in a heap before plunging into the surging brown river. The cold water gave her an instant energy boost, and without the weight of the dress, she was soon powering across the current with long powerful strokes.

This time, she beat everyone across, though by the time she crawled onto the opposite bank, she had been swept several hundred meters downstream. She scampered up out of the water and sat down, once again trying to catch her breath.

The rain had lightened considerably, but as she waited for the men to reach the bank, her heart rate slowed and she became thoroughly chilled. She could no longer see any of their pursuers from where she sat, and she wondered if they'd given up the chase.

Sweeney was the first to heave himself out of the water. He stumbled up the bank past her, and she heard him retching behind a bush.

"Welcome to Poland," she said.

Sweeney approached, wiping his mouth. "Thanks. Here, take this." He unbuttoned his shirt and draped the wet blue cotton over her shoulders. "Better than nothing."

She couldn't help but smile. "Thank you, Bobby. Mrs. Sweeney really did raise a gentleman." She pushed her arms into the wet sleeves and hurriedly buttoned it up.

John arrived next, towing Rip.

Despite being winded, Rip found enough energy to complain. "Man! I hate water. Nobody said anything about crossing no river."

"Hey, we made it!" John puffed. "Come on. Let's go find that chopper."

Mary suddenly felt as if she'd been Tasered. "Oh no! I left the satphone in the van!" She pounded her fists into the ground.

That's when she heard the helicopter.

Everyone jumped up at once and scrambled up the bank toward the sound.

At the crest of the hill, they found a road that ran almost due north, but they still could not see any aircraft, though it sounded close.

Sweeney stepped onto the roadway and squinted south down the road, then grimaced. "Wonderful. More company."

Mary had seen it too. Far off, a green military-looking jeep racing in their direction. She estimated it would reach their position in two minutes. "Polish border police?"

"Don't suppose it's our ride," John said.

Sweeney shook his head, causing droplets of water to cascade from his short blond hair onto his shoulders. "It looks like it's gonna be our ride one way or another. What do you want to do, boss? Keep running?" Mary realized he was looking at her, not John.

Just then the trees on the far side of the clearing began to quiver and sway, and a sleek blue French-made helicopter appeared above them.

Task Force Valor ran for the bird, yelling and waving their arms. The pilot saw them and flared hard. He snapped into a low hover two feet above the clearing. The side door slid open as the team stumbled through the rotor wash toward the chopper.

When Mary reached the door, she looked up into the smiling face of none other than Frank Baldwin, the team's tech sergeant.

"Frank!"

"Why, hello, ma'am. Where *are* your clothes?"

"Shut up and let me in."

Frank's grin was a mile wide as he extended his wrist to hers. "Yes ma'am. All aboard!"

The pilot fought to control the Dauphin helicopter as it dove through the wind-whipped rain for landing. Sweeney felt his stomach drop as the aviator felt for the ground through the maelstrom of spray thrown up by the craft, and was relieved when he felt the wheels thump down onto soggy earth next to the thin airstrip that had been barely visible as they made their final approach.

Once the engines powered down, Sweeney could just make out a white Learjet thirty yards outside the starboard window, waiting on the tarmac with engines running.

"There's our ride," Frank said, slapping Sweeney's bare shoulder.

"Ow, watch it!" Sweeney grumbled, massaging the spot. "I think I caught some shrapnel back in the dead zone."

Was that only yesterday morning?

"Sorry about that," Frank said with a grimace. "Don't worry, though. We'll take care of you. We'll have new clothes for you guys waiting in Frankfurt, so you won't have to ride all the way home looking like, er…that." Frank nodded at Mary, who was huddled across from them in Sweeney's tattered shirt, shivering. "Doc's there too. So he'll give you all a once-over."

John and Rip weren't much better off. Their ill-fitting and mud-stained costumes made them look like they'd been mining sludge for a week.

The female copilot stepped out of the helicopter and came around to pull open the side door. Sweeney wondered if the crew knew anything about the team's mission or if they'd been contracted to do the job. Not that it mattered. They were out of Ukraine alive, though in his case he couldn't even claim to have made it with the shirt on his back.

He unbuckled his seat belt and waited for John, Rip, and Mary to exit the bird, before stepping out into the frigid rain himself. He looked back in time to see Frank toss an easy salute at the pilots as he climbed out, then Sweeney turned and ran for the waiting Learjet, ignoring the cold raindrops that stung his neck and raised goose flesh on his arms.

The door of the plane dropped open as they approached, and a familiar figure stuck his head out the door, dressed in an olive-drab flight suit with a green aviator headset.

"Major Williams!"

The Task Force Valor commander waved for them to hurry and shouted over the roar of the engines. "Let's go, boys! The weather isn't getting any better!"

As soon as the team made it up the stairs and ducked inside the jet, Major Williams went around and embraced each one in turn, heedless of their soaked and soiled attire. "Thank God you made it! The chopper pilot kept trying to abort because of the weather. I had to practically threaten him with bodily harm to get him to stick around."

The Learjet's pilot, a squat black man wearing a U.S. Air Force uniform, stepped out of the cockpit and cast a wary eye at his passengers, then yanked the doorway up into place and slammed it shut with a thud.

After the noise and chaos of the last hour, the muted interior of the plane sounded like a mausoleum. Sweeney flopped into a plush leather chair near the back of the plane and let out a groan of relief— his actions mimicked by Rip, John, and Mary. Frank sat up front across from the major.

Williams raised an eyebrow at the haggard crew. "You folks look like you've been through the wringer. Buckle up and we'll have you in Frankfurt in less than an hour. There's drinks up here, but no peanuts." He tossed bottles of water to each team member.

"How about a cover-up for Phoenix back there?" Frank suggested, reaching into an overhead compartment and pulling down a stack of blue fleece blankets.

Major Williams took in Mary's half-dressed condition. "How in the world did you lose your clothes?"

"It's hard to swim in a full-length dress," she answered, blushing.

The plane's engines wound up and began pushing it down the runway.

Frank turned to inspect his exhausted teammates, who were half sitting, half lying in their seats, still recovering from the ordeal of the last hour. He burst out laughing.

Rip lolled his head around to look at the dark-haired tech sergeant. "You think this is funny, bro?"

Frank shook his head, still laughing. "I was just thinking you all make it look like this plane already crashed."

"Bite your tongue," Mary spat. "I won't be able to relax until we're back at Bragg."

"That could be awhile," Major Williams said, his tone sober. "We've got another tentative mission as soon as we can get out of Europe. Doc is waiting for us in Frankfurt with a C-141 standing by. We're headed there now. In the meantime I'll give you an update on what's been happening."

John looked as shocked as Sweeney felt. "You're kidding," John said. "Can't we at least take a shower and a nap?"

"We've got new uniforms and kit for you in Frankfurt. Maybe we can hose you off before you get on the plane." The major grinned. "Sleep won't be a problem. The flight from Frankfurt is at least ten hours."

"What's the status stateside?" Rip asked.

The major shook his head. "Not good. ITEB has been blowing up all over the place. The most recent is a bridge on the beltway around Washington DC and a casino in Las Vegas. There are shortages of fuel, natural gas, power outages—you name it. The whole country is going nuts, and the politicians are screaming bloody murder for us to find who is responsible."

"What about *posse comitatus*?" John said. "As U.S. soldiers, we can't operate inside U.S. borders, right?"

"You can't be deployed against U.S. citizens, that's correct," the major said. "But that won't be an issue here."

"Because the bombers are foreigners?" Rip asked.

Major Williams shook his head. "No, because we're not headed back to the continental U.S."

"We're not headed back to Bragg?" Mary blurted.

The major's sly smile answered the question before he dropped the bombshell. "Believe it or not, we're headed back to Panama."

THE CELL PHONE warbling on the dashboard brought Edgar out of a dream about the beautiful *sangre de toro* birds that chirped outside his rented villa in Cartagena. He blinked and then squinted against the bright sun outside, then remembered where he was—the last place he wanted to be. He couldn't understand why anyone would voluntarily take up residence in the sun-seared desert that was Las Vegas.

The text message that had just arrived was exactly what he'd been waiting for: directions to his meeting with the men he was now regretting having hired. He pried open his phone and read the message.

"Chevron. Alamo. Two hours."

Edgar grimaced, wondering what the message meant.

Ten minutes later, after consulting a telephone book borrowed from a convenience-store clerk, he had his answer. Alamo was a tiny village ensconced in the rugged no man's land seventy miles north of Las Vegas. He surmised that the gang members had gone there to hide until the flames of their recent handiwork had died down in the city.

Did they not realize the dangers they were exposing him to? Did they care? The city was in an uproar after the casino bombing—tourism had dropped to almost nothing overnight, and the police force was working double shifts to track down the culprits. And those were precisely the men he had to meet with.

The final instructions he'd received might have sounded simple—recover the remaining product and destroy it. But he knew MS-13 well—they were just the type of thugs who would find a way to make it *his* fault, and demand more money for it.

Nevertheless, he had to find a way to retrieve the remaining ITEB. Instead of launching the final "rain of fire" attack with the product he had left, the gringo had inexplicably instructed him to simply destroy it.

Edgar knew what the ITEB was worth—he himself had distilled it and sold it to the gringo. Though now that they had actually met, Edgar had to wonder what line of work the man was in to afford the ridiculous price he had paid. So far, however, Edgar had seen only half of the money. Something now told him he should have taken that portion and forgotten the rest, but his greed had gotten the better of him. If he survived to collect his pay, he would be able to really disappear in style.

He kissed the three rings on his left hand—*El Padre, El Hijo, El Espíritu Santo*—as he pulled the Expedition onto Highway 93 toward Alamo. He had an hour's drive to think of the best way to handle MS-13.

By the time he had driven across the desolate desert separating Las Vegas from Alamo, he had formulated a good plan. So many years in business had taught him the art of diplomacy—and where that failed, he wasn't averse to outright flattery. Yes, make the gangsters think they had done a great job, that they had earned their pay well even though they had failed to carry out the other objectives they were given. All that mattered was completing the job and escaping from this miserable country.

Alamo seemed larger than he expected as he pulled into town. Perhaps that was because the highway looked out from the side of one mountain range with nothing to block the view as far as the next range of scraggly peaks, with the entire town visible in between. Edgar was not used to such vastness.

He had scarcely rolled to a stop at the gas station when a young, jeans-clad punk emerged from the store wearing dark sunglasses and a red bandanna on his head. His emotionless face wore a wisp of a goatee. His skinny arms were adorned with various tattoos, and he walked with a ridiculous swagger that was doubtlessly intended to make him look tough, but in reality gave him the appearance of someone who had lost one shoe.

The kid approached his window. "You looking for Cholo?"

"*Sí.*"

"I'm s'posed to take you to him, yo."

Edgar pursed his lips. He didn't like this at all, but there wasn't much choice. He had to get to Cholo. He looked back at the punk. "Get in."

With the young gangster slouched in the passenger seat and giving directions with monosyllabic grunts, Edgar drove back south about five miles out of town. There, the kid indicated the entrance to what looked like a farm situated among old cottonwood trees that stood beside a small stream. A cluster of dilapidated buildings was visible from the road.

Edgar looked at the punk. "This is it?"

"You got it, *abuelo*."

Edgar wanted to backhand the kid. "I'm not your grandfather."

He drove the SUV down the bumpy dirt driveway. When they reached the shade of the trees, he spied Cholo's blood-red Imperial parked inside a wooden machine shed. The gangbanger was leaning against the open trunk, muscled arms crossed over what might have been the same white tank top he'd been wearing the last time they'd met.

Edgar stepped from the vehicle and conjured up his best politician's smile. "There you are, Cholo." He walked toward the leader, who hadn't moved and simply stared at him through dark sunglasses. "You did well, my friend." Edgar lied on both counts. "I have come to settle our business." On that, he was telling the truth.

Cholo acted as if he hadn't heard. Instead he reached into the trunk of the car and produced a bottle of ITEB, holding it up to the light. "Hey, *ese,* where did these bottles come from?"

Edgar stopped in his tracks, surprised by the question. Drops of sweat formed on his brow. "Where?" he answered. *Should I say? Does it matter now?* Probably not, he decided. "They came from Panama."

Cholo raised his chin a notch. "You got any more?"

"No, I…" Edgar didn't like where this was going. "I just came to give you what I owe you. But I need to get the remaining bottles back from you."

For a moment, nobody said anything. Tension hung like the

oppressive humidity in Cartagena before a rainstorm. At last Edgar knew for sure that bringing MS-13 into this had been a very, very big mistake.

Cholo shook his head, almost in slow motion. "No, I think we would rather keep it, you know? We can find good uses for it." He turned and placed the bottle back into the padded crate Edgar had given him.

Anger burned hot in Edgar's face. *How can I make him understand?* He took a step toward the thug. "Listen, you have—" He stopped midsentence when he realized he was now talking into the barrel of a large automatic handgun.

Edgar felt the blood drain from his face. He put his hands up in surrender and began backing toward the SUV. "Listen, Cholo, we can work a deal. Let me pay you and see what I can—"

At first, the explosion in Cholo's fist seemed to have nothing to do with the white-hot sledgehammer that struck Edgar in the abdomen. He clutched his gut and fell backward onto the dusty ground. He looked around for someone who would help him but saw only the impassive faces of the other gang members. The young punk who had led him there stood off to one side, desperately trying to maintain his tough exterior after watching what was probably his first murder.

It was not supposed to end like this.

Edgar looked down at the spreading stain around his midsection. He could feel every slowly fading beat of his heart as his lifeblood leaked through the three rings on his left hand. The searing pain made it impossible to breathe. He looked up and saw that Cholo now had the pistol in his waistband and was barking out orders in Spanish to his men.

This is what it is like to die.

But then the anger returned. Nobody crossed Edgar Oswardo Lerida, or Gustavo Soto for that matter. In his former life, when he'd been known as Oswardo, nobody would have dared do such a thing.

He could feel weakness entering his limbs as the blood continued to pump onto the ground. Blackness slithered around the edges of his vision. But his anger burned hotter by the second. He would teach them.

With great effort, he reached a bloody hand into his pocket and found the small plastic keychain he'd never gotten a chance to use back in Panama. It had remained with him ever since as a subtle reminder of his former life. The tiny transmitter in it had been designed to work over a distance of several hundred yards, but he knew he didn't need that much range now. The receivers for this device were embedded in the car tire valve-stem covers he had packed with only a gram of plastic explosive each. He'd dropped those innocuous objects into the box he'd given to Cholo. Each contained the explosive power of barely more than a child's firecracker, but just one was enough to cause a "car accident" by making a tire "blow out" on a dangerous curve. *But also just powerful enough to shatter a glass bottle.*

Edgar Oswardo Lerida raised a trembling, bloody hand and with great effort kissed each of the three rings he wore. *El Padre, El Hijo, El Espíritu Santo.* Soon he would know if any of the three existed, though he suddenly wished not to know. But if he was destined for hell, at least he would not be making the trip alone.

With the last of his energy he pointed the plastic keychain at Cholo's car. Then he closed his eyes and pushed the button.

The taste of revenge was incredibly sweet for the instant before it was swallowed by fire.

———

Nagar Singh shuffled past the six-foot birdcage and stopped to peer at the magnificent scarlet macaw inside. The bird eyed him warily, shifting its weight from one foot to the other.

"Hello, Nancy," Singh said. "Hungry?" His eyes twinkled at the resplendent creature. Its variegated plumage displayed such bright yellows, blues, reds, and greens that he often wondered if it had flown through a rainbow.

Squawk! The bird's answer made him smile. Nancy was always hungry.

The bird had become his friend in the week since he started his new job, as much as a bird and a man could *be* friends, anyway. They had a lot in common, Nancy and he. They were both more or less confined, though the bird had not chosen its cage.

Singh actually enjoyed the idea of living in this beautiful home, a new life in a peaceful and tranquil place. His new job had taken him to a remote mountainous region, far away from the smog, crime, and traffic of city life. Here, the air was clean and cool all year, and the verdant flora that stretched away from the large ranch house where he worked was always in bloom, as if stuck in perpetual springtime.

No more would he have to contend with the constant stream of picky and pampered hotel guests who hurried through their vacations at a frantic pace and expected him to move even faster. When his new employer had approached him about moving here, Singh had been all too content to leave his old job to younger men. Here he would spend the rest of his useful life simply keeping this magnificent house in order, a job made easier by the fact that there were so few visitors.

It was like heaven on earth, except that he was still a servant. He didn't mind that part, though. It gave him purpose.

Singh stole a glance at the helicopter that was parked even now across the lawn from the glass sliding door that framed a volcano in the distance. The flying machine looked like a fishbowl with a few skinny palm fronds attached to the top. When his employer had arrived, it had buzzed in like an annoyed dragonfly and scattered leaves and grass in all directions. A fearful sight.

He shook his head. "No, thank you, Nancy. I'm happy to leave the flying to you."

The bird shrieked again, but this time it began pacing back and forth on its perch, as if looking for a place to hide.

"What is it, girl?"

Squawk! Squawk! Squawk! The macaw was frantic now, jumping from side to side and flapping its wings.

Then Singh heard it: a sound like low, rolling thunder in the distance. He slid open the glass door and cocked an ear to the sky. The rumbling increased. Now it was an angry throbbing that echoed from one mountain peak to another across the secluded valley. Nancy was trying to fly through the bars of her cage.

It wasn't until he saw the black monsters appear over the top of the house that he recognized the very different sound of military helicopters. And suddenly a ride on the dragonfly didn't seem so bad.

Sweeney's stomach jumped into his throat as the Huey helicopter plunged through a break between two heavily forested mountains. He gripped the seat and held on, his jaw set, gripping the silenced Heckler and Koch MP5 submachine gun in his right hand.

In the briefing they'd been given on the flight from Frankfurt to Panama, he'd learned that an Israeli had been apprehended while trying to leave the country from Washington Dulles airport. An alert rental car agent had been cleaning up the man's rental car when he'd noticed that the saved route data in the on-board GPS showed the car had been in the vicinity of both ITEB explosions east of the Mississippi. He'd reported it to the authorities, who had picked up the man in the terminal. A search of his briefcase had yielded a cellular phone.

Apparently one of the incoming calls on the Israeli's phone had originated from a remote Panamanian ranch high up in the mountains near the Costa Rican border. Somewhere just ahead and below him right now. Someone in Langley felt it was significant enough to send in Task Force Valor.

Sweeney thought it was a long shot, but if the men responsible for the mayhem unfolding at home happened to be here, he planned to make them pay.

By what he could discern from the grim looks on the teammates seated around him, he might have to wait in line.

John Cooper, who was wearing an extra headset to listen to the pilots, looked up at him and held out a finger. "One minute!"

The chopper banked hard around a steep ridgeline, and then Sweeney saw it. A sprawling ranch house surrounded by manicured lawns, nestled in the bottom of the valley next to a crystal-clear mountain stream. Three other helicopters were already on the ground, and Panamanian commandos could be seen swarming across the grounds.

Sweeney's jaw clenched tighter. *They should have let us go in first.* Sure, it was their country, and he grudgingly understood why Panama's president wanted his own guys making the capture and arrest. But that didn't mean he had to like it.

Mary, who was sitting across from him, reached over and punched him on the arm, her eyes unreadable behind mirrored goggles. She had a headset similar to John's. She shouted over the *thrup-thrup-thrup* of the Huey's rotors. "They've got three guys in custody!"

Sweeney gave her a thumbs-up. "Let's hope there aren't thirty more waiting in the jungle!" His grip tightened on the MP5 submachine gun as the helicopter dropped into the clearing behind the ranch house and flared for landing.

The second its skids met earth, Sweeney followed Rip, Frank Baldwin, John, and Phoenix out the far side door. As he did, he caught sight of the major's aircraft above them coming in for landing.

The five ran for the back of the house, weapons at the ready but still on Safe. Four Panamanian Frontera police officers dressed in olive-drab fatigues and black Kevlar vests waved them over to a large glass double door.

They burst into a spacious parlor filled with more of the olive-suited Panamanian special police. In the center of the room, however, Sweeney spotted a set of leather couches arranged around a square glass table. On the couch, facing away from the door, sat three men with their hands held atop their heads by gun-toting policemen.

Sweeney watched as John began working his way around in front of the suspects—and then stopped suddenly. John's grim expression melted into one of disbelief. His mouth dropped open, and the color drained from his face. "Oh God, it can't be!"

Sweeney moved to his side, then gaped at the figure seated in the middle of the couch.

It was Michael Lafontaine.

To Lafontaine's left sat a slim young man with darker skin and wide blue eyes that had terror and confusion in them. To Lafontaine's right was an old man in a white turban.

Lafontaine's face bore a resolute frown, but his granite eyes showed none of the intensity that he was known for. Now they showed only sadness. "I'm sorry, John. I'm sorry you had to come here and see this."

Mary stepped forward. "John, do you know this man?"

But John was still speechless.

Rip answered for him. "This is Michael Lafontaine—he's John's godfather."

Mary's eyebrows shot up. "The one that is supposed to be dead?"

"That one, yeah."

John's face turned red. "*You* are responsible for this? You're the reason we've had to trek all over the planet tracking down this explosive?"

Lafontaine shook his head. "No, John. I didn't make the stuff. Actually, when I heard about your mission in Lebanon, I promised your father I would do whatever it took to help you. I started by getting in touch with some of my old contacts in this part of the world." He sighed, his eyes riveted on the floor. "That's where this all began for me."

Sweeney was confused. "Wait up. How were you trying to help, exactly? By the looks of what's happening in the States right now, your aid hasn't amounted to much that I would call helpful."

Lafontaine looked grim. "The arms dealer who was distilling ITEB was already shipping it all over. I contacted him and offered to buy the entire stockpile as long as he guaranteed he would take the entire remaining product off the market."

"Have you read the news lately?" Sweeney spat. "ITEB is blowing up everywhere!"

A fire ignited behind Lafontaine's expression. "And what effect is it having? Think about it, John. Finally, Americans are realizing how fragile their beloved economy is. They are realizing that Homeland Security is a farce. And the politicians—the same politicians that couldn't seem to get anything accomplished even when I was pumping hundreds of thousands into their reelection coffers—are now passing resolutions faster than any Congress since the Second World War."

Mary was incredulous. "You planned all this?"

Lafontaine turned his eyes away. "I did what had to be done. What no one else was willing to do."

"Even faking your own death?" Mary said.

He looked back at her. "Of course. The idea came from a book, actually. One I read long ago, where all of the difference-makers in society disappear and leave a corrupt culture to face the consequences of its own corruption."

"Atlas Shrugged," John muttered.

"Exactly. I did what I did for the good of the country. And besides, it was time for me to make a change." He looked at the young man seated next to him. "John, I'd like you to meet my son, Michael."

John cocked his head to one side. "Your son?"

Lafontaine sighed. "His mother and I had a relationship in the late eighties when I was stationed here. But I only found out about him a couple of weeks ago."

"And so you dragged him into this?"

The older man bristled. "He had no knowledge of the ITEB whatsoever. He will come to live with me here once he's completed college."

Sweeney snorted. "I hate to break it to you, Colonel Lafontaine, but you're going to be spending the rest of your days languishing in a Panamanian prison."

Lafontaine's calm expression returned. "Perhaps, except that Panama doesn't have an extradition treaty with the United States. And it recently passed a law stipulating that prisoners over a certain age may serve their sentences under home confinement." He took in the room with a sweep of his gaze. "Gentlemen, welcome to my prison."

John's incredulous look took on a tinge of disgust. "Colonel, I've always thought you were a great man, my entire life. But now I see that your sense of right and wrong has become corrupted. You've become no better than the terrorists you claim to oppose."

Sweeney could see the color rising in John's cheeks being matched in the face of Michael Lafontaine.

The colonel almost shouted. "How dare you!"

"No! How dare you, Michael!" John bellowed. "You've given in to the thinking that the end justifies any means. Tell me how that's different from bin Laden. Tell me!"

Lafontaine started to sputter out a response, but John stormed out of the room, stomping by a huge birdcage with a giant squawking macaw inside.

Sweeney watched him go. How could he help his friend?

Mary stepped forward and leaned close to Lafontaine. "Guess what, Colonel? Our government has already been on the phone with the president of Panama. And they are willing to make an exception for us in this case." Her voice dripped with contempt. "Since your crimes took place outside of Panama, your penthouse jailbird over there will probably get a little bit lonely."

Now it was Lafontaine's turn to go pale.

Sweeney never would have imagined wishing jail time on Michael Lafontaine, but now the thought seemed just right.

Outside Fort Bragg, North Carolina

Mary squinted into the bright afternoon sun, which was just beginning to fade to orange. The large orb dropped in the sky over Valley Pond, a thirty-acre lake just outside the edge of Fort Bragg's northernmost training area. The line of pine trees that ringed the lake's shore was broken only by a large plantation house nestled in mature hardwoods, and a run-down caretaker's cottage with a brand-new deck that overhung the water's edge.

In the grass next to the small cabin was a rectangular sand-pit volleyball court, now occupied on one side by the men of Task Force Valor in shorts and T-shirts, and on the other by four nimble women, who were beating them.

"Service!" Mary swung her arm back and expertly struck the volleyball with her open palm, sending it flying over the net. It headed for a spot right between Rip and Sweeney.

Sweeney, whose sweat-stained Army PT shirt was already covered in sand, yelled, "I've got it!" and dove for the ball.

He barely tipped it up to the team medic, Doc Kelly, who then set the ball just above the net for Frank. Frank was already in the air ready for the spike.

Mary took two quick steps toward the net. "Get it! Get it!"

But she needn't have worried. Major Williams's fourteen-year-old daughter, Denise, was already there. With a primal shout, the gangly teenager lunged upward with both hands over her head just in time to block Frank's attempt. The ball bounced harmlessly back over his head.

Rip and Sweeney both dove for it but only managed to end up in a tangled heap in the sand. The ball bounced before rolling out of bounds.

A chorus of female cheers went up from seven other girls on the sidelines—six of whom were Major Williams's other daughters, and the remaining one a beautiful black-haired teen who had just been introduced to Mary as Rip's younger sister, Gabi. The girl had apparently come to live with her older brother to get away from the gang influence in L.A.

On the court, Denise was being lauded with hugs and high-fives by John's girlfriend, Liz Fairchild, and another raven-haired Latina whom Mary had met in Panama: Fernanda Lerida. Mary joined in the celebration, patting the freckle-faced Denise on the back and pretending not to notice across the net the dejected commandos who were brushing the sand off their shorts.

Buzz Hogan sat in a lawn chair near half court, keeping score. "That's seven points for the girls' team, and three for these here high-speed special operators." He laughed.

Doc Kelly wiped sweat from his eyes. "Whew. The major was right. That Denise is a killer!"

Rip laughed. "Man, you're not kidding! Where's John? We need reinforcements!"

Liz shook her head. "He said he had to run to the store for some ice. But that was an hour ago." She shrugged. "Then again, he's easily sidetracked."

A sharp whistle sounded from the direction of the cottage. Major Williams, wearing a white paper chef's hat and his torso covered by an apron emblazoned with "May the Forks Be with You," waved from the deck. "Burgers are ready!" he shouted. "Come get 'em!"

"All right," Buzz said, rising stiffly from his chair. "Let's eat. We'll pick this game back up later."

"Awww, we had you all right where we wanted you too," Sweeney said, winking at Mary.

As the crowd drifted toward the cottage, Mary took in the beautiful lake, the trees, and the amber-tinged clouds in the blue sky. The scene was marred only by a single Black Hawk helicopter buzzing around high above, probably ferrying some troops around Fort Bragg for training. She sighed. *This is just what I needed.*

Sidling up to the other two girls, she smiled at Liz, whose gentle face and doe-brown eyes now reflected a slight concern. The two of them had really hit it off, even though they had only met several hours earlier. She put an arm around the athletic shoulders of her new friend. "Don't worry, Liz. I'm sure John's okay."

Liz smiled up at her. "Oh, I'm not worried. God's in control. If God can protect John through all the dangers of his job, I'm sure He can get him back from an ice run in one piece." Her grin widened. "I was just worried that he's going to miss supper!"

Mary laughed, impressed with the confidence and joy she saw in Liz. She looked past Liz, who was a brown-haired journalist, to the supermodel-thin Fernanda, whom she had met several weeks earlier in Panama. The lithe Panamanian had shown up unexpectedly at the party, and Rip hadn't stopped smiling since. "So, Fernanda, you came all the way here from Panama just to see Rip?"

The Latina's long black curls rippled down her shoulders as she shook her head. "Not exactly." Her accent was as beautiful as her appearance, though her tone was somber. "When we found out that my uncle Edgar had been found dead outside of Las Vegas, I came with my aunt to help identify the body. And since I had never been to North Carolina, I decided to stay an extra week and come see Rip."

Liz hooked her arm through Fernanda's. "She's my roomie this week in the luxurious La Quinta Inn while we help John pack up and find a new apartment."

Mary's eyebrows shot up. "He's moving? But this place is so beautiful!"

"Yes, and John loves it," Liz said. "But the man who owns this property is none other than Michael Lafontaine."

Mary gaped. "I didn't know that! Ooh. I guess that is a problem."

When they reached the cottage, Major Williams stood on the raised wooden deck and addressed the group in his best street-preacher voice. "Ladies and gentlemen, before we partake of this meal of fine southern barbecue and coleslaw, it is fitting that we offer thanks to God for His protection and provision during these last few months, which I'm sure you will all agree have been some of the most challenging of our careers."

A murmur of agreement rippled through the group. Mary noticed that even Sweeney gave a hearty "Hear, hear!"

The major doffed his chef's hat and continued. "But before we say the blessing, there's one minor point of business that needs to be attended to. If you will please direct your attention to the skies above us, you will notice a Black Hawk helicopter."

Mary looked up as the major pulled a Motorola walkie-talkie from his apron and whispered into it.

Then, high above, she noticed a black speck leaving the helicopter and dropping toward them. The speck grew larger until she could just make out that it was a man. A billowy gray parachute appeared above him with a *pop*.

"It's John Cooper!" Denise exclaimed, pointing skyward.

A cheer went up from the crowd, and Mary looked at Liz, who was gaping up at the descending commando, speechless.

The parachute traced a lazy arc across the sky, then dropped down and came across the lake straight for the assembled group. Before John had made it halfway across, Mary could see the wide smile on his face. She watched him pull on both toggles, which created just enough lift for his feet to skim across the surface of the water as he approached the shore, heading straight for Liz.

The group fell into a shocked silence when he deftly landed at the water's edge, only feet from them.

Sweeney and Rip were already there, collapsing their team leader's parachute as he dropped to a knee in front of Liz and held up a black velvet box, opened to reveal a diamond solitaire engagement ring.

"Hi, Liz. Wanna get married?"

Liz screamed. The crowd went wild. Mary teared up. When she looked up at Major Williams, she realized she wasn't the only one.

John was still on his knee, beaming. "Well?"

"Yes! Yes!" Liz cried, throwing her arms around John Cooper.

———

Once the excitement died down and everyone had gotten some food, Mary took her plate and Dr Pepper bottle and walked over to a Royalex canoe that lay inverted by the water's edge. She sat on it and put her plate beside her, savoring the smell of the barbecue and the beauty of the sunset, but not half as much as she savored the warm feeling in her heart. She wished she could always have that feeling, like everything was working out just as it should. Maybe Rip was on to something when he said it was better to not have to control everything.

I wonder if that's something I can learn?

She was happy for John and Liz. It was obvious by looking at them that they were deeply in love. Mary was jealous in a way too. Not that she wanted to be engaged at the moment—though that would be nice at some point. Instead she envied the way Liz could be so confident and so feminine at the same time. For some reason,

Mary had never felt very good at striking that balance. To her, to be strong meant being tough. Femininity meant being vulnerable, weak. But Liz seemed to be so strong and so feminine. How did she do that?

She watched the shadows lengthen across the lake and pondered what Liz had said earlier. *"God is in control."* Could it really be that simple? Was it possible the reason they'd gone to Ukraine had nothing to do with the ITEB but was so they'd be in the right place to thwart the catastrophe at Chernobyl? Did God work that way?

The canoe rocked gently, and Mary turned to see Sweeney sitting down beside her. The edges of his mouth curled into a slight smile that radiated the same vulnerability she'd seen when they'd shared the train car a week earlier. "Hey," he said.

She smiled softly at him. "Hey."

"The major says Lafontaine admitted to purchasing all of the remaining ITEB that was cranked out by Edgar Lerida's lab in Panama. The colonel claims he wanted to keep it out of the hands of terrorists." He gave a snort. "Whatever. Now that ITEB is off the streets, we're going to go back to being plain ol' Special Forces soldiers. No more CIA spook stuff."

Mary nodded, looking out over the lake. "For now. It really didn't end up the way I thought it would, you know?"

Sweeney nodded. "You remember when we hit that warehouse in Lebanon? On the way there, I was sure that was going to be the ITEB factory. I figured we'd mop it up and that would be the end of it. Things sure turned out to be a lot more complicated than that."

Mary nodded. "They always are, aren't they?" She looked over to see his blue eyes watching her and realized she wasn't just talking about the CIA. She shook her head. "I just can't believe Lafontaine was behind this. I got an e-mail saying they found out that the Israeli they arrested in DC used to work for him. Security coordinator or something."

"Yeah. It's kind of scary, actually. I mean, Michael was one of the most patriotic people in the country. If he can get his thinking that twisted, is there hope for any of us?"

Mary took a sip from her Dr Pepper. "John was telling me he thinks it's the same mind-set that caused things like the abuse at Abu Ghraib. Americans assuming that because we're the good guys, we can justify doing bad things because our ultimate purpose is to make things better."

"Hmm…" Sweeney appeared to think about that for a minute. "It doesn't work like that, does it?"

"Well, it shouldn't."

"So…" He cleared his throat. "Are you…? I mean, are we going to see any more of each other?"

She huffed. "After this mission, you've already seen more of me than I ever planned for."

Sweeney laughed. "You know that's not what I mean."

She shrugged and looked at him. "I don't know, Sergeant Sweeney. That decision is above my pay grade."

A look of frustration flashed in his eyes. "Just call me Bobby, would you?"

She tilted her head. "Are you flirting with me?"

"I'm trying to." He held her gaze. "But you're not making it very easy."

Now it was her turn to laugh. "Okay, 'Bobby' then." She reached out and ran a finger under the Arabic tattoo on his arm. "That says, 'Infidel,' doesn't it?"

He blushed a little. "I'm impressed. You speak Arabic too?"

"Not really. Just a few words. Why'd you choose to have that done?"

Sweeney's face darkened a little. "I don't know, really. Guess I was just…" His voice trailed off.

"Just what?"

"Nothing."

She frowned. "Now look, if you're going to flirt, you have to do it right. Step one is to open up, share a little bit of the real Bobby Sweeney underneath all those muscles."

He chuckled. "Tough guys don't impress you, huh?"

"Nope. Dime a dozen where I come from."

Sweeney sighed and ran a hand through his hair. "Okay. I guess I was going to say I got the tattoo to be rebellious. But saying it that way, it sounds like a stupid thing to do."

She raised an eyebrow at him. "Maybe. But I think it looks nice. A good conversation starter if nothing else, right?"

He rolled his eyes. "Sure. It definitely did that when I went home for my brother's wedding. Come to think of it, I've got some apologizing to do when I get back."

She tapped her chin with an index finger. "A man who can say he's sorry? Now that's impressive."

He smiled. "Great. Well, if you really want to be impressed, there's a place on post that rents four-wheelers. How about we go riding sometime?"

She pursed her lips. "You know, that sounds like fun. But I get to drive one of my own. That way we can really see who's the better driver."

Sweeney shrugged and gave a sly smile. "That can be arranged. And I promise to apologize when I beat you."

Author's Note

On Easter Eggs

In the world of entertainment, an *Easter egg* is an intentional message, inside joke, or other hidden meaning written into a story. One of the fun things about writing fiction is the chance to insert little personal messages to people you know. Most people will miss the messages, but they will cause a laugh when your friends read it. This book is full of them.

For example, *chamomile tea* shows up in each of the three Task Force Valor novels. While I was working on the first book, *Allah's Fire*, my editor challenged me to get in touch with my feminine side. I joked, "What, you think I need to include more girly stuff, like knitting and chamomile tea?" I observed how it would be dangerous to include chamomile anything in a novel, because it was far too feminine and would earn me an epic ribbing from all my manly Ranger buddies. She challenged me to live on the wild side. So, chamomile tea makes an appearance in all three novels.

If you look closely, you might see my friend Lynne Thompson chasing her son, David, through JFK airport. Lynne is "the official soccer mom" and author of *The Official Soccer Mom Devotional*.

Easter eggs can also bring deeper meaning to a story. For instance, each of the main characters in the story is named after one of the nineteen U.S. servicemen to have earned the Congressional Medal of Honor *twice*, with the exception of Rip Rubio, whose namesake earned "only" one. Phoenix was named for Mary Edwards Walker, a Civil War doctor and the only woman ever to receive the Medal of Honor.

This is one little way I try to honor real-life heroes with my fiction. I encourage you to go Google the names of the Task Force Valor team and read about the courageous exploits of their namesakes.

And if you're a friend of mine and notice something familiar when reading this book, there's a good chance I was thinking of you when I wrote it. Consider it a gift—hidden from most and meant only for you in thanks for your friendship.

About the Book

Writing fiction is hard, especially when it's a series written over the course of four years. Each book in the Task Force Valor series has been more complex, because each is constrained somewhat by the one before.

Gayle Roper and I came up with the original idea of a Special Forces Explosives Ordnance Disposal unit during a brainstorming session at her cabin in July 2004. The plot was influenced by real-life events and stories of the battles being fought by our troops in the war on terror.

In struggling to make the story authentic, I learned very quickly that I never wanted to write about a place I hadn't actually visited personally. I decided to go to Ukraine before writing book three.

In the summer of 2006 I went to Kiev and met with George and
Sharon Markey, two young American missionaries living there. They
welcomed me into their home, which they shared with a wonderful
Ukrainian couple, Stepan and Olenka Mankovska. Olenka was such
an incredible help in writing this book that I memorialized her effi-
ciency and skill in the story by naming the Ukrainian CIA agent after
her. In real life, Olenka is the mother of two and runs her own translation company.

My time living with the Mankovska family gave me great insight
into Ukrainian culture, especially when Olenka sent me to visit her
grandparents for a few days in the village of Peremyshl. I had the priv-
ilege of being one of the only westerners to ever visit this village. The
scenes in this book that take place there accurately describe what it
was like, except that Olenka's grandfather was still alive. He made it a
point to teach me how real Russian men hug. Apparently, in Ukraine,
nothing says, "Good to see you," like several crushed vertebrae.

My hosts didn't have a car. Like most of the other villagers, they
got around on foot or on bicycles, or by riding simple horse-drawn
carts.

My presence was a real curiosity. The neighbors kept coming by
to see "the American," as curious about me as I was about them. One
offered me a ride on his horse cart and very proudly drove me out to
the edge of town to see the paved road—apparently a real sign of
modern progress.

The man grilled me with questions about my life and looked
with great interest at all the pictures I'd brought of my home and
family. Looking at a photo of my front yard, he couldn't fathom the

concept of a lawn. "You don't harvest it for anything?" he asked, scratching his head as if growing something just to cut it down was quite silly. And I suppose he was right.

On Sunday we attended not one but three separate Eastern Orthodox services at small churches in surrounding villages. Upon entering, the first thing I noticed was that everyone was fanning themselves. Or so I thought. Then I realized they were making the sign of the cross—over and over and over and over. If one could make it to heaven simply by genuflecting (which isn't possible, by the way), these people would be at the front of the line.

The Orthodox tradition is filled with mysterious and ancient traditions, one of which has to do with church pews: there aren't any. I wondered if they had been removed to make room for the icons— there were so many of those that the church would feel crowded even if you were the only human being present.

Having an American at the services became something of a distraction, though everyone was very gracious. I got a fascinating lesson in Orthodox culture.

After church we went walking in the woods looking for mushrooms—a favored activity among the locals in the summer. After an hour or so we had several pounds of mushrooms, all of which I was convinced were highly poisonous. The one thing my guidebook said that you should absolutely, positively never do in Ukraine is eat the mushrooms. So when the aforesaid mushrooms showed up as the main course for dinner that night... Let's just say supper was scarier than my visit to the Chernobyl nuclear reactor. But I ate them, and they didn't taste half bad. Besides, I have all the kids I need already.

I signed up for a tour into the dead zone around Chernobyl. A tour company in Kiev offered a half-day venture, and I was surprised to find there were five other people who had signed up. We drove into the dead zone, our tour guide explaining the story of the tragedy that had happened twenty years earlier. Many villages around the reactor had to be buried, and we saw the mounds marking some of them.

Nature is thriving in the dead zone, and there are actually a few people who, like Alexi in the story, have moved back in and continue to farm there. We met one of them and asked him what his secret is for surviving in the dead zone. Among other things, he said to drink plenty of water and get lots of sleep. Sounds like a good plan pretty much wherever you live.

We toured the ghost town of Pripyat. It was one of the most amazing places I've ever seen. Imagine entering a fair-sized city and finding that all the people had suddenly vanished—leaving behind dishes in the sink and calendars on the walls, all the things we surround ourselves with every day. It was surreal. Among the everyday things, however, were scattered remnants of that terrible night when the reactor blew. I especially remember the gas masks—some of them obviously for children.

The greatest thing about writing fiction, for me, is the experiences you must collect in order to make your writing authentic. I hope that you were able to share in them with me by reading *Meltdown*. For photos of Ukraine, visit www.ukraine.livefire.us.

And visit www.livefire.us to continue the adventure.

Don't Miss the Action!

Read the other books in the TASK FORCE VALOR SERIES.

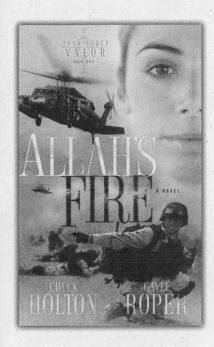

TASK FORCE VALOR SERIES — BOOK 1

Two Dangerous Missions Collide with Explosive Results

Reporter Liz Fairchild is determined to find her sister who has been kidnapped by terrorists in Lebanon. Sergeant John Cooper and his elite Special Ops team hunt down Palestinian extremists in possession of a new undetectable explosive that will change the "face of terror." As Liz and Task Force Valor's paths intersect, there is more at risk than their separate missions.

TASK FORCE VALOR SERIES — BOOK 2

The Global War on Terror Heats Up

The action and suspense continue in the second book of the Task Force Valor series. Sergeant "Rip" Rubio is on a mission to tackle both criminals and his own past as his sister slips into the gang culture. The story heats up as Fernanda and Rubio race to track down a lethal explosive with global repercussions. Will they save the world before it's too late?

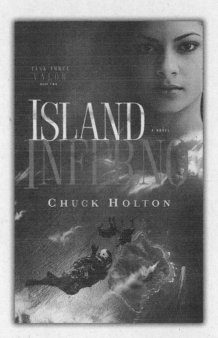